I REGRET
EVERYTHING

Seth Greenland

I REGRET EVERYTHING
A LOVE STORY

Europa
editions

Europa Editions
214 West 29th Street
New York, N.Y. 10001
www.europaeditions.com
info@europaeditions.com

Library of Congress Cataloging in Publication Data is available
ISBN 978-1-60945-247-6

Greenland, Seth
I Regret Everything

Book design by Emanuele Ragnisco
www.mekkanografici.com

Prepress by Grafica Punto Print – Rome

Cover photo © R_Koopmans/iStock

Printed in the USA

For Susan, Allegra and Gabe

CONTENTS

JEREMY
Trusts and Estates – 15

SPAULDING
The Iambic Pentameter Strategy – 29

JEREMY
The House of Regret Has Many Rooms – 39

SPAULDING
The Rubbish in My Attic – 58

JEREMY
Another Facet of the Dreamer – 73

SPAULDING
Bucketful of Buddhists – 87

JEREMY
The Rumpus in My Head – 97

SPAULDING
A Starving Prisoner Gorges Herself on Your Language – 117

JEREMY
You Are Not Africa – 131

SPAULDING
Drunk, Maybe, But Not Numb – 139

JEREMY
In Want of a Country House – 146

SPAULDING
Just Kill Me – 161

JEREMY
Literary Monsters – 165

SPAULDING
Only Poets – 172

JEREMY
Remover of Obstacles – 178

SPAULDING
The Dark Carnival – 190

JEREMY
A Single Organism of Happiness – 197

SPAULDING
And Then It Got Weird – 222

ACKNOWLEDGMENTS – 253

I REGRET
EVERYTHING

Judge: What is your profession?
Brodsky: Poet. Poet and translator.
Judge: Who said you were a poet? Who assigned you that rank?
Brodsky: No one. Who assigned me to the human race?

—from the trial of the poet
JOSEPH BRODSKY

It would be easy to say my troubles began when a mysterious woman walked into the office but that would ignore the time freshman year in college when Aunt Bren called to let me know my mother had removed all of her clothes in the furniture department at Macy's and been taken to Bellevue. Besides, a sentence like *my troubles began when a mysterious woman walked into the office* veers into private-eye territory and my work did not in any real way resemble that of a private eye. As an attorney with a trusts and estates practice, courage and love of danger did not thrum in my breast, only caution and prudence. Clients relied on me to structure their assets in such a way that by the time they were no longer living, every opportunity had been taken to protect their heirs, charities, and legacies. Generation-skipping trusts, real estate trusts, blind trusts, wills, codicils, prenuptial agreements, and tax planning were my territory. I counseled captains of industry, advised widows and offspring. Life with an unstable parent taught me there were times a person's affairs were a baffling wilderness. It was my job to tame the anarchic trees, mutating vines, and proliferating stinkweed into a fragrant, orderly garden through which the beneficiaries could one day stroll.

Running parallel to my legal work, albeit at a more leisurely clip, was my career as a poet. These seemingly divergent fields appear irreconcilable but there was more overlap than one would think. If a poet crafted something eternal out of the chaos of the universe, so, too, did the writer of a last will and testament. All of an individual's doubts, certainties, accomplishments, failings, accumulations, divestments, judgments, values, and, finally, wishes for the future were distilled into the lucid prose of a binding document. There was no brief to be made for the aesthetic magnificence of such a text, but as something that wrung order from the unruliness of life, it had its own subtle beauty.

Like the law, poetry was a competitive endeavor. There were hierarchies, cliques and claques; the same kind of snaky infighting and competition found in most professions. I lost a pitched battle for the editorship of the literary magazine at Sarah Lawrence to an (admittedly, equally qualified) African-American lesbian who employed a virtuosic campaign of implication and innuendo to convince our well-meaning colleagues that my heterosexual orientation marked me as a congenital oppressor. There was a terrific collection of talent on the staff yet few of the aspiring scribblers had the stomach to make a profession of it (my former nemesis went on to become a consultant for McKinsey). To me literature was more than just a viable if challenging vocation. It was a mission, a statement about the manner in which I intended to live: heightened, luminous, and free of the constraints that bound my more timorous classmates. My student loans were Himalayan but there would be time enough to pay them back.

In the poetry racket, anyone that aspired to be taken seriously had to get an MFA. I was accepted to the program at the University of Iowa but dropped out in the spring of my first year due to an entirely avoidable imbroglio with my advisor. Immediately, I returned to New York and got a sublet on the Lower East Side. A job as a proofreader on the lobster shift gave me time to write and with a handful of published poems meant to compensate for a nonexistent MFA, I applied for university teaching positions. But this youth-inflamed enthusiasm proved to be temporary because after much sobering cogitation on the realities of academia (teaching posts were not forth-coming), a growing uncertainty about devoting my entire life to a quixotic dream, and my former graduate school advisor's vow to do everything in his power to prevent me from ever obtaining employment, I was forced to change course.

Despite my professional shift from literature to law, I kept a foot in both worlds but with a twist. Although my given name was Jeremy Best, my poetry was published (in the kind of liter-ary review whose prestige exists in inverse proportion to its cir-culation) under the name Jinx Bell. Simple. American. And the same initials as my real name. This might strike one as odd, or at the very least eccentric, since we live in an age whose defin-ing characteristic is an unrestrained mania for self-promotion. But for me, keeping this aspect of my existence private height-ened its value. Imagine having thousands of gold coins hidden in a safe. I was rich and the world none the wiser. My co-workers and clients had no idea I was a poet.

On a humid June afternoon a scrim of rain obscured the buildings across Third Avenue just north of 63rd Street. My twentieth-floor office was standard for a senior associate, a boxy white-walled space overlooking southern Manhattan. There were no framed degrees, no art on the walls. Nestled in the corner of a bookshelf next to the annually issued com-pendium of all New York Surrogate's Court rules, regulations, and statutes in the trusts and estates area known as "the Greenbook" was a row of first editions signed by famous poets, the sole intimation of my other life.

A hefty Indian-American woman, thirty years old, stood in front of my desk. She wore a loud floral print sleeveless dress from which a white bra strap protruded. Reetika Mehta, mem-ber of Actors' Equity and currently appearing at Thatcher, Sturgess & Simonson as my secretary. We had been working together for five years. As a poet with a little bit of money, I believed in supporting other artists. I fantasized about creating a grant-giving organization—the Best Foundation—but since that hadn't yet happened, Reetika Mehta was my beta version. If she was in a show at a nonprofit theater, I would buy a ticket and make a generous contribution. Whenever there was an audition, if at all possible, it was break a leg and off you go.

Reetika informed me that one client was coming in to discuss a bequest to the New York Philharmonic, another to set up a trust. A mother and her adult son wanted to talk about a Fifth Avenue co-op they had inherited.

"They're the co-owners per the will, her husband, his father," Reetika said. "Mrs. Fitzwater wants to sell, her son doesn't."

This was our routine. Because I did not like surprises, Reetika briefed me a day ahead of time. Since I had not married and currently did not have a girlfriend, I welcomed the intimacy my job afforded me. A trusts and estates attorney traffics in people's deepest desires, secrets, and fears. This father favors his daughter over his son? I will glean it. That wealthy wife loves the child of her first marriage more than her current husband? She might not tell me outright but I will know. The anxious uncle of the profligate nephew, the adult child fretting over a mother with incipient dementia whose age-spotted hands still hold the financial reins in a death grip, the devoted husband with a mistress of thirty years' standing that he does not want to leave out of his will? Each saga was revealed.

"Can't the Fitzwater family see a therapist?"

"I'll suggest that in an email." Reetika raised an eyebrow and I nodded in acknowledgment. Her presence brightened the essential dreariness of a law office. I rooted for her to get cast in a show but lived in fear of her leaving. Reetika could have been a lawyer but she chose to battle it out with auditions, improv classes, and the relentless disappointment that accumulates in any creative career. It was brave, admirable, and an irritating reminder of my own failure to walk the tightrope without a net.

A few minutes later, while in the middle of drafting a letter to the heirs of my client Brenda Vendler, recently deceased, to inform them of the modest financial bequests coming their way, I looked up and saw the figure of a young woman standing in the hall outside my office. She asked what I was doing, but not in a way that suggested she actually cared.

"Working on the disposition of a will."

"Your own?"

"Why would you ask that?"

"Because you're so old." Her smile was like a basket of kittens just learning to use their claws. "Is it boring?"

She leaned against the doorjamb then glanced down the hall as if she were expecting someone. Turning her attention back to me, she said, "I'm Spaulding Simonson." It took me a moment to realize this was the daughter of Ed Simonson, managing partner of the firm. We had met at a party her father threw for new associates. She must have been fourteen at the time.

"I know."

That revelation was taken entirely in stride, *Of course you know, everyone in this place knows, why shouldn't you?* "You're Mr. Best, right?" I was amazed she could recall the name of an adult casually encountered in the context of a function her father probably forced her to attend. Her voice had dropped an octave since then and had a slightly rusted quality, like she was just getting over a cold contracted on the slopes of Aspen. She was tall, maybe 5'8", and wore a loose green cardigan sweater over a white tee shirt, black leggings, and ballet slippers. Her hair, the burnished gold found on coins and in youth and thereafter in bottles, fell in thick ringlets over her shoulders and down to the middle of her back in the manner of a silent movie ingénue. Light freckles dusted her pale cheeks and chocolate eyes peered from behind tortoiseshell glasses. A multihued purse that appeared to be constructed from the kind of handcrafted fabric rhapsodized over in design magazines hung from her shoulder.

"You have a secret identity," she said.

Before I could react—How could this exemplar of adolescent cold blood, one whose cultural vectors pointed toward Williamsburg and obscure Internet file-sharing sites, possibly know about my other life?—Spaulding slinked into my office and settled on the couch against the wall perpendicular to my desk.

"You're Jinx Bell."

This was the point when a more circumspect man might have said he was busy, wished her good luck with school and the rest of her life, and told her to please close the door on the way out. Instead, I asked how old she was.

"Nineteen. You?"

"Thirty-three."

"Halfway to dead."

My mind flew back to my apartment that morning. Compartmentalization was something at which I excelled, thoughts of death kept in abeyance. Now they burst from my subconscious like a whale breaching the ocean surface. Here's why: I killed a Minotaur. All right, it was a dream. But it felt real. Walking along the beach in Montauk where I had spent childhood summers with my parents, this hairy behemoth came at me and I beat him brutally with a club until whatever spark animating his vainglorious existence was extinguished. Then I woke up, thrust off the sweat-soaked sheet, and fled my bedroom as if it were a crime scene. The dream made no literal sense because I was a coward, incapable of attacking anyone with a cutting remark much less a blunt object.

Gray dawn pressed against the windows. In my living room I took in the surroundings. The apartment was a large one-bedroom on the third floor of a renovated brownstone. Unlike my office, decorated to suppress the individuality that might lead someone to know me in a deeper way, this space was a perfect reflection of my tastes. The ceilings were nine feet high, the floors polished oak, the moldings original, lovingly restored. A Turkish rug acquired on a trip to Istanbul anchored the room. A tall bookshelf ran along one wall. It contained roughly half of my two-thousand-volume library. An Andy Warhol lithograph hung over the fireplace, a portrait of my father in his younger days.

Despite the early hour, hip-hop music throbbed from the apartment next door. When the landlord had informed me that the new neighbor was Croatian, my Slavophile—Dostoevsky! Prokofiev! Borscht!—ears pricked up. He was a fortyish man named Bogdan who entertained at odd hours and had a great fondness for international interpretations of urban music and hashish, which regularly wafted from beneath his door into the hallway. Several times, when the BOOM-THUNKA-THUNK of the bass abused my ears at 2:00 A.M., I knocked on his door and requested it be turned down. Invariably, he would be stoned, but the druggy membrane would barely filter the enmity he exuded like body odor. His look seemed to say, I'm in America now and I can do whatever the fuck. The volume would be lowered, but a day or two later the same thing would occur and again I would ask him to be more neighborly. The last time I stood at Bogdan's door in the middle of the night I saw three dark-suited men who looked like they had just returned from performing a contract killing in Chechnya. They eyed me like I was a capon. I threw in the towel and purchased earplugs.

Showered and shaved, I ate a breakfast of yogurt and half a banana while I labored over a new poem. After an hour, when it became clear I had written myself into a corner from which no escape seemed possible, I put down the pad. To ensure the early morning wouldn't be a total waste I dashed off two checks for five hundred dollars each, one to a local food bank and the other to the New York Public Library Annual Fund.

Then I walked from my apartment on a tree-lined street in Carroll Gardens through a Brooklyn bouillabaisse of vigorous mothers pushing baby-laden strollers with gym-toned arms, medicated children of high achievers shouldering bursting book bags, and sullen hipsters slouching sleepy-eyed toward coffee shops, to the F train.

While soaping myself in the shower I had noticed a lump in my groin, a slight swelling just to the left of my pubic bone. Anatomy was not my bailiwick. The area to the left of my business was terra incognita. Swelling anywhere was not good, but what was swollen usually reverted to the mean before long. Unfortunately, because my livelihood required the constant projection of worst-case scenarios, I found myself battling the nagging notion that this symptom spelled The End. My mother had been treated for lung cancer and although she was a lifelong smoker I feared a similar fate.

"Mr. Best, hello?" In my reverie, I had forgotten about Spaulding.

"Sorry, what?"

"My therapist told me it's okay to joke about anything."

"What were you talking about?"

"I said you were halfway to dead."

Halfway to dead—delivered with a smile, like it was amusing, which, under the circumstances, it was not. It was audacious, though, and announced a will to engage in an exchange that might provide passage from the drab confines of Thatcher, Sturgess & Simonson to worlds uncharted. It invited a comeback, a rejoinder that would raise the temperature of the room and alleviate the tedium of the day. But in the time it took to review the situation and game the possible outcomes only an idiot would conclude there was anything to be gained by even an innocent flirtation with Ed Simonson's teenage daughter. So I gazed at her evenly and waited. If she wanted pop and fizz it was not being served. When Spaulding realized no response was imminent, she absently ran the tip of her forefinger along the sleeve of her sweater, ignoring me completely. She wore rings on several fingers, including one made of silver and shaped like a chevron on her right thumb. Her purplish nail polish was chipped.

"It was inelegant," she said. "Do you like that word?"

"Inelegant is excellent."

I returned my attention to the liquidation of the Vendler estate. It held a Montauk saltbox anyone might covet and I pictured myself cradled by a chaise with a book in my lap lounging on a buttery summer day. This was a stalling tactic because Spaulding's presence required, strike that, *demanded*, attention. I had no intention of giving in so easily.

Kevin Pratt strode past the office door with an armful of files. A sixth-year associate, he was a hale and fit former college squash player and looked like the kind of person who never suffered a head cold. Over six feet tall with a wide chest, he walked on the balls of his feet, which gave him the aspect of a faintly menacing rabbit. At Thatcher, Sturgess & Simonson he was the closest thing I had to a friend. Pratt glanced in and stopped when he saw Spaulding upholstered on my couch. I asked if he had met Ed Simonson's daughter. He looked her over appraisingly and reported he had not.

Spaulding possessed the sensor that tells a woman when someone is doing a sexual Dun & Bradstreet on her and gave a polite smile that Pratt, had he any sensors at all, would have read as an invitation to go away. My colleague was competitive when it came to women. In his state fair, Spaulding was a blue ribbon.

"Do you want a tour of the office?" he asked.

"Maybe later," she said, in a way that meant never. "I'm having a private conversation with Mr. Best. Nice meeting you, Mr. Pratt."

Spaulding wielded the power inherent in being the managing partner's daughter, while at the same time mocking that power. There was a captivating lightness to her manner, a sense that the entire scene was being staged for her enjoyment and she appreciated the effort everyone was making. Dismissed by the duchess, he departed.

"I've got a lot to do," I said.

She rose from the couch and rounded my desk. Reflexively, I hit the key that returned my monitor to the screen saver, a color photograph of Lake Winnipesaukee surrounded by flaming autumn foliage selected for its banality. She stood behind and to the left of me, no more than a foot away. There was a pleasing scent. Her hair? I tried not to notice autumn and pine and the savory tang of fresh ginger cookies because it was June and humid and Spaulding.

"These are all poetry?" She had removed a delicate volume from the shelf: *Lord Weary's Castle* by Robert Lowell, pub. 1946.

"Be careful. They're first editions."

Spaulding returned the book to its place. "Whose will are you working on?"

It would have been a relief to have described my desire for Mrs. Vendler's house, for a quiet place to write, somewhere to pursue my destiny away from the kingdom of her father, but what I said was, "I can't talk about it, although nothing would give me more pleasure. Well, that's an exaggeration."

The mellifluous laughter sounded like a cascade of pearls and caught me by surprise. Spaulding moved away from me, then turned and relaxed into the sofa.

"I read your poem in *The Paris Review*," she said. These are eight words guaranteed to freeze the blood of any poet while he awaits the follow-up. Whether the verdict is positive or negative, one develops an instant case of acute stress response, otherwise known as fight or flight, and further brain activity ceases until the situation is resolved. *I liked it* or *I hated it* doesn't matter. What matters, and matters deeply, is the stating of some, *any,* opinion. It violates the laws of the universe to say *I read your poem* followed by nothing. This is to stare into the yawning void itself. "That's why I came to talk to you, but if you're really tied up, we'll do it another time. Okay, so."

I waited. She placed her hands behind her neck and with an outward flick of fingers delicately fluffed her ambrosial curls.

"It was good."

I could have smoked a cigarette.

Then she stood up to leave. "You can stay a minute," I said, trying to convey with a mixture of insouciance and feigned impatience the strain her continued presence was going to be. At this I failed spectacularly. Of all of my bad qualities, vanity is perhaps the one of which I am least proud. So if someone wants to make "The Valley of Akbar"—the title of my poem—the center of attention, the experience has the voluptuous quality of a Roman orgy. Spaulding returned to her previous attitude on the sofa, and held me in regal regard. "Finish your thought," I said.

"I already did."

Was she going to make me interview her, to extract another morsel of a compliment? I had to finish dealing with Mrs. Vendler's estate and prepare for a client meeting. There was no time to dither with Spaulding. "So you read *The Paris Review*?"

"They had it at my school. My English teacher subscribed and he knew who you were. He didn't believe you worked with my father. And, yes, I read it. Why do you use a pseudonym? Don't you want to be famous?"

"No one wants to hire a poet to do what I do. The stereotype persists. Clients want paragons of probity."

"Then you probably shouldn't say 'paragons of probity,' since it sounds kind of poetic."

"In the law, dullness is a virtue."

"A boring lawyer didn't write that poem of yours. You slice a terrorist's balls off and give him breast implants? All in *terza rima*? Pretty punk rock."

"It was supposed to be about empathy."

"Weren't you afraid the ayatollahs would get all *jihadi* with you?"

"I don't think they're the *Paris Review* demographic."

She thought about this and nodded. It was not only unusual for me to have a spontaneous conversation with a reader who had responded to my work, it had never actually happened. And that she knew *terza rima*—the *a*, *b*, *a* rhyme scheme popularized by Dante in *The Divine Comedy*—was aphrodisiacal. Spaulding swung her feet to the floor, placed her elbows on her knees, and lit me with her eyes. "What else have you written?"

"I've published poems in literary journals you've probably never heard of and I'm finishing a collection."

"Finishing?"

Was that a skeptical brow furrow? Hard to tell. People think lawyers play fast and loose with the truth but this is not my modus operandi. The truth is easier to remember, and so it is what I habitually sling.

"Soon."

"So, Mr. Best." I waited. Like a deer hesitating on the misty shoulder of the Taconic Parkway, she seemed to be deciding whether or not to proceed across. "I think Edward P. Simonson is kind of busy today." There was a brief pause in the conversation, then, "Want to take me to lunch?" Her voice was barely above a whisper, barely above a thought, really, and I wasn't sure I had heard correctly. "Never mind, forget it."

"What?"

"That was crazy." She hesitated, then out flew, "If you took me to lunch you could tell me about the poetry collection you haven't finished."

I laughed, which was something I rarely did at the office, and Spaulding's cheeks flushed. There was some kind of interior struggle going on that made me root for her.

"Much as I'd savor your disdain, I've got a lot of work to do."

From somewhere there came an exasperated exhalation of breath and I looked up to see her father's bulky form in the doorway. "Spaulding," he said in a voice redolent of regattas and swizzle sticks, "What are you doing here?"

"You were in a meeting."

He told her to wait for him in his office. She rose languidly, said goodbye, and strolled past her father. Before departing she turned and mouthed, "I won't tell him you're a poet." It was hard not to grin. When Ed apologized for his daughter's unscheduled visit I assured him she had not been a problem. Ed was fifty and had the fleshy look of an ex-athlete.

"Your billables for May were the same level as they were in April," he said. Ed's tone was beige but I knew that my April billables were more than acceptable. That was his setup. Now came the attack: "Kevin Pratt did well in May." I nodded, giving nothing away. This was a favorite tactic of his. He would suggest that perhaps one was not performing at the highest level, stoke interoffice rivalries, and then wait for a reaction. In these moments I coped with his presence by composing nonsense couplets:

Simonson was my savvy captor /
He spoke fluent Velociraptor.

Then without another word he was gone, presumably to play the same kind of mind games with his daughter. Between Ed's gamesmanship, Spaulding's pheromones, and what I had discovered in the shower, it was difficult to concentrate. The rain had stopped so I told Reetika I was going for a walk.

In Central Park two elderly violinists were playing a Bartok Duo. Wisps of steam rose from puddles. Pedestrians strode past. The only other people who stopped to listen were an older lady wearing a sun hat and clutching a WNET tote bag and a nanny whose charge was asleep in a pram. The music was lovely, the hurly-burly of the city faded, and for a few moments there existed no thoughts of meetings or clients, the future or the past, only the soothing tones of the timeless melody. When they finished I dropped a crisp twenty into an open instrument case and turned quickly away so the musicians would not see that I was weeping.

SPAULDING
The Iambic Pentameter Strategy

That year went from heinous to outstanding and back to dreadful. My mother's third marriage broke up so she was more unavailable than usual. My father was over a decade into his second one and no closer to divorcing this wife who treated me like I had the Ebola virus. Then there was the month I spent in "rehab" which was really a mental hospital but my parents insisted we call it "rehab" since being marinated in drugs and alcohol didn't have the same stigma as crazy. Oh, and my older brother Gully who lived in Seattle where he was learning how to build sailboats only came to visit once while I was recuperating.

I was living with my mother in Manhattan and planning to enroll at Barnard in the fall. It was good to be back in the city. I had gone to Spence until my parents divorced and they shipped me off to school in Switzerland. It wasn't that they didn't love me. But parents have their own needs and everyone's needs were equally important as my mother explained to me after polishing off her third gin and tonic in the Swissair departure lounge when I was twelve and flying to Europe alone for the first time.

My mother lived in the co-op on Riverside Drive that she and my father shared until she threw a kitchen knife at him one particularly festive Thanksgiving and he moved out. How she got full custody of Gully and me after that episode was something no one's ever been able to explain and didn't say a lot for Edward P. Simonson's interest in having us around.

In the divorce my mother's big win was the apartment, a three-bedroom on the tenth floor of a doorman building. I hated it. Don't get me wrong; the place was total real estate porn. Big rooms, lots of sun, a river view to die for, wood floors, all the original details. North of us the lights of the George Washington Bridge twinkled. But my mother was there with her four cats. What's funny about this is that I'm an animal lover, but four cats for one person seems excessive. Oh, and I'm semi-allergic, which she was convinced must have been in my imagination. So, four cats plus my mother are five reasons I didn't want to be there. Six if you count her boyfriend Dodd who was usually draped over the living room sofa like a ratty afghan.

Let me tell you about my mother. Her name is Harlee Joy Spaulding. I know. Har-LEE. It was Janet Spaulding when she was growing up in Rye, but Janet failed to capture her uniqueness so she christened herself Harlee at Vassar where she majored in art history. She could babble endlessly about Minimalism but when it came to stuff like knowing how to talk to me about anything other than the perils of addiction, forget it. During the 1980s she had worked in an art gallery in SoHo but then she married my father to pursue a life of child-rearing and cocktails. She was in recovery again, sober less than a year, which meant I was supposed to no longer be worried about coming home to find her passed out at four in the afternoon. But the thing is, you never stop worrying.

Harlee was a beautiful woman and that goes a long way toward explaining how she managed to swing another two marriages even if both imploded because of her drinking hobby. I ignored the not-my-real-dads as best I could. There were step-sibs in the mix but since I got packed off these kids were like apparitions who appeared when I was home for the holidays and floated in and out of my adolescence like little ghosts. For husband number two she moved us to the Upper

East Side and for number three it was Tarrytown. Like a true New Yorker, she never sold her own place. The Riverside Drive address was her life raft and she always swam back there.

Since my release I had been living at "home" which meant reluctantly cohabitating with my mother, her feline menagerie, and occasionally Dodd. Harlee was hinting she might marry him. She was going to be fifty soon, so her hormones were conspiring to help her make worse decisions than usual.

—After a certain point, Spall, you can't set your sights too high.

She wasn't sure Dodd was marriage material since he got downsized from some mid-level job at a bank, went to massage school, and had recently started work at a day spa called Harmony. She was always making him give her "sacral adjustments." Ten minutes after we met Dodd told me it looked like my shoulders were out of alignment and asked if I wanted one. Like that was going to happen.

—From her perch on the couch my mother said, Dodd, can you believe this girl had to wear a brace and stay home from school for an entire year when she was eleven because of spinal curvature and now she's turning down free treatment?

A typical day: I got up late, hopefully after Dodd left for the spa. Coffee, black, and a piece of wheat toast with apricot jam. My mother would be in the living room listening to Joni Mitchell on her iPod, drinking quarts of coffee, and working on a sweater or a blanket, yarn snaking from the tote bag she carried with her everywhere, knitting needles pumping like pistons.

—Morning, Spall, she'd say.

—Hey, I'd say.

—Everything good?

—Awesome.

—Get enough sleep?

This was passive-aggressive because I was sleeping like a bear so it was her way of telling me she didn't approve.

When I stayed home I read novels: Camus, Houellebecq, and *The Sickness Unto Death* by Kierkegaard, not a novel but more my Bible since it said that if you don't get right with God you're in despair. I wasn't a God person but it worked as a metaphor. My copy had a lot of underlining. And I read poetry. I dug the 20th-century poets who knew how to rock a rhyme. Blank verse was supposed to be cooler and rhyming poetry allegedly for dorks but it was a soothing representation of order in the universe and that was something I craved. Last winter I learned to use it as a coping technique, the Iambic Pentameter Strategy. In challenging moments I would formulate words, sometimes nonsensical, occasionally borderline poetic, that in five-foot lines would mimic the human heartbeat—

ba-Bum / ba-Bum / ba-Bum / ba-Bum / ba-Bum.

It worked like a breathing exercise for a yogi.

And there / is Dodd / again / upon / the couch.

Arranging this reality in iambic pentameter made it easier to deal with.

When I went out I'd sit in Central Park, usually Strawberry Fields, and think about John Lennon and how he was lucky to get assassinated. I know that sounds weird so don't get mad but look, how could he ever follow The Beatles and once he was dead there was no pressure. Or maybe I'd go to the Met and hang around the Egyptian pavilion in silent communion with the art lovers. I'd study the carvings on the ancient stones or stare at the sarcophagi and consider the mummies that were buried in them. Here's a profound thought: The mummies were just like me three millennia ago, people who woke up, ate breakfast, suffered through their day, had dinner, then lived to be about my age and died. If I were an Egyptian, I'd be old. The typical life span today is nearly four times as long. That's a lot of afternoons to fill. So a few times a week I laced up my Chucks and took long walks. To the northern tip of

Manhattan where the East River veered from the Hudson and shells filled with rowers pulling long oars in soothing rhythm glided past. To the Promenade in Brooklyn Heights where with a pen and paper I'd sit on a bench and sketch the boisterous skyline. Fifth Avenue from the arch in Washington Square Park all the way up to Harlem was the best for dog watching because you'd go from toy poodles to pit bulls on one long stroll.

—Where were you walking? my mother would ask when I arrived home.

—Nowhere in particular.

In my rambles around the city, I thought a lot about Happiness. Whenever I saw my father he reminded me life was about goals. Maybe I would be happier, he suggested, if I had a goal.

—Goals, Spall, he said. You choose one, work toward it, and then before you get there set your sights on another.

How was anyone ever supposed to feel satisfied? No wonder half the country was on antianxiety medication. But it was complicated since goals per se were not a bad thing.

—Dig the furrow and the harvest will take care of itself, my father said.

He liked to use farming metaphors even though he went to boarding school. It's the Protestant work ethic the country was founded on and woe to you if you didn't get with the Calvinists who ran this place. Even if you wanted to be a glassblower. There was a lot of pressure to be a really good glassblower, to have a shop and a catalogue and blow a shitload of high-quality glass. I wasn't that competitive. Like my brother Gully. He was building sailboats and my dad thought that was fine as long as he wound up building the boat that won the America's Cup. But Gully didn't care about being the guy who built the boat that won the race. He just loved boats. It's why he was living three thousand miles away in Washington State. So he didn't have to meet our father for lunch and hear about how an individual needs goals.

—Spaulding, have you gained weight?

Edward P was seated behind the yacht-sized desk in his law office with its view of rainy southern Manhattan. The drop-in wasn't planned but if he had an issue with that it was hard to know. As a rule, if a father asked his daughter if she'd gained weight it's *quel faux pas* but he was probably concerned I might develop anorexia to go along with my other less than optimal qualities so his observation was probably meant to be encouraging. Once you'd been labeled as a person with psychological issues it was hard to figure out how you were being perceived. Was someone walking on eggshells because they didn't want to trigger an episode or did they mean what they said?

—You told me the same thing last week. The meds cause water retention, remember?

—Well, you look . . . terrific? Am I allowed to say that?

This was typical for us. My father was not the easiest adult to talk to. He'd say something that could be misconstrued, then I'd respond in some slightly defensive way at which point the exchange usually ended, unless he had swallowed a couple of Scotch and sodas. Then Edward P became pretty voluble, although, to be clear, he stopped after two and, unlike my mother, never threw a single knife at anyone. He worked like a coal stoker in a Dickens novel, played indoor tennis in the winter, sailed in the summer, and seemed devoted to my two half-brothers who were twelve and ten, probably to make up for not being around much when Gully and I were kids. He was carrying a few extra pounds and when I thought about how being a lawyer stressed him out it was hard not to be concerned. When my parents broke up I spent every other weekend with him and one month every summer. At least that was how it worked before I was sent away to school. Now that I was technically an adult, all bets were off.

—So, Dad, I had this idea. You know your ex-wife's cats?

—Sure, he said, rolling his eyes.

—I can't live in that zoo anymore. Would it be okay if I moved in with you guys? It would only be until school starts in the fall.

—You can't make it through the summer?

—Dad, I said. My sinuses.

—Duly noted, he said.

—I'm going to die.

I realized maybe this was a little tone-deaf considering what I had put him through this past winter.

—What are you doing this summer? he asked, not bothering to answer the question about moving in with family number two.

—Not a lot, I said. I enrolled in a creative writing workshop at Barnard summer school.

—You need to get a job, or an internship sort of thing. You need a plan, Spaulding. A goal. We've discussed this.

—I want to be a writer.

—Look, kiddo, any kind of career in the arts is a long shot. There's a lot of rejection and a person needs to have a thick hide. You have so many great qualities but a thick hide?

—I'm nineteen years old. Don't crush my dreams.

—In the event you can't find anything you can intern here at the firm a few days a week, get a feel for the place. You have a good brain, Spall. You'd probably make a fine attorney.

—I'd rather be a lighthouse keeper.

—Then do something you like.

—Are there any jobs where I can read all day?

—If you don't find one you can run the copy machine here.

—Seriously?

—Do I look like I'm kidding?

—What about moving in with you guys? I promise to keep taking my meds.

The rain had started up again, splashing against the windows. I gazed around the quiet order of my father's office, the well-lit paintings of sailboats, the clean desk of a tidy mind.

—Let me talk to Katrina.

Hurricane Katrina, the wife. I knew that's what he'd tell me. My father and I were like two bad musicians trying to find the beat. Someone was always a little ahead or behind.

—You're welcome to stay here until the rain stops.

Several of his colleagues were waiting for him in the conference room and he excused himself. After he left, I put my feet up on the couch. Because of my shyness, often mistaken for snobbery, meeting anyone I wanted to talk to was hard. My parents did not have writers as friends so I never encountered any. And it would have been challenging to have sought them out since my school was in Montagnola near the Swiss-Italian border, not great if you wanted to expand your horizons although lovely if you were a sheep. If you're wondering what drove me to stand in Mr. Best's doorway, there you are.

What did Mr. Best make of me when I appeared, when I entered the room, when I posed on his office couch? Could he tell how horribly self-conscious I was? Such a crippling case of nerves it felt like kernels of corn popping in my stomach. When I met someone new, I felt like a marionette and instead of being in the conversation I'd see another me, meta-Spaulding, equally uneasy, pulling strings. Could he tell? And had I really asked him to take me to lunch?

Dr. Margaret Noonan, who I'd been seeing twice a week since my release, and who insisted I call her "Dr. Margaret," had told me to approach social situations like I was playing a character named "Spaulding." This Spaulding was deep-space cool and confident. This Spaulding could star in a movie about the other "real" Spaulding and win an Oscar. In my father's office these words cycled through my brain:

The ner- / vous girl / asserts / her fool- / ish plan.

But Mr. Best was so friendly, talking to me like I was a person and not throwing me out. I made a mental note to discuss this with Dr. Margaret during my next session. I had initiated a conversation and nearly gotten through it without embarrassing myself. Why did I ask him to take me out to lunch? When it came to trying to understand my behavior, Dr. Margaret was helpful but whenever I talked to her about anything creative she saw it as an extension of my therapy.

—I'm working on this poem about flying over everybody.

—So you can't be seen? Or so you can be seen?

I don't know! But I didn't want to talk about it. My parents forced me to go to therapy. Dr. Margaret was nice and everything, but I would have rather been at the dentist. I thought it might be helpful to have a casual conversation with an actual writer and that's what I was thinking I would do with Mr. Best. At least that's what I was thinking until I stepped into his force field. Yes, force field. It sounds overdramatic (and intergalactic) but that was the effect of the confidence, authority, and ease he exuded.

It wasn't his physical attractiveness, because while he was nice enough looking—dark hair, medium build, a shade under six feet—he wasn't exactly a runway model. Mr. Best just seemed to have it figured out. Here was someone with a goal and a plan. He had a job where he made money and an art life, too. I wanted to know what he knew.

Facebook showed several Jeremy Bests in New Zealand, Australia, England, and America but mine did not have an account. Needless to say, he was a stranger to Twitter, LinkedIn, and Tumblr. In fact, the online profile of my Jeremy Best was remarkably low-key. A search engine only turned up membership in some professional societies. His alter ego, Jinx

Bell, had a similarly inconspicuous Internet presence: a couple of poems in literary journals, the edition of *The Paris Review* where his work had appeared, and that was pretty much the extent of it.

But he was a published poet, an artist, and that was impressive. Did he want an apprentice?

JEREMY
The House of Regret Has Many Rooms

The day before Spaulding's appearance, Ed Simonson and I were having lunch at the University Club. He had invited me out to discuss a delicate matter and the mealtime din made it easier to speak confidentially. Ed speared his last oyster, put it in his mouth, swallowed, and chased it with a sip of lager. I thought of him as the Raptor. It wasn't a nickname I shared with anyone.

"I've been looking over what you've done on the Vendler estate." Like all good attorneys, Ed Simonson was inscrutable. His expression did not indicate whether he thought the work was high quality or I was going to be asked to resign. Had my designs on the client's Montauk home been telepathically surmised? The finest attorneys have an ability to peer into the souls of their adversaries. Did he think of me as an adversary? "Solid work there, as usual."

The Vendler estate was routine. Was this what he had wanted to talk about? I ate a spoonful of chowder and waited for him to continue. A woman laughed at a nearby table. Across the room a couple appeared to be having an argument. Thirty seconds passed. There was a vacant look in Ed's eyes. He was either deep in reflection or had suffered a small stroke. To occupy myself, I removed a monogrammed Mark Cross fountain pen from my pocket and examined its sleek design. The old-school pen was an affectation I allowed myself because no client who employed a firm like ours wanted to sign anything as serious as a will with a ballpoint. Ed still hadn't moved when the waiter cleared the appetizers and set our entrées down.

"How long have you been with the firm?"

"Five years."

Five years was the point where lawyers at Thatcher were given an early indication of whether they would be made partners. Most were informed they should quietly begin looking for a new situation. You're welcome to use your office, phone, and stationery, they were told, but your future is not at This Firm. Was that the purpose of the lunch? I had a sense that Ed liked me on a personal level and was struck with the realization that this was his way of imparting the bad news gently, as if sea bass in a Béarnaise sauce was going to compensate for professional disaster.

Clearing his throat, Ed mentioned Dirk Trevelyan, an older client who had minted gold on Wall Street. Was he going to suggest Trevelyan might have something for me when I left my current job? Why had he asked me how long I'd been at the firm? It was a question to which he already knew the answer.

"His current wife is a talented artist apparently. *Quite* a talented artist." It was difficult to discern why Ed repeated the phrase, repetition not being a rhetorical device he favored. "You've done the drafting and the amendments for Trevelyan's will so you know that his art collection is positively extraordinary, the Utrillo, the Brancusi, and that little Kandinsky he's got."

I told him that we had arranged for a professional photographer to take pictures of each piece for the purpose of cataloguing the estate. It was important that he know just how on top of my game I was.

"Well, the second Mrs. Trevelyan found it all very inspirational. Trevelyan keeps her on a short leash financially and the lady has expensive tastes that apparently led her to borrow money from some unsavory characters. She was in for over seven figures when she decided to pay them off with Dirk's Kandinsky."

Ed sliced a piece of tuna, put it in his mouth, and chewed mechanically. It was as if the story had made his appetite vanish. Seeing him eating reminded me there was food on my plate and I took a bite of the sea bass.

"She gave it to them?"

"And the old man has no idea. Because . . . you're not going to believe this . . . she painted a copy and that's what's on the bedroom wall."

The enormity of the betrayal sat there, neither of us saying anything. Ed took another bite of his tuna, then absently picked up my Mark Cross pen and tapped the table a couple of times before wrapping both of his hands around it and squeezing.

"How did you find out?"

"Mrs. Trevelyan came to see me. Jeremy, this is sticky. Do you know what that little Kandinsky is worth?"

"I think we had it valued around five million."

"In all my experience, imagine . . ." He shook his head, whether with respect for Mrs. Trevelyan's skills or consternation at her husband's position, it was hard to tell.

"Where is she now?"

"Mrs. Trevelyan flew to Bora Bora this morning. She didn't want to be around for the fireworks."

"What are you going to tell him?"

The waiter stopped by to refill our water glasses and ask how we liked the food. Ed told him everything was perfect and turned his attention back to me.

"By the way, the partnership committee is meeting later this summer. You're aware we don't consider associates for partnerships until they're in their seventh year at the firm, but because of the job you've done and the nature of your clients your name is in the hopper."

"Really?" I said, stupidly.

"Your work has been exemplary. No promises, though. But if you don't get it this go-round, right now I'm not telling tales out of school when I say your future at T.S.&S. is bright."

"I'm remarkably glad to hear that."

"One thing to be aware of, Kevin Pratt has a year of seniority on you. He's an excellent attorney and Trusts and Estates can't absorb two new partners." This was the Raptor on full display—dangle a reward, snatch it away. Or not. It was impossible to tell what he was thinking other than he enjoyed befuddling the associates. "It may just be a numbers game."

"So, Trevelyan. What are you going to tell him?"

"I'm not going to tell him anything, Jeremy," he said, going in for the kill. "This is your chance to shine."

A day after the lunch with Ed my memory of our encounter commingled with images of his droll daughter and the perplexing question of why the Bartok Duo had brought me to tears. Was it the crippling beauty of the music? Fear that the swelling I'd discovered indicated cancer when it was probably just a swollen gland? The answer remained obscure but the desolation I experienced felt bottomless. This is why a person learns to compartmentalize. I was on my way to see Dirk Trevelyan and needed to focus.

It had rained again since I had returned to the office from my afternoon stroll in the park and great puddles massed in the gutters. I delicately stepped over one, taking care not to get my wingtips wet, and slid into the backseat of the waiting town car just before the clouds opened again and rain battered the windshield. The Jamaican driver greeted me in a mellifluous baritone. A peaked chauffeur's cap crowned his short dreadlocks. He introduced himself as Joseph and his serene aspect guaranteed me a quiet hour in which I could work. When he eased the car into traffic I opened my briefcase.

We hadn't driven half a block when I looked out the window and through a curtain of rain spotted a soaked Spaulding marooned under the awning of a boutique. I told Joseph to stop. At the curb, I rolled down the window.

"Would you like a ride?"

Spaulding brightened when she saw me and with her sweater over her head like a cowl ran to the car. I swung the door open and she slid in, raindrops coursing down her face, the lenses of her glasses dripping.

"It's as if the sky was pregnant and her water burst," she said.

"That's disgusting," I said. She laughed. "Where are you going?"

The moisture must have released the molecules in the residue of her shampoo or the soap she had used that morning and caused them to effervesce because a lovely natural scent now misted the backseat. In the office I thought I'd sensed pine and ginger. Now what? Orange peel? Cinnamon? I had no time to waste on this—*Orange peel? Cinnamon? Get a grip, Jeremy.* Her hair was damp. She took her glasses off and brushed it out of her luminous eyes.

"Would you mind untucking your shirttail? I need to dry my glasses and I'm kind of wet."

This was not the kind of request made of a person one barely knew. The driver's dark eyes regarded me from the rearview mirror. Was he amused? Did he know this girl was the managing partner's daughter? I was never someone who treated anyone working for me as if they were invisible and while Spaulding's request would have unnerved me were we alone, Joseph's presence heightened my discomfort. But it did not heighten it enough to stop me from removing my shirttail from my pants. Spaulding took it and dried her glasses, polished the lenses, held them up to inspect, then rubbed them once more, her tapered fingers mere inches from my lap. It was an intimate act and while it occurred I realized I wasn't breathing. When she finished I tucked my shirt back in and inhaled. Her bouquet filled my nostrils. She arranged the glasses on her face and thanked me. I composed myself, cleared my throat.

"So, Spaulding . . ."

"Yes, Mr. Best?" A spray of mischief in her eyes.

"Where are you going?"

"Where are *you* going?" When I told her I was off to see a client in Westchester she asked if she could come. "I don't have to be anywhere and I really don't want to hang around my mom's apartment."

The late spring rain veiled the sidewalks, the store windows, the buildings, turning them into a shifting wash of slate gray. The windshield wipers beat a rough cadence. I needed to get myself in the right state of mind to tell the client what was going on with his wife and didn't want to be stressed. Equanimity was my stock in trade, the quality my clients expected. This girl was distracting.

"Where does your mother live?"

"Can't I go to Westchester with you?"

Unlike the moment when Spaulding appeared at my office door, when I could have said I was too busy to talk, now that she was seated next to me in an air-conditioned town car hydroplaning uptown in a downpour, asking her to leave felt cloddish. What harm could come from a ride to the country? At a red light, a man and a woman huddled under a large black umbrella swam in front of us. It was a monsoon out there. I couldn't drop Spaulding off on a corner. She settled into the seat. The light turned green.

"I'll be good," she said.

Our passage through a puddle at the intersection of 72nd and 3rd sent a sheet of water sailing into the air like a celebration. I took out a folder containing Dirk Trevelyan's last will and testament, flipped to the paragraphs pertaining to his current wife, and began to make notes. Spaulding produced a

Moleskine notebook and a pen from her purse, glanced at me, and started to draw.

As we rode north on the FDR Drive, Spaulding looked up and asked, "What do you think of my father?" The kind of question that can only lead to a bland answer. Ed Simonson could be tough, profane, avuncular, frightening, and solicitous, occasionally within seconds. But delving into any of these complexities with his daughter would serve no purpose.

"He's a terrific lawyer," I said. "We don't socialize, but I like him."

She turned her attention back to her notebook, scratched a new line. My unwillingness to engage on this subject did not seem to bother her. "He'd like me to follow in his footsteps."

"That's what my father wanted. He was an attorney, too."

"A big shot Manhattan lawyer?"

"Andy Warhol did his portrait."

"Get out! Did you get along?"

It had been a long time since I had spoken to anyone about my father. Maybe I needed to be distracted from health worries, or from trepidation about my assignment. Whatever it was I didn't shut the conversation down.

"My father left my mother when I was ten. He wasn't a traditional parent, the kind who took a child to ball games or the movies. He wasn't a traditional lawyer either. Back in the eighties if you were the kind of artist or designer successful enough to be allowed in the VIP room of a trendy nightclub and forward thinking enough to have a will, chances are Philip Best wrote it. He was a regular in the social columns, went to all the big art openings, the best parties. If it was the kind of thing you couldn't take a kid to, he loved it."

Joseph eased the car over the Willis Avenue Bridge. Spaulding looked at me, waiting. It was hard to know whether it was the open way she listened or my repressed need to talk about this, but I plowed on.

"His life was fabulous until this famous artist he worked with died. My father was the guy's executor. The paintings in the estate were worth millions and the heirs accused him of shady dealing. It turned into a big mess, there were lawsuits and he nearly got disbarred."

Spaulding closed her notebook and touched my sleeve. "Oh god, that's awful."

"Then he introduced me to Tim."

"Your dad was gay?"

"If you're asking me if Tim was a woman, the answer is no."

"Poor mom."

"She would definitely have agreed with you. I remember asking if I was supposed to call Tim 'Uncle Tim' but my father said, no, I could just call him Tim. He had zero idea I was being sarcastic."

"How often did you see him?"

"The court mandated Wednesdays and alternate weekends and that's what he did . . . I shouldn't be telling you this." And yet. It's these kinds of exchanges that are the currency of further intimacy and against my better judgment that is what I was after. "He and Tim had this exquisitely restored Queen Anne house on three acres in Bucks County and I'd spend those Saturdays and Sundays in the country with the two of them. All the physical affection he had denied my mother and me was heaped on Tim. They would hold hands, or my father would put his arm around Tim's waist when they walked in their garden. He hung on to Tim as if were he to let go the poor guy would blow away like pixie dust. He basically ignored me and when I was about sixteen the visits just fell off and I'd see him a couple of times a year."

"What about now?"

"He's dead."

Talk of death quiets the living and Spaulding didn't press on. She didn't ask how he died or where he was buried or if I missed him, just continued sketching in her notebook. I returned to my papers. We floated past Yankee Stadium, a pallid smudge on the gray horizon, and angled to the Cross County Parkway, then north on the Hutchinson River Parkway, a haze of sodden flora. Past the deserted Saxon Woods Golf Course the rain abated. For twenty minutes I concentrated on how exactly ownership of a London apartment my client co-owned with his wife could be shifted entirely to him until I sensed Spaulding's eyes on me. I looked over at her and saw that she was slanting her notebook in my direction. On the page was an exquisitely crafted pen and ink drawing of my profile, eyes down and intent on my client's travails.

"This is good."

"I took drawing classes when I was a kid. You can give this to your girlfriend."

"I don't have one."

There was nothing meant by this, it was a simple statement, a fact. But for some reason it was followed by a slightly awkward silence.

"Well, then. Never mind." With her phone she snapped a picture of the portrait. Then she asked for my phone number and programmed it into her device so she could send it to me.

"Hey, what should I call you? Mr. Best? Jeremy? Jinx Bell?"

"You can call me Mr. Best."

Ordinarily, I didn't adhere to that kind of formality, but Spaulding was a perfectly designed temptation. "Mr. Best" was a border fence. She would stay on her side, I on mine.

"Really? We're going to be all BBC costume drama?"

"Indeed."

"Does that mean you have to call me Miss Simonson?"

"Or Lady Presumptuous."

"Oh, Mr. Best," she said in a flawless British accent. "Your reserve is absurd!"

"Quite," I replied, and back and forth we went in clipped cadence until the joke was exhausted.

A munificent sun illuminated the vast acreage of Dirk Trevelyan's property, its rolling lawns a vibrant green that seemed to glow in the storm's aftermath. It was the kind of vista that made one wonder if nature actually favored the rich. A stolid-looking middle-aged woman with cropped straw-colored hair and wearing a maid's uniform opened the door to the grand modernist steel and glass edifice. I introduced myself and she beckoned me inside. Spaulding was in the car with strict instructions to stay with Joseph.

The floor-to-ceiling windows overlooked the patio and beyond that an ovoid swimming pool into which a five-foot artificial waterfall splashed from a raised Jacuzzi that appeared hewn from stone. Topiary in the shapes of animals and several large-scale abstract sculptures dotted the immense back lawn. Old-growth trees cast pools of soft shadow. The sleek room had a desk with two computer monitors, one of which displayed a financial news site, the other lists of securities, and the walls were hung with photographs of Trevelyan with two presidents, several prime ministers, the mayor of New York, a former pope, and the hockey player Wayne Gretzky who, like my client, was Canadian. Behind the chair in which I sat there was a small Picasso. Whether it was real or the handiwork of the second Mrs. Trevelyan was impossible to know without calling in an authentication expert.

Dirk Trevelyan was in his seventies and had taken every available opportunity to arrest nature's pitiless course. A facelift, whitened teeth, and a high-quality series of dyed hair transplants were the immediately noticeable renovations. Seated in his ergonomic desk chair, he regarded me with the concentration of a superannuated praying mantis. It was not difficult to imagine him springing forward and devouring my head.

Another maid, this one considerably more attractive, entered bearing two tall glasses of lemonade on a silver tray. When she departed, he said, "It's not that I don't want to take care of my second wife, but Marianne, my first wife, is the mother of my four children and I want to be more generous than I was in the will, you see." Trevelyan's voice was a smooth purr. "The second Mrs. Trevelyan and I, we've only been married for five years and unfortunately, well, I rewrote the will when I was in a different frame of mind than I am today." I nodded sympathetically. Dirk Trevelyan was not our only elderly—how he would blanch at *that* adjective—client whose mind was clouded with the erotic fog emitted by a younger second wife. "But I acted unwisely when I put several properties in the second Mrs. Trevelyan's name."

All of this was going to be moot as soon as he learned of his current spouse's transgression so there was no point in letting him go on. "Excuse me, Mr. Trevelyan," I said. "But there's something you need to be aware of before we go any further." His startled expression let it be known that he was not a man accustomed to being cut off mid-monologue. His dark eyes held me like pincers.

"And that would be?" The aggravated tone confirmed what his look had suggested.

Setting the lemonade on a coaster, I leaned forward and launched into the story, keeping my voice as free of inflection as possible. Trevelyan listened with no expression, his head tipped slightly back as if the unpleasant facts were exerting centrifugal force. When I finished he didn't say anything at first. In the backyard a gardener was trimming a hedge. Several crows launched from a tree. I glanced at the alleged Picasso, a figure with contorted limbs playing a stringed instrument, and again wondered at its provenance. When I looked back at Trevelyan the muscles in his face were slack and his shoulders visibly sagged. The breath seemed to have gone out of him. He sat perfectly still. In a tone equal parts incredulous, angry, and mortified, he rumbled, "The Kandinsky is a forgery?"

"That's what your wife told Mr. Simonson."

"And why did Simonson not come up here to inform me himself?"

"You would have to ask him." Again, I waited. Outside the window two of the crows, black wings beating, battled over the corpse of a small rodent. A financial news reporter mutely blathered on one of the computer monitors. I took another sip of lemonade, and relished the coolness in my parched throat. Trevelyan pressed the tips of his fingers to his temples.

It was hard to know if my solicitous expression changed when I looked out the window and saw Spaulding on the lawn with Joseph's cap tipped rakishly on her head. Near a giant bush trimmed to the shape of a giraffe, she proceeded to execute a series of ballet steps. Although her movements reflected the hazy memories of a girl who wore a tutu as a child, she wove them into a coherent if slightly awkward dance that transported her across my field of vision. Step, step, leap, plié, relevé, leap, spin, plié, leap, stumble slightly . . . recover. It was hard not to smile. She came to rest, arms loose at her sides, facing the house. Spaulding must have seen me seated with Trevelyan because she executed a bow worthy of a ballerina who had just performed *Swan Lake* before springing upright and cantering off.

"Your masters sent you into the lion's den, didn't they?" Trevelyan looked at me then followed my eyes out the window. To my relief, Spaulding remained out of sight. Addressing the internal politics of the firm, or Ed Simonson's reluctance to undertake an unpleasant job, or what his daughter was doing capering around the back lawn would not make the task at hand easier. "You've caught me a little off guard here, Mr. Best. I'm not exactly sure what to say, much less do."

I dutifully expressed my chagrin, then laid out the options

and described the ramifications of each, periodically glancing out the window to see if Spaulding was going to perform an encore. This took about ten minutes, during which he asked no questions. By the time I finished and drained the remainder of the lemonade, Spaulding had still not reappeared.

Trevelyan rose from his chair and said he could use a little afternoon sun. He could have used a morphine drip.

I wondered whether his lack of generosity with wife number two reflected an underlying psychological condition. And was her betrayal its florid result? All of his treasure did not establish the simple loyalty of the one who was supposed to be closest to him. Ah, but was he not culpable, too? Was he not responsible for his own fate? Wealth and wisdom were different continents.

We strolled toward the back of the immense property. Trevelyan stared straight ahead. He hadn't uttered a word since we had left the house. I hoped Spaulding would not materialize like some wood nymph, necessitating introductions. After what seemed like several minutes had passed, he turned to me and said, "I want to divorce her." This was not my territory, but if he wanted to talk about his marriage there was no point in stopping him. "And I suspect I can deduct the value of the painting from what I owe her in the prenup and that should make us about even." Turning toward the house he announced, "I built that pile of tin for my second wife. It was designed by one of the leading architects of Europe, a protégé of Louis Kahn. The apple orchard wasn't here. I trucked the trees down from New Hampshire because I knew she enjoyed painting them. I had never collected sculpture before, only paintings. These sculptures? They're all for her. I'm thirty years older and I'll predecease her, but I thought if I could craft an environment where she would be surrounded by beautiful things she loved . . ." He trailed off and gazed toward a gap in the clouds through which a glorious angel slide indifferently poured. Nature does not favor the rich. They are as capable of misery as the rest of us.

"Have you ever been married?"

Whether it was the heat of the day, the tart taste of the lemonade that recalled childhood, or the long pauses between everything Trevelyan said, the simple question set my mind reeling. I had never had a relationship with a woman last longer than a baseball season. When the firm hosted a dinner, finding a suitable female companion for the evening was never a problem but when it came to sustained relationships, I was a disaster; a master of the unreturned phone call, the forgotten birthday, the middle-distance stare.

And meanwhile, where had Spaulding gone?

"I've managed to avoid it," I said.

"What's the point of that? Marriage is grand!" A laugh escaped his lips, full-throated and brief, and he told me he was fortunate because at least he'd been in love. "Who cares what we leave behind? What matters is what happens while we're here. I used to be obsessed with the idea of legacy, but now? Do you know who Diogenes is?"

Although this seemed like a non sequitur, I nonetheless immediately declared my affiliation with the Sarah Lawrence classics department. I held up my left hand and showed off my class ring, an amethyst set in a gold band with my graduation year engraved on it.

"An abiding keepsake, Mr. Best. Lovely. This is why Diogenes, a man who lived in a giant pot, was the most sublime of the Attic philosophers. When Alexander the Great asked him what gift he would like to receive . . ." Here, Trevelyan looked away, as if searching for something eternal beyond the topiary.

"Diogenes told him to just stop blocking the sun."

"Thank you, Mr. Best. Yes! Mind you, he was living in a pot. I'm more of a romantic."

"But you'd be fine in a pot with someone you loved and could trust."

Trevelyan clapped me on the back as if I had passed a test. We discussed in further detail how the will would be reconfigured and he coolly instructed me to draw up the necessary amendments. The movement in my peripheral vision was only the murder of crows.

He told me he'd like the original Kandinsky back and I informed him the firm knew how to deal with these matters. A man with no return address would talk to the second Mrs. Trevelyan, glean the details of the transaction, and, if Trevelyan was willing, pay off his soon-to-be-ex-wife's debt in order to retrieve the painting. Yes, these guys exist and some of them work for top law firms. No one's arm gets broken but order is restored. His eyes sparked when he heard this. He'd write the check.

Saying goodbye in front of the house a few minutes later, he assured me that I had a dazzling future. "It was gutless of Simonson to send you to do his dirty work. You'd think the thousand-dollar-an-hour guy would have the balls to do it himself."

There was nothing to be gained by agreeing so I offered what I hoped was an enigmatic expression. Was Spaulding going to perform a curtain call? I glanced nervously around waiting for her to spring from behind a shrub.

Trevelyan said that if there was ever a favor he could do, *any* kind of favor, I should not hesitate to ask.

"Take the jet to Bermuda for the weekend sort of thing."

"I could never do that."

"You're a gentleman, Mr. Best. Don't let it stop you. Be bold!"

Briefly I considered discussing the establishment of the Best Foundation but as it only existed in my mind's eye could not steel myself for The Ask. Being bold was a challenge for me.

Trevelyan clapped me on the back again, wheeled, and strode back into his house, a man with things to do. As we drove off the property I asked Joseph if he had any idea where Spaulding was.

In his iced tea voice he told me she had asked to be taken to the train station. The peaked cap was back on his head. "It's hard to say no to that girl."

On the Major Deegan Expressway headed south toward Manhattan, as I scrolled through a series of work-related emails, my mind kept returning to Spaulding. The last person I had dated was a modern dancer named Cree whom I met at a retirement party for one of the partners where she was working as a server. We went out several times, which led to forgettable fellatio followed by desultory cunnilingus during which, to keep from getting bored, I used the tip of my tongue to spell out the third article of the New York State Tax Code. Our pillow talk consisted of Cree telling me she wanted to try online dating.

Spaulding, on the other hand . . . why was I even thinking about her? Perhaps it was because she embodied so much of what was missing in my life. Audacity, enthusiasm, a brio that would be addictive if . . . if . . . if . . . If what? If I were to let something develop? This train had to be stopped. I pulled out Trevelyan's will and began to dictate amendments into a pocket recorder but my attention glided as if on casters from my client's miscalculations to my own.

The house of regret has many rooms. Sometimes, there is an awareness that a wrong decision was made, but it's not that big a deal and life continues, as it would have had another option been pursued. Then there are massive regrets: the kind where one thinks, If I hadn't made that choice, life would be completely different (read, significantly better). Isabel represented the second kind, a maw, a Grand Canyon, a black hole of regret. The Australian wife of my graduate school advisor, she was an anthropologist and I made the mistake of falling in love with her. She was around my age, at least ten years her husband's junior. Tall and slim with long chestnut hair tied back with a strip of leather, she had lovely hands that she used to fabricate her own jewelry and the silver earrings she made were set off by her burnished skin. She rode horses, had an easy laugh, and could drink whiskey like one of the Pogues. Presumably, these were among the things that had attracted her spouse, an Irish poet whose fondness for cannabis was only exceeded by his lechery and who had enough charisma to be something of a rock star in the insular world of poetry. His name was Milo McLarty and rumors abounded about too-close relations with female students.

In graduate school I volunteered at an animal shelter and one Saturday afternoon Isabel stopped by to inquire about adopting a dog. There was a one year old she liked, a chow/German shepherd mix, and when I lent her a leash so she could take him for a walk, she asked me to join her. She had spent six months in India researching polygamy and was planning to do her thesis on the subject. This led to a discussion of our own love lives. She joked that her husband was in favor of polygamy but from the way she spoke I could see she wasn't really joking. It was near the end of my first year in the program and I'd been there long enough to know Milo's shenanigans were an open secret. Isabel and I became so engrossed with each other that no one kept track of the time and the shelter was closed when we got back. She didn't want to bring the dog home because Milo had not been informed one was on its way so I offered to bring him to my place for the night. This I did and in due course she and Milo adopted him. Or, more accurately, Isabel adopted him, Milo got angry, and when she told him she needed the company when he was out fucking his students, he smacked her in the face.

Isabel and the dog fled the house and found their way to my

doorstep. I offered her my bed but she insisted on sleeping on the couch. This arrangement lasted for about ten minutes, or until Isabel crawled in next to me, followed by the dog. Of this I am not proud. But I will tell you, with no Clintonian parsing of words, we did not have sex that night.

The next morning, after listening to multiple messages from Milo begging her forgiveness, discoursing on his desire to change his evil ways, and imploring her to come back, she returned home, leaving the dog with me. It was a cold peace with the unhappy couple and a few days later when she called to ask if I would meet her for drinks, I accepted. Many ounces of Johnnie Walker into the evening an indiscretion occurred, which is to say in my humble graduate student digs we copulated like a pair of deranged macaques. When Isabel and I drunkenly decided to inform Milo of this via a late night phone call, my continued presence in the graduate program became untenable.

One night, about a week later, Isabel showed up at my apartment. She brought a small gift, a sculpture of Ganesh, the Indian god with an elephant head. Our sex was epic, she said. We laugh a lot, she said. It was a spring night. The windows were open and I could smell the dogwood trees. Here was a beautiful, accomplished woman who was willing to throw her lot in with me. There was a research opportunity in Africa, did I want to go out there with her? I could teach English, write, travel.

"Ganesh is the remover of obstacles," she said.

To an analytical person, the condition of romantic love is not something one arrives at simply. It's easy to define it as nothing more than a series of chemical reactions taking place in the brain. And there was my unfortunate family history. But Isabel temporarily overwhelmed rational thought and I loved her in the messiest way. Here is the tragedy: The idea of making the kind of grand declaration that running off together would represent felt operatic to me. When the opportunity arrived, I couldn't do it.

Regret expands. It matures. It accrues strength and mass. It is a living organism.

Isabel got divorced and I enrolled in law school at Columbia. From time to time I would get postcards from polygamous hotbeds like Gabon and Burkina Faso and would write back with the considerably less compelling news of what I was doing. But our correspondence eventually petered out. As for the dog, I managed to place him with the family of a computer science professor.

SPAULDING
The Rubbish in My Attic

The teacher's name was Mr. Davenport and he spoke in a near whisper.

—Poetry, he gravely intoned, is the voice of the divine speaking through us.

Somewhere in middle age, he had retained enough youth in his features that it was easy to see the boy who had been picked on in the schoolyard. His hair was as disheveled as short hair could be. Myopic eyes peered through heavy glasses. His robin's-egg shirt was wrinkled and his jeans sagged in the ass, not in the hip-hop style but like a guy whose pants don't fit. The shoes he wore appeared to have been swiped from a nun. I liked him instantly.

—The best poems, he told us, are about feeling, emotion, what's in your heart. It doesn't mean check your intellect at the door, you need to know the difference between a trochee, a dactyl, and a spondee, but it does mean you need to be in touch with the rubbish in your attic. And don't be scared to write about it.

The rubbish in my attic terrified me, the pitchforks, pre-scriptions, rags, resentments, and breath mints, but maybe my attic was a gold mine.

The classroom was on the fourth floor of an old brick build-ing on the Barnard campus at 118th Street and Broadway. It was the third week of what had been a blistering June. The windows were open but no breeze circulated the tropical air. Sweat pooled at the base of my back. A suitcase rested next to me. Edward P had somehow performed a miracle and convinced Hurricane Katrina to let me spend the summer living with them. My mother was at the gym when I left so I taped a note to the refrigerator.

Dear Harlee, I'm off to spend a few weeks at your first husband's house in Connecticut. Please don't take this as a reflection on you or how I view our relationship. It's more about the cats. Why don't we try and have a regular dinner or something? Hugs, Spaulding

Was it insensitive to leave a note as opposed to waiting for Harlee to return from her workout and then having a long discussion about the need to balance my needs with her needs? Au contraire. It was totally sensitive because now she didn't have to pretend she wanted me to stay.

Mr. Davenport asked us to go around the room and tell everyone our names, what we hoped to accomplish in the workshop, and then say something true about ourselves that no one would suspect.

There were eight girls and two guys. Dylan was doughy with a mop of dark hair, a slightly bulbous nose, and lips that were always pursed when he wasn't asking questions in an effeminate voice. He would hold his hands in front of him and wave his fingers as if he were conducting an invisible orchestra. Despite his large frame, his Polo shirt hung over his pressed white pants like a dress.

—The thing about me no one would suspect, Dylan said, is that I was raised as a Jehovah's Witness.

A few of the girls stared at each other like they didn't see that coming. If you look at someone and imagine they're the opposite of what you think you have at least a fifty percent chance of being right.

Lucas went next. He was short with unkempt curly blond hair and a superior vibe. Red skinny jeans and a faded Sonic Youth tee shirt. In a voice that sounded like he'd been gargling with rocks for thirty years he informed us that despite a perfect score on the SATs he was going to school to become a luthier, a word he dropped as if we should have known it. (Thank you, dictionary app! Luthiers make stringed instruments.)

I only mention the guys because the girls were all more or less alike, brooding, neurotic lovers of mid-20th-century female poets, stayers-at-home, readers-of-books. My tribe.

When it was my turn to speak, here is what came out of my mouth:

—The thing about me that you might not suspect is that I spent a month in a locked ward at Payne-Whitney. Show of hands, anyone else?

They stared in mute wonder. Dylan leaned forward, interested.

—The problem with writing workshops, Mr. Davenport said, is that they can feel like group therapy sessions and since I'm a writing teacher and not a therapist, that's not something we want to encourage.

Then he moved on to the next student, probably a good idea.

I'm not sure what I was trying to accomplish by advertising that information. I thought about saying it then watched myself say it like I was both in the audience and onstage. I wondered if that sense of two selves was good or bad and what did it say about my mental health? But lots of successful poets were mad, bad, and dangerous to know (Lady Caroline Lamb re: Lord Byron), so maybe I was just trying to make everyone think I was more legit.

Alone at a café on Amsterdam Avenue, I sipped an iced coffee and texted Mr. Best.

Asked my workshop leader if he'd like you to talk to the class and he said yes. Can you?

* * *

According to Wikipedia so you know it's totally true, Death

Valley is the lowest place in America, Mt. McKinley the highest, and suburban Connecticut the dullest. All right, I made up that last part. Nothing had changed around here since the locals were burning witches. As white as it was when the Continental Congress convened in the late 18th century. Yes, material advances had been made, but it was still the place where the ruling class burped and scratched safe as a bottle of gin in a locked cupboard. This was where my father's second wife and their two sons spread out in a mock-Tudor house on a shady street in Stonehaven, a town founded back when the citizenry didn't have to hide the way they felt about Jews.

In the late afternoon the temperature was still prickly. The cab I took from the train station to my father's house was a converted squad car. The driver was a beefy guy from Poland. A rivulet of sweat sliced the side of his stubbled head. He said the local police liquidated half of their vehicles so they could get cooler ones. Then he told me Stonehaven was the safest place in the world.

Every time I visited I was amazed all over again by the almost throbbing lushness of the landscape. The city makes some people feel claustrophobic but that is nothing compared to the anxious sensation all of these trees evoked. Forbiddingly tall, their long, ropy arms were thick with leaves that squelched the light. Packed cheek by jowl, it was easy to imagine them whispering to each other, spreading rumors. There was a reason so many fairy tales took place in forests. Castles showed up a lot in those stories and Edward P's house might not have had crenellated battlements and a moat but it was a honker of a home.

In order to get my father to allow me to live there I had to promise to religiously take my meds. I intended to keep the promise but it was imperative that I begin to cut down. I hadn't written any poetry since the winter and it was necessary to throw off these chemical blankets that dulled every sensation.

Dr. Margaret and I discussed this at our previous session and she agreed to let me try. Today was my third day on a lower dose. Maybe that was why the trees seemed like they could animate and pursue me down the road.

And maybe that's why I began to obsess over the reason Mr. Best hadn't texted me back. Had I been too forward sending the text in the first place? Should I not have emailed him the pen and ink drawing I did in the car? Maybe he wrote his poems on an old manual typewriter and was at war with the 21st century. And dancing on his client's lawn might not have been the greatest idea either. What one person considers adorable another might see as bipolar. All of this was agitating me when the cab turned onto the street where my father's family lived.

On the side of the road was a shady-looking guy in his twenties dressed in worn clothes shuffling down the sidewalk in the opposite direction with his hands stuffed in the pockets of dirty jeans. He had a beard and scraggly blondish hair. Despite the heat of the late afternoon he wore a flannel shirt. It was hard to tell if he was homeless or a hippie. As we drove past, he looked right at me and I noticed that he was cute in the way of certain serial killers, the kind who when they get caught their neighbors say, he seemed so normal! This one had regular Nordic-type features like so many of the androids around here. Instead of looking away I kept staring and noticed his eyes had pinwheels spinning in them. Not pinwheels literally, but they were frantic, the type of eyes that let you know someone is nuts. That's how you tell. It's always the eyes. A guy can look like Brad Pitt but if he's got those eyes there's duct tape, rope, and a shovel nearby. He kept walking and after we had passed him I turned around and there was the house of my father's second, more perfect family.

I rang the bell and waited. With my suitcase next to me, I felt like some poor immigrant steaming toward Ellis Island a hundred years ago with a stomach-churning combination of fear and hope. A housekeeper I didn't recognize let me in. She was a stocky black lady with an island accent. She told me no one was home. I mentioned I was Edward P's daughter and she looked like I might be trying to pull a fast one on her. I inquired whether anyone had mentioned I was coming. Apparently, they had not. Well, I thought, we're off to a terrific start. When this lady, whose name was Delia, appeared reluctant to let me cross the threshold, I flashed my school ID and pointed out that her boss and I had identical last names. She took a hard look at the card, squinted at my face like a TSA agent, and compared it once again to the photograph on the card before grudgingly allowing me in.

Edward P and Katrina's room was at one end of the upstairs hall, my ten-year-old half-brother Cody was in the bedroom that overlooked the backyard, and my twelve-year-old half-bro Marshall was in the bedroom with a street view at the end of the hall opposite the adults' room. Beyond Marshall's bedroom the hallway made a right turn. At the end of that passage was my room. It was above the kitchen door and faced the free-standing garage.

My phone vibrated. A text! It was . . . Harlee.
Good luck!
Succinct. Hard to blame her for that when I had bounced without warning. Beneath my window a car door slammed. I began to unpack.

—So they're making you stay in the maid's room?

Marshall stood in the doorway and watched me put my clothes away.

—Yeah, it looks that way.

It had been nearly a year since I'd seen him and he'd grown a couple of inches but was still shorter than me. He had spaniel eyes set in a pale, sensitive face and long brown hair that fell over his forehead.

—Our maid doesn't live here, he said.

—That's a good thing since apparently I'm in her room.

—I'll trade rooms if you want, he said. I don't want to be so close to my parents.

—That's two of us.

In the backyard I could see Cody playing some kind of war game with a friend. He was wearing a Knicks jersey that hung to his knees. The boys were running around with toy rifles shooting each other. Cody was the more physical of the two siblings, the one who jumped around a lot and broke things. Marshall was ethereal, the kind of kid whose delicate quiet held a promise of something interesting occurring later.

—What happened last Christmas? You were supposed to come stay with us.

He got right to it, didn't he? Still at the age where he wasn't thinking ahead in the conversation, or wondering if a question was okay to even ask.

—Yeah, well, it's like this, Marshall. There were a few problems that had to get taken care of, so I went someplace and took care of them.

—What kind of problems?

—They thought I was crazy.

—Are you?

—Depends what you mean by crazy.

He looked thoughtful, like he was formulating a definition in his head of what it meant to be insane. The jagged pieces appeared to be coming together. The evidence in front of him had to be puzzling. How did he view me, this troubled interloper, this trespasser in his private space?

—And now you're good?

—Sometimes I bark at the moon.

He thought about probing further but decided against it. Instead he wandered into the room and flopped on the bed.

—Do you have any weed? he said.

—I'll pretend I didn't hear that.

—I've never actually smoked it.

—Me neither.

—You're lying.

—You caught me, dude. You're better off knowing that people lie and life sucks and figuring out how to deal with that reality.

He nodded his head like he was actually considering what he'd just been told. That was an appealing quality. He wanted to *know*. Marshall looked at me like I had answers. I didn't want to disappoint although that was where my main talent seemed to lie.

—My parents let me plant a garden. Want to see?

Beyond the slate patio with its perfect furniture and gleaming grill was an immaculately tended lawn ringed by white birch trees. Marshall led me across the grass and behind the garage. In this place that couldn't be seen from the house, he had turned over the nearly black earth and planted flowers. Already two months into the growing season, the plot was a rowdy palette of floral mayhem. There didn't seem to be any discernible pattern but it was pure beauty. Flowers were easier for me to embrace than trees.

—That's marsh marigold, he said, pointing. That's blue phlox and that one's New England aster.

—Marshall, I gushed, this is freaking amazing.

He walked to the side of the garage that bordered the neighbor's property and beckoned me to follow. A slatted wood fence separated the two yards and there was about three feet separating the garage and the fence. He was standing next to two marijuana plants.

—Know what this is?

Before I could answer, a woman's voice called his name. His shoulders drooped.

—My nemesis, he said. To the voice, he called, We're out here!

Hurricane Katrina was standing in the middle of the yard

wearing a tight tennis dress. Edward P's second wife was forty-two. Slender and athletic, her perfectly dyed honey blondness was gathered into a tight ponytail that allowed her to show off gold hoop earrings with diamond accents. She was attractive in that *Vanity Fair* way common on Madison Avenue and spring-wound, like if someone pressed a hidden button she'd shoot thirty feet in the air.

—Spaulding! she said. How are we doing?

—We're doing fine.

—Welcome to Stonehaven. We're glad you're here.

Edward P met Katrina when she sold him the Stamford condo he moved into after he left us. Six months later she was living in it with him, her selling skills not limited to realty. She has that instant smile salespeople have, the kind that turns on with a switch. It's a little disconcerting. My mother and I were in a fancy boutique one time and the saleslady saw me as a street urchin, you know, not in an adorable way but like I was going to steal a brooch, until she realized who I was with, then she was all super-smiley and can I help you? That's Katrina's skill. She could probably turn it on at her own mother's funeral since the smile seemed unconnected to whatever she was actually feeling.

Katrina asked me how I liked my room and when I told her I was just happy there were no cats in it she looked at me like I had said something strange then let me know I should feel free to decorate in whatever way pleased me but not to paint the walls. She told Marshall the two of them had to leave for an appointment in a few minutes and in the meantime he should wait for her in the kitchen.

—I have to go see my psychiatrist, he announced with more brio than you would think that particular information warranted.

This proclamation blindsided Katrina and after he departed she paused, as if to decide whether it required further elaboration or clarification on her part. Concluding it did not, she said,

—We're certainly glad you're here.

—I am, too.

—Now that you're living with us, Spaulding, it's important to remember we have a few rules.

This was imparted with a short laugh, an attempt to suggest bonhomie that only heightened the nervousness she projected. She was talking in a loud voice. Hard to tell if I made her nervous or she wanted the neighbors to hear how she was laying down the law with her wayward invader.

—We'd like you home by eleven o'clock each night. You'll be expected to keep your room clean and make your bed every day. And no drugs or alcohol.

—What about my meds, Katrina. Are you okay with those?

That came out with more bite than I'd intended and Katrina's smile flaked a little.

—We want you to have a restful time while you're staying with us.

—*Restful?* It was difficult not to bridle at the word but if this woman talked to me like I was a mental patient, you couldn't blame her. The rules won't be a problem, I said. Then she left to dominate Marshall.

It was sadly predictable that Hurricane Katrina was never particularly glad to see me when I was growing up. Who wanted to be reminded of someone else's past when it contained problems that weren't over, which is what another person's kids represent. Today she was making an effort, probably because of what had happened over Christmas.

After putting my stuff away, I placed my iPod on the dock and cued up Joy Division. Then I lay on the bed, stared at the ceiling, and considered ways I might worm myself into Mr. Best's life. While not a raving beauty by any means, boys found me attractive and I got hit on with some regularity. But my exchange with the perfect Katrina made me feel lumpy and unformed. Some people have the power to make you feel crappy about yourself. It's fine when you see them in magazines or on the Internet. It's harder when they're across from you at the breakfast table.

Mr. Best had the opposite quality. When he smiled it made me picture a cabinet with a healing light inside. The cabinet opened just a crack and troubles vanished in the radiant glow. When it closed you lived for the moment it swung open again. Did he think I was attractive or did he consider himself too old for me? Why did I make that joke about "halfway to dead" when he told me his age? I kept thinking about Mr. Best, if I'd done anything to intrigue him, whether I was flickering in his consciousness, if he even gave me a momentary thought, and as I began to absently massage my breasts it occurred to me that on my first evening in Stonehaven I should probably wait until everyone had gone to bed before masturbating. It had been forever since I had touched myself, and it was disorienting to be contemplating it now. Before the incident I would think about sex a lot. The absence of desire was not something you noticed but when it returned your thoughts converged like filings on all the magnetic places. Were the effects of the meds starting to dissipate?

In the bathroom down the hall I threw cold water on my face. The mirror was a comfort because, instead of reflecting back the scaly visage of a hideous ogre, I saw a relatively pretty nineteen-year-old girl whose false smile could pass for real in low light. Yet Mr. Best didn't seem the slightest bit interested. He still hadn't responded to the text, which didn't really surprise me. Maybe I'd send him a book, or some of my poems with a note asking him to tell me what he thought. I could send him the book first, to soften him up. It's not good to ask people for stuff right away.

The glimmering landscape faded and Edward P arrived home. He appeared in my room with a bottle of beer in his hand and welcomed me to Connecticut, then asked me to join him in the driveway.

—Just got it today, Edward P said. What do you think?

—It's cool, I said since that's what he wanted to hear.

The gleaming red Tesla glowed prosperously in the outdoor lights. Cody sat in the driver's seat, a maniacal glint in his eye, hands gripping the steering wheel, wrenching it side to side. Marshall stood next to Edward P and me in front of the car, regarding his brother as if he were a chimp in a cage. Moths flitted around us in the warm evening.

—Marshall, our father said, don't let me catch you driving this thing.

—Why would I want to?

Edward P looked at him curiously. He didn't quite know what to make of Marshall. Cody's uncomplicated aggression was more understandable to him.

—And Spaulding, that goes double for you.

—Can you teach me how to drive?

—Sure, he said, with no enthusiasm. Are you sure you're ready?

—What's that supposed to mean?

Edward P looked at me uneasily. He didn't want to get into it but I could tell he was wondering if I was stable enough to get behind the wheel of a car. I'm fine! I wanted to yell, to pound on his chest. That whole thing last Christmas was a great big holiday-wrapped mistake! Dr. Margaret told me that the only way I could ever convince anyone would be with behavior, not words. Hurricane Katrina appeared at the kitchen door and announced that dinner was ready. Edward P told Cody to get out of the car.

—One more minute, Cody said.

—Get your little butt out of there now, Edward P commanded.

Cody dejectedly followed the order. After slamming the door he spotted a moth that had landed on the hood of the car and promptly crushed it.

—Goddammit, Cody! Can we wait a day before we screw up the paint job?

Edward P took out a handkerchief and wiped up the remains of the insect as my chastened little brother slinked toward the house.

—Sucks to be a moth, Marshall said.

By the time we sat at the table the incident was forgotten and the usual awkwardness returned. Katrina had made crab salad and turkey burgers that we ate quietly while she and Edward P talked about an upcoming reunion of his college sailing team that they planned to attend as a family.

—You're welcome to come, too, Spall, my father said.

—We'd love it if you came, Hurricane Katrina said.

—Maybe I will, I said, because I thought that's what normal sounded like.

—I hate sailing, Marshall said.

—That's enough, Marshall, my father said.

I made a point of clearing the table and helping with the dishes without being asked. Marshall jumped up to assist.

—They always make me go, he said when the two of us were in the kitchen. And I just want to leap off the boat.

We finished cleaning up and Katrina ordered the boys to take showers. The kitchen was large and airy with an island in the middle and a breakfast area that looked over the backyard. Katrina sat in a bar chair at the island and tried to talk to me which was nice but we didn't have a lot in common. Her life revolved around looking after the boys, playing tennis, and selling houses. She told me she wasn't crazy about sailing either but did it because you have to do things together when you're married. When Marshall and Cody reappeared in their pajamas Katrina asked me to tell her if I needed anything then went upstairs. My brothers and I were in the den watching some movie with aliens and robots—they watched, I coped—when the text arrived.

Dealing with forged Kandinsky. Can't make plans.

Even though he dodged my bullet, the return text was a major mood elevator. My mother had taught me about painting and as my brothers continued to stare at the plasma screen in the den I rifled my brain for something clever to say about Kandinsky but all I could come up with was,

He's no Kokoschka, though he has fans.

At least it rhymed. I immediately texted back hoping Mr. Best would notice we had just collaborated on a quatrain. And got no response. But that was fine. Maybe he wouldn't commit to coming to the class, but texting allowed me to believe there was some kind of connection.

The sight of a giant robot trying to strangle a dinosaur transfixed Marshall and Cody but my thoughts kept skipping back to Mr. Best. It was impossible to not think about him. He was charming the way a poet should be, not in some tacky self-loving rap star way but like someone who drinks ouzo and smokes unfiltered cigarettes and publishes their work in literary journals under a pseudonym is charming, and super talented. (Not just my opinion either since the editors of *The Paris Review* agreed.) And for a guy who was formal and kind of stuffy, he was willing to share personal details like that story about his father. I thought it was a little peculiar that he asked me to call him Mr. Best but there weren't a lot of people in my life I had any desire to talk to and if that was the price I was happy to pay it.

When the movie ended Marshall and Cody scampered off to their rooms and I returned to mine. It felt like a monk's cell. There was a narrow bed, a chest of drawers, a desk, and a chair. I had brought *Middlemarch* but didn't feel like reading because Mr. Best . . . because Mr. Best what? Invaded my thoughts? Loomed in my vision? Hovered over my bed? Yes, all of those phrases. It was after ten o'clock, what was he doing? Composing a poem? Eating dinner? What did his apartment look like? What kind of neighborhood did he live in? What kind of food did he eat? How did he take his coffee? When did he start writing poetry? He said he didn't have a girlfriend but maybe he met someone in a bar earlier tonight and now they were having sex. Maybe he was alone in his apartment. Did he know girls who did booty calls? Would he make a booty call later? The questions floated to the surface like bubbles from a diver's tank as I pictured him in every permutation of each increasingly sex-crazed scenario. Mr. Best with one girl, Mr. Best with two girls, Mr. Best with a guy. Gay . . . That hadn't even occurred to me.

To slow my mind, I concentrated on the whiteness of the walls. They were the white of the arctic, of endlessness. Pictures, artwork, something was going to have to get slapped up there. Just nothing that would set me off. The pen and ink drawing of Mr. Best would look good but might be hard to explain to Edward P.

I lay down on the bed, closed my eyes. I felt old for a teenage crush. These sensations would have to be reined in. Sensations? What was going on? It hit me that whatever silly infatuation I felt for Mr. Best was strong enough to penetrate my weakening chemical armor. Numbness was a fort. Something to retreat to, a place to feel safe by feeling nothing. It was a place without risk and bother, a trial run for a nullity I yearned to escape. The love I felt for Mr. Best would be my means.

I dug my fingernails into my palms.

Outside / my win- / dow dy- / ing crick- / ets cry.

JEREMY
Another Facet of the Dreamer

E verything good?" Dr. Tapper asked. A kind man with a full head of side-parted white hair, he was fleshy, full but not fat. Dr. Tapper always looked like he had just consumed a delicious meal. I had left work early and gone to his office at Columbia Presbyterian Hospital on York Avenue, where Andy Warhol had died unexpectedly. After several days the swelling in my groin had not receded.

"Excellent," I said, as if there was any other answer. How else could I be? The last time medical drama intruded into my life was when I was stricken by mononucleosis in college. Getting mono was like owning a copy of *Nevermind*. At one time or another everyone had it. After three weeks in bed I was fine. Since then, nothing. I exercised, didn't smoke, drank moderately, and never had sex without a condom, so no pesky microbes could have been lurking in my system waiting to explode into something embarrassing or fatal. Seated on the examination table with my boxers around my ankles and Dr. Tapper phlegmatically probing the area immediately to the left of my flaccid penis I was a picture of apple-cheeked health.

Perhaps because I was naked my thoughts turned to Spaulding. That morning she had stopped by my office to bring me coffee and the welcome news that she would be interning at the firm. She was wearing cream linen pants and a faded lavender blouse. Her hair was loose and when she leaned over the desk to set the coffee down I noticed an almond-colored birthmark on the left side of her neck.

"My class is meeting this afternoon. Will you come talk?"

I told her that today wasn't going to work but I would try to get there soon. My gaze seemed to unsettle her slightly. It occurred to me for the first time that perhaps her confidence was something of an act. "Pending my poetry schedule, poets' lives being the most hectic."

One of her front teeth was slightly crooked and when she opened her mouth to laugh I noticed an orthodontist had fitted her with an expander. This imperfection along with the tortoiseshell eyeglasses compounded her owlish allure.

"Can I ask you one more question?" Not waiting for a response, she continued, "What do you do when you're stuck, when you're trying to write and nothing . . . ?"

"Write emails. On your computer, your phone, whatever device you're partial to. It doesn't matter to whom. Just pretend there's nothing at stake, you're writing to a friend who's going to punch delete after they read it. Let the words hit the screen."

Spaulding nodded as if trying to decide whether I was putting her on. This was exactly my technique and I told her so.

"Who do you write to?"

"Friends, mostly, most of whom I haven't seen much lately. They've gotten married or they live in other cities."

"I'm going to try that. Is it all right if I send one to you?"

"Sure."

There was a brief lull in the conversation and then it looked as if Spaulding was trying to decide whether she'd overstayed her welcome. Without moving, she appeared to lean toward the door. Was she too young? Eloquent arguments can be made to the contrary but here's the simple answer: Probably. All right, that's an equivocation but she was still the boss's daughter, which felt even more reckless. I was seeing the doctor later and who knew what he was going to tell me? I thought about that comical ballet she had performed on Dirk Trevelyan's lawn, the vitality that flames in youth.

"That was quite a performance you gave yesterday."

"I wanted to thank you for the ride but I couldn't interrupt the meeting."

"Please don't do anything like that again."

"Totally. Bad doggie, no biscuit."

I shrugged and rolled my eyes and motioned for her to sit. Smiling apprehensively, she sat on the couch and asked what I wanted to discuss. "Art, poetry, the usual stuff lawyers gas about," I said. We talked about the writing class she was taking and I told her I'd be willing to read whatever she wanted to show me. This prospect both surprised and excited her. It wasn't so much a charitable impulse as a way to generate interaction that would not be overtly suspicious. Evidently, I was a little more taken with her than was wise but what risk was there in looking at poems?

Reality intruded when Reetika needed Spaulding to do an errand. Before departing she took a postcard out of her pocket and laid it on my desk. On it she had written *For Mr. Best Lawyer/Poet/Art Guy*. It was a reproduction of *Composition VII* by Wassily Kandinsky. A golden move and astonishing given her age. She glided out of the office without looking back.

Dr. Tapper stared at my scrotum as if it held the answer to the riddle of time. The impassivity displayed when he squeezed my testicles suggested what he held in his hand were radishes and our encounter taking place in the produce aisle at Trader Joe's. It was difficult to banish the notion of some kind of tumor wreaking havoc down there. Testicular cancer would be ironic when the one poem Jinx Bell was known for was about a terrorist mastermind having the contents of his ball sack excised. Would mine suffer the same fate?

The room was bright, optimistic. It was easy to pretend

this exam was an item on a to-do list, something to take care of before picking up the dry cleaning and going home. Dr. Tapper, having exhausted the garden of earthly delights that was my groin, now spent an inordinate amount of time kneading the sides of my neck. Swollen lymph glands, he finally announced, let's have some tests shall we, nothing to worry about. Then this: Maybe we can get them done today, I'll make some calls.

It was Friday, traditionally a busy workday because clients often wanted to talk to me before the weekend. And the pressure on associates to be present at all times was intense. Partnerships were a Hobbesian competition and any unexplained absence gave the competition an advantage. *Where was Best at 4:00 in the afternoon yesterday? He wasn't in his office. Anyone see him?* In the eternal jockeying for position that goes on in any major law firm the associates knew who was present and who was unaccounted for. The decision to cancel my afternoon was not made lightly.

Scans were performed, blood and marrow drawn. The weekend crawled by. There was a party at Dirk Trevelyan's Sutton Place townhouse that I was happy to attend (and flattered to be invited to). Vociferous in his praise whenever he introduced me to other guests, several of whom were attractive women, Dirk showed me off, telling everyone they would be lucky to join my roster of clients. But I was alternately beset by thoughts of Spaulding and a burgeoning fear of death that revealed itself like sparks in an endless darkness, little pinpricks of terror, so I left the party after an hour.

On Sunday Pratt and I attended a Yankee game. The park setting, the clean lines of the field, the orderly manner in which the game proceeded, made me for minutes at a time stop imagining the stealthy anarchy raging inside me. It wasn't anything I could discuss with Pratt, delicate feelings an Achilles' heel in our profession. The Yankees walloped the Red Sox, a good sign. On the subway ride home I switched trains at 14th Street. In the station a jazz band played a ballad that sounded incongruously soul stirring in the crowded subterranean setting. I was going to give them fifty dollars but when I noticed the bass player was a woman I doubled it. I always doubled it for women. Was that some kind of reverse sexism? I didn't care. I was old school.

* * *

"Do you have any family, Jeremy?"

"An aunt and uncle, but we're not close. Why?"

It was Tuesday and I was back in Dr. Tapper's office. The test results were in.

"It usually helps to have family when you're facing this kind of thing."

Every horrifying possibility immediately lined up shoulder to shoulder for my frenzied inspection. With great effort I affected a placid exterior.

"What's going on?"

"You have a non-small cell lung carcinoma, which in plain English is lung cancer. Unfortunately, yours is stage four."

This news hit with the force of a falling building, a roar of crumbling drywall, bricks, and dust. Stage four? How was that possible? I had looked to the future with a certain amount of optimism because there were decades left. In a second, that naïve certainty evaporated. Terror ran a fingernail down my spine. Bile dripped in my gut. Tapper looked on with professional compassion.

"I've never smoked."

My second thought was that my most recent donation to the American Cancer Society should have been larger, as if that somehow might have made a difference. It's funny how, when humans are confronted with the implacability of science, we so often turn to superstition. Dr. Tapper seemed relieved there was no overt display of emotion. "Fifteen percent of everyone diagnosed with this is a nonsmoker." He sighed. "And you've got slow-growing metastases in the groin, liver, neck . . . all over." *All over.* A terrible choice of words in so many ways. "I'm sorry."

"Is there a stage five?"

"No, there isn't. Look, I want to be honest with you. The only course of treatment is extremely aggressive chemotherapy. There are side effects you need to be aware of. We can discuss them if you want to go that route."

"How much time would that buy me?"

"Hard to say, but you need to consider quality of life."

"There are no exceptions?"

"Sometimes there are outcomes for which there is no scientific explanation, and for that reason we don't like to make predictions. The statistics for your disease are . . . they're not great."

"What about spontaneous remission?"

"You work in trusts and estates, don't you? So you know anything can happen. I can recommend an oncologist."

I asked how long he thought I had without treatment.

"It's impossible to predict."

Although Tapper tried to look sympathetic, there was no good way to pass along this news. Did I want an oncologist? Needles in my veins carrying gallons of toxic chemicals that would sicken me and proceed to not work at which point the wasting away would begin in earnest and oblivion rush forth seemed like a terrible way to spend what could be my last summer. I didn't care. Save me! Whatever would run like a marauding army through my cells destroying everything in its wake sounded impossibly great. He told me to call after I had thought about it and to not worry if he took a day or two to return the call because:

"I'm going to Italy for two weeks."

Oh, I've thought about it in the time you've taken to tell me you're going to Italy! His words were innocent enough, they've been said before by many people. But they stuck in my craw like fish bones. *I* have cancer, but *you* are going to Italy. *You* will be drinking Nebbiolo. *I* will be . . . well, you know what I'll be doing. More than anything I wanted to be going to Italy. Where I would be going: Not Italy.

"I spent my junior year in college there." My voice sounded like it was coming from another room. Tapper prattled about Tuscany. It was impossible to listen. How could I be certain his diagnosis was correct? Before I allowed myself to drown in a sea of melancholy, I would get a second opinion. And I asked how soon I could meet the oncologist.

On York Avenue people swirled around me as if this were just another day, confident the sun would set and the moon would rise and they would return to their apartments and make dinner or order takeout, spend time with the family, make a phone call, send a text message, watch a movie, listen to music, play video games, read a magazine or a novel, make love or pleasure themselves, brush their teeth, wash their faces, go to bed, sleep untroubled or wrestle with vexations, then rise tired or rested, yearning or satisfied, and repeat, all as if nothing was wrong and convinced it was without end. Didn't they know the whole world was different now?

The hellish aura that enshrouded me was cleaved by the chirping of my phone. Reetika informed me that Dirk Trevelyan was eager to get an update on the Kandinsky situation and to sign his new will and that a Claude Vendler, nephew of the client that owned the Montauk house, had called about the disposition of his aunt's estate. Their lives were spectacularly irrelevant.

Going back to the office was not an option. Colleagues could gossip about my absence all they wanted. A man in my situation needs to believe he is immortal and if he finds himself in midtown Manhattan this belief might be strengthened by a long walk to Brooklyn. To know it was still physically possible, that I was not compromised, weakened, *dying*, that the six miles from Tapper's office to home were a simple stroll and would prove the planet had not spun off its axis.

I joined the throngs of office workers on the daily march. My brain, heart, liver, and lungs, my sight, hearing, sense of taste, and smell were all present and accounted for and my skin seemed to absorb every external stimulus and turn it into energy. Never had I felt healthier as I marched south. In the East Village I stopped at the Strand Bookstore. Here was my first thought upon entering this temple of literary culture: If Jeremy Best/Jinx Bell were to ever have a book of poetry published he would not live long enough to see it on a shelf in the Strand. It was the saddest thought ever to occur to anyone. But the sight of the shelves had its usual brightening effect and drew me to their musty bosom where I posed like Kirk Douglas in *Spartacus*, hands on hips, chin thrust forward, in front of the B's. There, between the collected works of Anna Akhmatova and *The War Poetry of Homer Brant*, was the place reserved for my work, the place where it would abide for eternity. It wasn't there yet but it would be. If I could finish the poems I was working on and get them published as a collection.

Before leaving I bought several books about cancer, cancer memoirs with titles like *Sexy Cancer* and *Cancer, Baby!*, and a book in which the author claimed to have cured himself of a horrible disease through ingesting a mountain of vitamin C.

As I approached the Brooklyn Bridge surrounded by oblivious pedestrians an email arrived from Spaulding. *Spaulding!* For some reason this struck like the appearance of the first evening star low in the desert sky.

SpauldingS1@gmail.com
JBest@TSSLAW.com

Dear Mr. Best,
Since you advised me to write emails if I felt stuck, I hope you don't mind if I send you this one.

Poetry is good to read when you're feeling lost or misunderstood or just effed up because the poets like you who are talented enough to publish what they write see the world in a way that is usually at least as twisted as the way I see it. This sent me to my copy of the Norton Anthology. With the list of poets in hand, I googled them one by one and printed out their portraits. My half-brother Marshall (he's 12) walked in and asked me what I was doing. When I told him, he wanted to know if he could help so I said sure, why don't you find some scissors and glue.

The two of us began cutting the poets' heads out one after another and then taping them in rows on the walls of my room. Marshall was working on a picture of Anne Sexton, moving the scissors like a pro.

—I like your shoes, he said. What kind are they?
—Ballet flats.
—Can I try them on?
Without a word, I took them off and handed them to Marshall, who removed the sneakers he was wearing and slipped into them. His smile was starlight.
—I wish I could wear these to school.
—Fly your freak flag, dude.
—I sneak into my mother's closet sometimes and try hers on. She has an awesome shoe collection.

Marshall kept the ballet flats on. The job took us four hours and by nine in the evening all of my walls were covered. There's an English wall and an American wall. There's a suicide section. There's a European wall. The printer in the house didn't have the capacity to render color so all of the faces are black and white and shades of gray.

Marshall was smoothing out some wrinkles on Emily Dickinson's face when Hurricane Katrina (his mother) materialized. The hallway was carpeted so we didn't hear her stealth approach. While she silently registered her shock at my interior decoration, Marshall slid the ballet slippers off.

—This is kind of surprising, Spaulding.

She ran her fingertips over W.H. Auden's nose, trying to determine how his photograph had been attached to the wall.

—You told me not to paint.

The advantage of having someone think you're unstable is that they don't want to provoke you. Katrina looked at me like I was a knot she could never unravel.

—It's totally cool, Marshall pronounced. I want to do my room like this.

—That isn't going to happen, Katrina informed him. Then she said it was bedtime and he needed to brush his teeth.

When my co-conspirator left he kicked up his back foot with a flourish his mother either did not notice or chose to ignore.

So that's life up here in Connecticut, not that you asked but I thought you might find it amusing. I've attached some pictures so you can see for yourself.

Any thoughts on when you might visit my class? I mentioned it to the teacher again and he's still into it.

Yours, Spaulding

P.S. I'm sending you a few poems. Can't wait to hear what you think!

Although it was somewhat discomfiting that Spaulding's missive had gone to my work email, I smiled for the first time in days. But to savor this welcome volley for even a moment was almost impossible. Spaulding, Spaulding, uncompleted poems, premature death. My thoughts were like a troupe of drunken acrobats, flipping and flailing. At home I tried to watch television, a ball game, a sitcom . . . I stared at the wall. I thought about my funeral and took a sleeping pill. From the sounds assaulting my apartment, it was clear my neighbor Bogdan had guests.

BOOM-THUNKA-THUNK, BOOM-THUNKA-THUNK.

The endless infernal bass loop vibrated in my bowels as I twisted the sheets in my king-sized bed. The bedroom was large and airy. There was a bureau with a clean surface and several bookshelves packed with sturdy hardbacks. The only decoration was a series of starkly framed black-and-white photographs of the World Trade Center under construction—steel skeletons rising toward the heavens, hard hats on beams floating thousands of feet above the earth—that I hung as a reminder of the ephemeral nature of things. This was a concept far easier to contemplate in the abstract.

Was I, in a few short months, going to be lying in a hospital bed surrounded by—by whom? No one. Or worse, strangers. Why had my personal life been such a disaster? When my mother died, we were barely speaking to each other, something that tormented me. My father had wanted some kind of relationship but his emotional needs were too complicated. There wasn't even an ex-wife I could lean on. Girlfriends had come and gone, some had wanted to get serious but I'd always acted as if there was plenty of time to make a choice. What an idiot I was.

The coolness of the air conditioning, instead of inducing relaxation, made me feel like I was already lying in the refrigerator of a funeral parlor.

And my colleagues? None of those friendships, if that's even what they were, felt like they would outlast our employment at the same firm. There was one friend from college that lived in the city, Margolis, a playwright, but we barely saw each other. What had my life become? Work, which was the immersion in the intimate details of other lives. Writing every day. And a casual social whirl with a series of people who could never penetrate the membrane that surrounded me.

I envisioned my organs closing like shutters in an empty house, unable to swallow, unable to see, hearing muted sounds in the distance until, finally, a faint murmur, someone's voice fading, fading, and then . . . and then? I stopped thinking about *that* as the inner seas pitched and heaved and my mind went reeling in the opposite direction, further and further back, to a summer rental in Montauk at the untamed eastern end of Long Island, and my first conscious memory. The day is beach bright and I am in a playpen in a room that opens onto a modest backyard. It is square-shaped with wooden slats and my small hands clutch the railing. I am calling out to my mother who is on the other side of the room folding laundry. She smiles at me. She wears capri pants and a fitted blouse, her hair in a bun. She is twenty-five years old. Her hands reach down and lift me up. In the air I am a conqueror! I am eternal! I will live!

BOOM-THUNKA-THUNK, BOOM-THUNKA-THUNK.

My feelings for my neighbor, murderous though they were, energized me. I got out of bed, collected myself, and, in a satisfying bit of psychological alchemy, logged in to my personal email account and channeled the rage I felt toward Bogdan into a measured response to Spaulding.

> *Dear Rhymester,*
> *Your brother sounds like a terrific character for a short story. And I love your poet room idea although please don't tell your father I said that. If your parents make you take the pictures down maybe it could be an installation at the Whitney Biennial. Have you ever been?*
>
> *You write well. Your prose is limber, you've got an eye for the mischievous detail, and you're funny, which never hurts.*

I don't even mind your non-use of quotation marks around dialogue. It worked for Joyce. Steal from the best, I say.

Keep writing emails. It's a great way to flush the plumbing before the clean water starts to run.

Thanks for the Kandinsky postcard. It's taped over my desk at home.

The etiquette for signing off in an email is always baffling and I spent a couple of moments trying to land on the one that would convey the combination of engagement and distance I was after. This meant *xo* was out. So, too, were *Best wishes*, *Always*, *Fondly*, *All best*, *Yours*, *Yours truly*, *Sincerely*, *Cheers*, *Ciao*, *Warm regards*, and, obviously, *Love*. But all I wanted to do was conclude an email. Could I not just say that I was done?

My decision:
Goodbye, JB
P.S. In the spirit of reciprocity, I've attached one of my poems.

It helped to write to Spaulding but my mind would not rest. Some draw on years of meditation practice to calm themselves in times of stress, others on prayer. I had a more personal technique to access the still center of the spinning world. During the year I spent in Italy, a film studies professor screened an obscure Italian movie from the 1960s called *Gianni and the Pope* about an old man from the provinces who travels to Rome in order to stand in St. Peter's Square and see the pontiff before he dies. But Gianni gets diverted to the demimonde of artists, dancers, musicians, whores, and hustlers and has an entirely different experience from the one he imagined.

I slid the DVD of the film into my laptop.

A prostitute named Lara escorts Gianni on a nocturnal journey through the sleeping city. He's infatuated with her and the sequence vibrates with a low-key sexual tension. Lara finds a stray kitten and sends the pliant Gianni to search for sustenance. When he returns with the bottle of milk he has miraculously located in the middle of the night, he sees her staring over the river, cradling the kitten. He approaches and places his hands next to her alabaster face but does not touch. He lowers his hands to her bare shoulders and rests them there. She kisses his cheek and together they turn to watch the river flow through the starry Roman night. Gianni falls asleep and Lara steals his wallet and runs away. When he wakes up he is bereft. Yet in those fleeting seconds when his heart is full of this wholly unexpected experience he is suffused with a profound sense of contentment and that's the moment that comes to mind when I remember the film. Not the disaster he awakens to but the moment of peace. Those fleeting seconds of utter quietude stilled my tempestuous thoughts (among them: Dr. Tapper was going to Italy but I wasn't?) and finally I slept.

My sleep was broken. I had the dream I dreamt the night before I met Spaulding. Again I was on the beach at Montauk attacked by the Minotaur and as before I fought back and beat the monster to death. But when I woke up this time the operative emotion was not guilt. It was rage. At the world. At myself.

There is a school of thought that says every character in a dream is another facet of the dreamer. The Minotaur dwelt at the center of a labyrinth where he was eventually slain by the hero, Theseus. Was I Theseus or the Minotaur? And if I was the Minotaur, was I trying to kill some part of me over and over?

Three mornings a week I rode the train into the city with my father. The train car was as quiet as Dr. Margaret's waiting room. Edward P was either working or buried in the *Wall Street Journal*. After Did you get a good night's sleep? and Are you taking your meds? we didn't talk much. At the office I would sort mail, go on caffeine runs for the attorneys and summer associates, and spend endless hours in the copy room sacrificing entire forests to bound volumes of briefs.

The other summer interns were all super-ambitious college kids so I mostly kept to myself, ate lunch alone, and whenever possible snuck away to read *Middlemarch*—Why couldn't Dorothea Brooke leave that horrible marriage? I know it was the 19th century, but still!—or scribble and revise poems. When I would walk past Mr. Best's office, I'd say hello the rare times the door was open and he'd wave when he saw me but I didn't go in and he didn't invite me. He seemed preoccupied with something and I wasn't going to ask.

In Connecticut Marshall was my sole distraction and ally since Cody was away at sports camp. He was in rehearsals for a local summer theater production of a play about global warming and when he was around I helped him learn his lines. Sometimes we'd work in his garden. Under the pounding sun, flowers were planted and weeds pulled. My fingernails were a mess and my neck got sunburned because I would forget to put sunscreen on, but the time outdoors with

Marshall made the trees seem less forbidding until finally I could sit in a chair by myself in the backyard and read and write like a person.

The poem Mr. Best sent me was . . . what can I say . . . intimidating? I printed a copy and carried it in my wallet. At the office, when I told him what I thought about it, he thanked me and nodded. I didn't want to be too forward. It was enough that I forced him to take me up to Westchester that rainy day, so after giving his contact information to Professor Davenport I decided to temporarily back off.

That weekend in Connecticut, I baked a white cake. All of us had dinner together on Sunday night and we ate my cake for dessert. Katrina only had one bite because she was about to start a cleanse and was convinced the sugar would aggravate her system but my effort was appreciated. To my surprise (I can admit when I'm a bitch), she was not the termagant my crazed boarding school imagination had turned her into. She made sure the refrigerator had stuff I liked (stinky cheese, edamame, ginger ale), took me to get a cut and color at her place with her guy, and was not remotely an ogre.

The lower doses seemed to be working. Lines, fragments, half-formed ideas poured out of me and filled notebooks. The workshop met just before the July Fourth weekend and I wanted to read. The story of getting locked up in a psych ward was oversharing and I needed to send a signal that while I might not be the most fun person, I wasn't mental either. To accomplish this I read a couple of new poems. One, about sailing with my brother Gully when a wildly flapping mainsail knocked me off the boat, was actually kind of goofy. Another was about being surrounded by walls covered with the faces of popes. Everyone was surprised to learn I wasn't Catholic but intrigued when I said the poem was about male privilege. And then there was "Addicted to Beauty."

Beauty in the Rue Morgue,
Beauty in the Cathedral
Beauty, She Wrote
The Simple Art of Beauty
Beauty on the Orient Express
Why are we addicted to Beauty?

The latter one got a gratifying response, particularly from the girls.

The classroom wasn't air-conditioned and we baked like croquettes. All of the windows were open and a fan that could barely be bothered to swivel lobbed dust motes lazily in our direction. Mr. Davenport was eviscerating a short story Lucas had written about a family vacation to Howe Caverns when Mr. Best strolled in and nodded deferentially to the class. This was as welcome as a sea breeze. We had been told there was going to be a special guest that day but Mr. Best and I hadn't exchanged more than a few Good mornings in the past week. He looked at me with that smile that takes you in and comforts but at the same time creates an invisible barrier. His summer suit was freshly pressed, his tasteful tie carefully knotted, shoes buffed. The entire presentation reflected a dignified cool to which the rest of us could only aspire.

Mr. Davenport concluded his demolition of Lucas then invited Mr. Best to preside from a chair next to his at the front of the room. When he settled in Professor Davenport announced:

—We are very honored to have a famous poet with us today. Mr. Best laughed when he heard that and said Hardly. *Hardly.* It was the perfect response.

—My name is Jeremy Best, he said. I publish under the name Jinx Bell.

The class nodded like this was the coolest thing they'd ever heard. A couple of them probably started to come up with pen names of their own. The professor wanted to talk about "The Valley of Akbar."

—What drew you to the subject matter?

—There was a time when a poet was publicly engaged in the life of his nation, Mr. Best said. When people paid attention, when poetry was relevant. By writing about subjects like terrorism, torture, militancy, militarism, and America's role in the post-9/11 world I'm trying to connect the art form to our time. Actually, that's bull. I just write about what interests me. I don't know that poets will ever have a public role again but for me poetry is something that must be read closely because the finest work demands a radical empathy. What do I mean by that? Because a poem is a distillation of what the poet thinks about a particular subject it requires the reader to engage with it in the deepest way possible and to locate the aspect of the poem that speaks to her in the deepest way. This takes a degree of awareness that some people aren't willing to commit to. That's modern life. There are probably apps that can help them. But if we can get people to read poetry at all it can have an effect on how they communicate, make them more conscious of what they think and say. That part's not bull.

Mr. Davenport nodded. The workshop nodded collectively. What else do aspiring artists want to hear but that their efforts have meaning?

—Look at Abraham Lincoln. He thought like a poet. Mr. Best stepped to the whiteboard at the front of the room and quickly wrote,

That from these honored dead we take
Increased devotion to that cause for which
They gave the last full measure of
Devotion.
That with determination we resolve
That these dead shall not have died in vain

That this nation under God will be
Born anew
And on this day we vow that government of the
People by the people for the people
Shall not perish from
The Earth.

He timed the words by clapping his hands and the rhythm in which he read them to us made them physically penetrate our bodies the way a good song will. The hushed classroom had become a secular church. No one thought about how hot it was or that no air was circulating. Mr. Davenport stared at Mr. Best. The kids stared at him. The words were Lincoln's but Mr. Best's rendering took wing and with him we were airborne.

—I don't know if anyone noticed, but I did a little rewriting. Lincoln's words are better, but I'm making it more consistently rhythmic. You see, he continued, it's not a poem but it scans like one and these are some of the most familiar words in all of American history. But if Lincoln really understood meter, he wouldn't have dropped the word "and" into "of the people by the people and for the people" since it ruins it. That extra word takes you out of the rhythm. See, "people—by the—people—for the—people" is perfect iambic pentameter with an enjambment that rolls into Shall Not Perish From The Earth. Do you know what enjambment is?

No one breathed. If Mr. Best was really rewriting President Lincoln the class didn't have the slightest problem with it.

—It's when the thought of a line of poetry doesn't end with the line but continues to the next line, all right? You don't need me to tell you that that's gorgeous, poetical language. Or look at the Second Inaugural.

Here Lucas piped up:

—With malice toward none, with charity for all, with firmness in the right as God gives us to see the right . . .

The frayed tee shirt he wore heightened the effect of the words. Lucas blushed but when he finished the class broke into applause and Mr. Best clapped the most enthusiastically of all. In that moment, Mr. Best looked more comfortable than I'd ever seen him. His face radiant with Lincoln's language, at the response to it in the classroom, at the pure pleasure that words could elicit. When he looked at me and grinned, I was done.

—President Lincoln is all well and good, Mr. Davenport said, but what about your own work. What are you working on now? Anything you'd care to share?

Mr. Best hesitated. The class leaned forward as if tugged by an invisible thread. It was easy to see how much everyone respected him. He hadn't been there more than twenty minutes and already the room was crowded with disciples. Everyone waited. The only sound was the quiet whirring of the balky fan.

—These are notes, he said. This isn't a poem, just shards of language that might coalesce into something. Or not.

Maybe I imagined it but I thought Mr. Best looked at me before he began to read.

—*Sylphlike sign from swirling stars. Nubile harbinger of exaltation. Sanguine tigress. Devilish herald of destruction. Dawn of my demise. You fueled my filaments with a concatenation of bad thoughts, bad behavior, and bad tidings. And a jiving jazz quartet.*

He paused for a moment and then looked at Mr. Davenport.

—I'm not exactly Abe Lincoln, he said. The class laughed. Everyone was wishing Mr. Best were the teacher.

—Fueled my filaments is excellent, Mr. Davenport remarked.

—Those are some lines I've been playing around with. It's like an artist's sketch. And then I'll refine it. I have no idea what "jiving jazz quartet" is doing there. It's an anachronism but I like the way the words flow.

Dylan asked what concatenation meant.

—It's a series of interdependent things or events, Mr. Best said. And you bring up a good point. Ten-dollar words. SAT words. Some people think they're pretentious but an unexpected word choice is a good way to pull the reader's attention in. They're fun to play with. And the people who think they're ostentatious can go fuck themselves.

When the laughter died down, Mr. Davenport asked if Mr. Best had one piece of advice for everyone in this room. Mr. Best thought a moment.

—Buddhists have a ceremony called Life Release, he said. They'll go down to a dock, buy a bucket of baitfish, and release them into the water. They do this to earn merit, to have good karma. Now picture a fish releasing a bucketful of Buddhists. That's what a good writer does. Avoids clichés. Perceives the familiar in new ways. Makes you see the little Buddhists swimming.

Mr. Best left before the class was over and we went back to critiquing student work. It was impossible to pay attention. That fragmentary poem . . . Sanguine tigress? I *loved* the phrase and only wished it was about me. A sanguine tigress was something to aspire to if you were a medicated minx. A sanguine tigress with talent enough to summon a bucketful of Buddhists.

When the workshop concluded, I approached Lucas and Dylan and asked if they wanted to go out drinking that night. Getting a buzz on would put a glow on the train ride back to Stonehaven. To my amazement, they were up for it. We headed for a bar in the East Village with Yoshi, this other girl from the class they hung out with. The guys had bogus IDs, so they were drinking beer, Yoshi got a Diet Coke, and I had orange juice. There was a vintage video game in the back and when Dylan and Lucas got up to play I asked Yoshi what the deal was with Lucas and her. They were just friends, she told me, Did I like him? He seems all right, I said. His poems are okay. You should get with him, she said. He likes you.

I'm horrible at small talk and wasn't sure how long I could keep it up. Meanwhile, Yoshi fiddled with her iPhone, texting, Tweeting, showing me a new app she was "totally in love with." I glanced toward where the guys were playing the video game. Lucas looked inviting in his skinny jeans, his tight tee shirt, and his black Vans. The lean muscles under his tee shirt (at least a size too small) twitched as he manipulated the joystick. His hair was light brown bordering on blond and had grown so long in front that he periodically flicked his head to keep it out of his green eyes. He reminded me of a guy from some nineties band. Although I wasn't convinced Lucas liked girls it was easy to picture having sex with him, but harder to figure out how to care about it since the only guy I could think about was Mr. Best.

Yoshi was working as an intern at an art gallery in SoHo and was keen to tell me about it. She laughed easily and her manner invited confidence. She'd been seeing some guy, an electronic musician, and there was a story about him trying to teach her how to run a music software program during one of his sets and her being too drunk to remember the cues because an hour before the performance she had put a tampon soaked with vodka in her vagina. But at the point of the conversation where I was supposed to share some personal information, I froze up. It wasn't like I could talk to her about this older lawyer guy I was obsessing about. She had just seen him in the classroom. Would she have thought it was wrong? Or gotten wet? Either way, I didn't want to know.

Girlfriends were never something I was good at. Or boyfriends. Human relations were vexing. There was a picture of me in a school yearbook where I'm seated at one end of a sofa looking at the camera. At the other end two of my classmates are making out, totally oblivious of me. When I write a memoir, it's the cover.

I finished half the orange juice and produced the flask I had taken from my father's house, unscrewed the cap, and topped off my drink then poured some in Yoshi's soda. She was impressed even though that wasn't the effect I was going for. Just because my mother was a recovering alcoholic didn't mean I couldn't enjoy a cocktail. To get drunk was the idea. After a few sips that started to happen. Yoshi talked about living with her mom over the summer because her parents were divorced and she didn't like the woman her dad had married. Here was more common ground and there was yet another gap in the conversation I could have filled with some kind of personal revelation. That's when Yoshi said,

—So who was that dude who came to the class today? Do you know him?

It was important that Yoshi not suspect I held any feelings one way or the other for Mr. Best, much less that I thought I was in love with him. It wasn't something anyone else needed to know. So I made a point of pausing for the briefest moment before I opened my mouth to make sure there was no animation in my face.

—He works at my dad's law firm.

—Are you two a thing?

—What? No! He's as old as something that's really old!

So much for the cool approach. Did my voice squeak? Yoshi's expression was unchanged so I probably didn't sound like a complete idiot.

—So? I'd totally fuck him.

—I hardly know the guy.

—Would you?

—No!

The boys finished the video game and returned to the table. We talked about bands, websites, and where we wanted to live after we graduated: Lucas/Brooklyn, Dylan/Brooklyn, Yoshi/Los Angeles, Spaulding/Doesn't Know.

—So much for avoiding clichés, I said

—You're implying Brooklyn's a cliché, Lucas said. That's kind of judgy.

—I don't know, Dylan said. If I can see the Buddhists swimming does it matter where I live?

—I can totally see the Buddhists swimming in Brooklyn, Lucas said.

While the conversation was happening about half the contents of the flask was consumed.

When Yoshi and Dylan went over to talk to this guy they knew who played drums in some band, I was alone at the table with Lucas. He'd had a few drinks, too.

—So, you think we should hook up? My friend has a loft in Williamsburg and I have the key. We can pretend it isn't Brooklyn if you don't want to be a cliché.

I laughed and told him I secretly liked Brooklyn but was saving myself for marriage. It was hard to tell if he knew I was joking and just didn't want to get with him. That's when Yoshi and Dylan returned to the table.

—Some rando was creeping on me, Yoshi said.

If I had to guess, I'd say she was imagining that. But here's the thing, you never know. It's so hard to figure out exactly what someone else has really experienced compared with what they think they've experienced. It's all so subjective. Maybe some rando had been creeping on Yoshi. I kind of doubted it, though.

There was a party on Ludlow Street with a deejay from Atlanta who was recording with Kanye, did I want to go? I said I had to walk my dog or he'd poop all over the house. The disadvantage of going off meds that flatten you out is that when your feelings start to return it can get awkward. It was nicer to make something up as opposed to saying what I felt which was I'm not comfortable, this is making me anxious, and we're done for the night.

In a café on Rivington Street I sat at a window table and ordered a glass of sparkling water. The visit to Spaulding's class had been a wise decision. Seeing her in the collegiate milieu reinforced her youth. It was a helpful reminder to refrain from a reenactment of the debacle that had forced me to withdraw from the MFA program. After talking to the fledglings I had returned to the office and put in several more hours at my desk. Chemotherapy would begin the following morning and I needed to make sure my workload did not become unmanageable.

Since receiving Tapper's diagnosis and getting it confirmed by a dour oncologist at Memorial Sloan Kettering whose farcical walrus mustache made him no better at delivering bad news, I trudged to the office every day where an infinity of trusts and estates documents awaited. There were modifications in the morning, appendices in the afternoon. All thoughts of my potentially deteriorating health suppressed.

I wasn't sure what my reaction to the pretty poison was going to be. Would I be too feeble to change a light bulb, or would a relatively normal life be possible? To get some exercise, and because I didn't want to assent to the idea of extinction, I had decided to walk downtown. I passed a tent encampment in Union Square thronged with citizens waving signs, railing against the horrors of war, greed, and racism. It was vivifying to see people who assumed the world could improve.

The recently opened café had distressed wood floors and a pressed-tin ceiling that had probably been manufactured in Korea last January. There was a mahogany bar and behind it a dazzling array of spirits killed time in the soft amber light. I wasn't able to enjoy their company since I had sworn off alcohol for the duration of my treatment. When the waitress arrived, I thanked her for the sparkling water, took out my phone, and opened the poetry file.

A few stanzas and I was ready to march up to Union Square and offer my legal services that evening. There isn't a critic of my work harsher than I and after no more than thirty seconds spent scanning the lines all confidence drained. Spaulding had admired one of these poems but what did she know, she was nineteen. On the other hand, living in Europe had rendered her more sophisticated than the garden-variety American girl so perhaps my self-laceration was unjustified. Could I trust her assessment? Sipping the water, I pondered my situation. What was making me persist? My position at the firm was secure and a partnership likely. But was that the accomplishment for which I wanted to be remembered?

While I ruminated a text arrived from Spaulding.

Are you anywhere near the East Village?

The taxi dropped me off on East 7th. Across from Tompkins Square Park, a rowdy crowd of drunken frat boys erupted from a bar like a sweaty lava flow and oozed west. A delivery truck rumbled past and revealed a girl across the street. A blanket of hair swung down as she canted her head to the side and wobbled, holding the lamppost. In a bell of light was Spaulding. She unpeeled from the lamppost and took a few uneven steps toward First Avenue.

I watched to see what she would do. It did not look as if she could find her way to the corner. She shuffled a couple of steps to her right, then back to the left, a private dance to silent music. She put something shiny to her lips—a flask, how 1920s!—inclined her head back, and took a long pull before slipping it back in her purse. Spaulding was framed in the violet-hued window of a trendy boutique called Tiny Bubbles. Behind the pane were two mannequins in retro-punk regalia gazing eyeless toward the street. She didn't notice my approach.

"You texted," I said.

"Mr. Best," she said, drawing out the *r* in mister and extending the *s* in Best. She was a little drunk. "I hope you didn't mind. You killed it in class today. Thanks for coming. To class, I mean. And here."

"Let me buy you some coffee."

"I'm not drunk if that's what you're thinking." She reached into her purse and removed the silver flask. "Want to go dancing?" She shimmied her shoulders and laughed. Then she belched. Which in no way compromised her attractiveness. "I do not have a drinking problem. My mother does."

There was a whiff of whiskey on her breath. A nervous energy radiated from her, as if my presence had created a charge. When she unscrewed the flask, I grabbed it. This was a surprise. What mullah had appointed me East 7th Street Taliban? To retaliate, to be cute, perhaps to exasperate me, she put the cap of the flask in her mouth. I had a vision of her choking and me having to perform the Heimlich maneuver, failing, and being forced to inform Ed Simonson of his daughter's incomprehensible death on the sidewalk in front of the retro S&M mannequins in the window of Tiny Bubbles. So I stuck the fingers of both my hands in Spaulding's mouth, a disarmingly intimate act, and pried her teeth open. This made her gag—had the cap dropped into her esophagus?—but her mouth unlocked and I removed the saliva-soaked thing, wiped my fingers on my suit pants, screwed the cap on to the flask, and stuffed it in my pocket.

And then she threw up. Without warning a bilious blast

spattered the sidewalk and would have caught my pant leg full-on had I not danced out of the way. She put her hands on her knees, doubled over, and I instinctively leaned forward and held her hair as another spasm shot forth. I slipped behind, not letting go of her cashmere-soft hair as, still bent over, she dry-heaved several times. There were flecks on my shoes. She spat to clear the detritus from her mouth then straightened up. It was disgusting but her damaged magnetism was sensual beyond measure.

She pushed her curls out of her eyes and looked at me apologetically.

"Well, that was elegant," she declared. "I'm really sorry."

When I silently pointed toward the corner, she dipped her head in a performance of chastisement and began walking. A few minutes later we were seated in a café just off Lafayette, the kind of place where the barista could do a Lucian Freud painting in the foam of one's latte. A group of NYU kids prattled meaningfully at a nearby table. I sipped black coffee while Spaulding emptied several packets of artificial sweetener into a quadruple espresso.

"I'm apologizing again," she said. "Thanks for looking after me."

When I asked her what she was doing in the neighborhood she said, "What's your favorite word?" This brought me up short and I didn't answer right away. "You're a poet," she reminded me. "You should have one. Mine is darkling." It was not a word I knew and I asked what it meant. "As an adverb it means in the dark and as an adjective it means menacing, but I like to use it as a noun even though it's not a noun in the dictionary."

"So what does your personal noun mean?"

"It's like a kid who always sees shadows." I nodded. A plausible definition. "Someone takes a ten-year-old darkling to *The Nutcracker* and she thinks all these charming children dancing around the stage are going to wind up divorced with substance abuse problems and Herr Drosselmeyer looks like a child molester."

"Was that you?" Spaulding smiled but didn't answer. Again she asked if I had a favorite word. "I've always liked quotidian," I said.

"Which rhymes with obsidian."

"And the trumpet of Gideon."

"And the bar at the Parker Meridien where I drank gin with a scholar Ovidian."

The exchange happened so quickly it was like watching a close-up magician work with a deck of cards. Her internal rhyme was a delight.

"Ovidian?"

"Ovid? The ancient love poet? A scholar Ovidian."

I laughed and she joined me before we both lapsed into slightly embarrassed silence. Spaulding sipped her espresso.

"Did you know Ovid's father wanted him to be a lawyer?"

"Nothing changes," she said.

Reaching into her purse she pulled out a Moleskine notebook with something wedged into its pages that turned out to be a passport. When she began to write I asked if she always carried her passport.

"It's a habit I got into when I was living in Switzerland."

"Because you might want to make a quick escape?"

"I used it to get into bars."

Headlights blurred the window. The air smelled of expensive muffins. There were crumbs on our table from whatever the previous occupants had been eating and I cleaned them off with the back of my hand. She returned the notebook and passport to her purse, shifted in the spindly wood chair, and leaned forward. She asked me if the poetry collection I was writing was my first one. I said it was and told her about the novel I had abandoned and the piles of rejection letters.

"And that's why you became a lawyer?"

What was I going to tell her? That I became a lawyer because I didn't have the courage to run off with a woman I was in love with and pursue another kind of life? Should I have told her I had no idea I had been in love with this woman until the series of events that led to my withdrawal from graduate school was in the past, that I was a lawyer because it better suited my penchant for self-abnegation?

"Shouldn't you be home scribbling a sestina?"

This took her aback and when she asked in an attitudinal way if I was kidding, I told her no, not really. She drained the espresso and rose from her seat. What had I done? I couldn't let her leave.

"I read your poem."

Her expression shifted, suddenly focused. It's always a crapshoot when someone offers her stuff for evaluation. Whether she really wants to hear what one thinks is impossible to know.

"I liked 'Addicted to Beauty.' Slightly derivative, which is understandable." She didn't convulse at derivative, a word no artist wants to hear. That impressed me. "You're scavenging and repurposing but the idea has wit. And 'Last Christmas' showed promise." She asked if I had any advice. "What you have that no one else does is Spaulding Simonson's voice. Cultivate that. If you think you might have gone too far, you haven't. A client of mine said something in another context that stuck with me. Be bold."

"I'm not bold enough?" There were steel pins in her tone. The quadruple espresso had sobered her up. She was still standing, ready to flee.

"It's bad form to ask a writer if anything is autobiographical but since you're on the inexperienced side and perhaps could benefit from some of my mistakes I'm going to ask if any of 'Last Christmas' was autobiographical."

"Are you asking if I tried to kill myself?"

"That's what I'm asking."

Spaulding sat down. Thirty seconds passed. I signaled the waitress for a refill.

"At boarding school I started to have these panic attacks where my heart would start beating like a hummingbird's wings and it was hard to concentrate on what I was supposed to be studying because it felt as if every solid surface was beginning to disintegrate. The idea of flying home for Christmas was freaking me out. Can you imagine a major panic attack at thirty thousand feet?"

"That would be tricky to navigate."

"So my mother flew to Switzerland to come get me. She wasn't happy about having to make the trip. I didn't want her to come anyway, I wanted my father but he had a meeting in Chicago that he couldn't cancel. You really want to hear this?"

I assured her that I did. She glanced toward the kids at the other table, preoccupied with their own concerns. I wanted to tell her that they were probably no less complicated than she, that everyone had troubles and we distinguish ourselves by how we respond, but I spared her the lecture.

"After my mother cajoled me out of my dorm and got me to her hotel the first thing she asked was whether I wanted to go shopping in Zurich or Geneva. That's the level she worked on, like you're staring at the emptiness at the center of existence and she's all, 'Spall, look at these earrings!'"

Before I could stop myself, I laughed. She didn't seem to mind.

"I told her I didn't want to go shopping while I was having a breakdown. She said, 'Spall, I'm trying.' And I'm like, 'I know you are and your version of trying just makes me incredibly sad.' And then I started to cry and couldn't stop."

Spaulding ran her finger clockwise around the rim of her

espresso cup and looked down. An older couple doddered in clutching playbills from the Public Theater. They flopped at a table against the wall. The kids at the other table were going over their check, figuring out how much each of them owed. I began to doubt my observation that Spaulding's life was no more complicated than theirs.

"You don't have to tell me any more if you don't want."

"At one point she said to me, 'Spall, you know I've been sober less than six months this time and I don't really want to lay this on you but I think the episode you're having might be threatening my sobriety.'"

"What a narcissist."

"I know, right?" She looked at me for affirmation and I shook my head in sympathy. "So my mother called a doctor and they shot me up with what felt like a horse tranquilizer and somehow got me back to New York. I couldn't get out of bed. I didn't bathe or even wash my face or brush my teeth. The Adderall the doctor had prescribed jazzed me up and Xanax flattened me out. I started to hallucinate. I can't believe I'm telling you this. You'll probably never look at me again."

"That's not true."

"I've only told the story to my therapist." She took several gulps of water. "The thought of going back to boarding school when the break was over terrified me and I don't mean *terrified* the way some kids might say they're terrified of a history test. The kind of terrified where you can't stop shaking. I didn't want to be in Switzerland, but I didn't want to live in my mother's apartment."

"Where was your father?"

"He came to see me when he got back from his trip. He's like, 'Buck up, Spall, you're going to be fine. These panic attacks you're having? There are other ways to get attention.'"

"Ed's a raptor."

"What?"

"Your father is not a nurturer."

"That night I called my brother Gully who was supposed to be flying in from Seattle for the holiday. He was the only person I could talk to. The call went direct to voicemail. Apparently, the universe wasn't going to let me reach Gully, a conversation with either of my parents was pointless, and I wasn't going back to Switzerland so I swallowed too many Xanax and chased them with Champagne. Gully found me and called an ambulance. They pumped my stomach and I spent the next month in a mental hospital. I wasn't even really trying to kill myself."

With a fervor that shocked me more than Spaulding, I gripped her forearm. She tensed. "That's the cruelest thing you can do to anyone who loves you."

Spaulding yanked her arm away. Her eyes scorched. She glared at me, then got up and marched out. I threw some bills down and caught her on the sidewalk. She forced a smile, the gleaming white, slightly crooked teeth. I wished I hadn't touched her. A police cruiser rolled past. For a moment I thought Spaulding might flag it down but I don't think she even noticed. I asked her where she lived and she told me not to worry about it. She took a mint out of her pocket and popped it in her mouth.

"Please don't grab me like that."

"I'm sorry. Spaulding, listen, I'm going to take you home, okay?"

"Naughty, Mr. Best!"

"To your place," I said, trying to act like an adult. "Or your mother's place, or wherever it is you actually sleep at night."

"I'm not sure I've forgiven you."

I had the urge to caress the small of her back with my fingertips. That thought was immediately tried, sentenced to ten years' hard labor, and exiled to Siberia. I rested my hand on her shoulder in a manner that suggested general concern for humanity. She didn't seem to mind. A cab materialized and I held the door. The driver was a middle-aged man from somewhere a language of all consonants was spoken. Slipping into the seat, she said, "Grand Central Station."

I slid in next to her.

"What are you doing?" Spaulding reasonably wondered as the cab moved away from the curb. Her indignation had cooled and she did not seem displeased with my presence. Although no plan had formed, I said, "Making sure you go home."

"That isn't necessary, Mr. Best."

"I know, Spaulding. And I don't want to because, honestly, you're kind of a pain. But you're probably still hammered and could pass out in a park and be kidnapped by gypsies." My mouth was running because I wanted to keep her engaged. There was a sense she could leap from the vehicle. Why was I doing this? If the Raptor heard I had escorted his inebriated daughter uptown after a night of Mephistophelean revelry, would he thank me for saving her from the predations of the city? Ed was a cunning Manhattan attorney; he would presume the worst.

"I don't need you to tell me how cruel I am," she said.

"You're right. Over the line. But you need to consider your legacy. We all do."

I settled in for the ride. As we edged uptown she was twirling a lock of hair and gazing out the window. The cab was quiet.

"Does it suck being a lawyer?"

"Not as much as living in a refrigerator carton under a bridge."

"A ringing endorsement."

There was no use pretending otherwise with her. It wasn't like she needed to hear my version of the speech about working hard and being diligent. To what end? So she could end up like me, in her thirties and trying to convince herself she'd made the right decision.

"Everyone has their tragedy, Mr. Best."

"What does that mean?"

"The awful thing that comes to define their lives. Like when your brain says lawyer but your heart screams poet."

I pointed out that everyone needed to make a living. "And why is that?" she asked. "So you can have a fancy apartment and drive a sweet car and go to work every day where you spend all your time helping rich people not pay taxes?"

"Only a terminally unimaginative drone grows up wanting to exist in a world where the word *hour* is invariably preceded by the word *billable*." I did not say that out loud because no one talks that way, but for some reason I still felt the need to justify my existence. "What I wanted to be," I extemporized, "was an artist, someone who spends his days mining the unconscious for material to be transmogrified from the base metals of random memory and fleeting impression into the spun gold of extended and satisfying verse. And like Baudelaire and Rimbaud, one was after the affections of those who could appreciate it, but in a less homoerotic way." That, alas, I did say out loud. *Transmogrified? One was after? Homoerotic?* From which distant outpost in the cosmos of my head had those locutions beamed? Spaulding had just shared her darkest secrets and I was making a speech to the *Académie Français*. Could I not just talk to her? Had my circuits shorted and rendered my words pompous and off-putting? And why was I telling Spaulding this? Did I want her to repeat it to her father? That I had taken her on a cab ride and performed a pseudo-intellectual fan dance replete with highfalutin literary/sexual references thrown in for her delectation? "The sex wasn't a goal, really," I continued, heedless. "Sex is nothing but a time killer, something to do when the conversation is exhausted." I was chittering like a magpie.

"What are you trying to tell me?"

Excellent question.

"That people measure males by how much sex they've had and I am more interested in the approbation of others than is healthy." Apparently, I couldn't stop.

"Did you just start therapy or something?"

"Therapy exists to prepare us for death. I'm already prepared," I lied.

The cab crawled across 14th Street. Spaulding rested her head against the window. Streetlight shadows strobed her hair. Spaulding's palm rested on the seat. Two fingers delicately beat an unheard rhythm. Then the most extraordinary thing happened. Her head pivoted in my direction and she leaned in. A quick kiss caught the corner of my mouth so it wasn't full-on and it ended as quickly as it began. Her lips tasted like grapes. She reclined against the seat, staring straight ahead. My heart kicked. She shifted her eyes toward me without moving her head.

"Will you try to put your bonus in my partnership?"

Her laugh filled the back of the cab and was as brief as the kiss. I was dumb. It's a well-known power move to intentionally create discomfort in another and at this Spaulding was a preternatural master. She smiled, keyed up by my embarrassment. The conversation was supposed to remain on the level of saucy banter. I had no intentions in this area, repressed, unacknowledged desire being distinct from intent, Your Honor.

"Did I really say that?"

No easy response presented itself. On the surface it was a horrible idea, but I was painfully drawn to the exquisite torture of Spaulding Simonson, her possibility, her skewed view, her reverence for words, and the way she looked nestled in the dim light of the taxi.

"Spaulding, please know I'd . . ."

"You'd what?"

Every wrong choice I'd ever made raged back at me and I retreated to the rumpus in my head.

"Will you at least let me see some of the poems you're working on? I loved that fragment you read to the class."

"Sure, sure."

It was late and the neighborhood should have been peaceful but the sidewalks were teeming. The crowd seemed rattled, as if they weren't moving entirely of their own accord. None of them looked like they had to be anywhere in the morning. They sported unisex ensembles of loose pants or shorts, large tee shirts, dreadlocks, and tattoos. Random cries could be heard as they moved uneasily uptown.

We stopped at a red light. Someone was bellowing words I couldn't make out and this was followed by a rhythmic chant. There were shouts and it was not the sound of exhilaration but of fear and anger and suddenly a gaunt bearded man darted in front of our cab and ran across the street. A sprinting policeman trailed him, his gut straining against his too-tight summer shirt. The trajectory of this chase led the pair across the avenue where the bearded man plunged into the sidewalk throng quickly followed by the cop. It was easy to tell by the yelling that the riled multitude was not going to help the policeman. Spaulding grabbed my bicep and squeezed.

"Make a gesture, Mr. Best. Break a vase."

There was more yelling behind us, louder this time. I looked through the rear window of the cab and saw a phalanx of mounted policemen herding people uptown, away from the circus at Union Square. The crowd was spiky and there were curses and screaming and I saw a man fall down in front of one of the horses. When I glanced at Spaulding to gauge her reaction to the spectacle, she was gone. Then there she was among the police and the horses gesticulating for the cops to get away from the man who was on the ground. It was a mark of astonishing bravery or madness, the kind of thing I could never imagine doing, and it was in that instant I knew. Our lives are lived with the illusion of control and then there are moments rare as wisdom when we abandon the pretense that we are masters of our fate. Despite all of my finely honed instincts of self-preservation, the chorus of inner voices imploring me to run in the opposite direction, and every iota of common sense, I had fallen in love with Spaulding Simonson.

Just as she launched herself at a police officer the horde closed and it was impossible to see what was happening. I threw twenty dollars on the seat and flew out of the cab. The mob had swallowed Spaulding as if she hadn't been there at all. Bodies whirled ever closer, mouths agape, random shouts of escalating confusion. I became acutely conscious of my clothes: Paul Smith suit, white Comme des Garcons shirt, gray Sulka tie, Brioni shoes. A target between my shoulders was the only thing missing. A short man with a neck tattoo leered at me. A sallow grin split his dirty face and displayed a broken front tooth. He extended his grimy hand, palm up. "Help me out?" he said before the momentum of the pack pulled him off. Someone crashed into my shoulder and I looked to see a large dreadlocked man disappear behind me as if being chased. There was another bump from the opposite side sending me back in the other direction and then—*Yuppie fucker*—a brick serrated my right cheek—the pain blinded—and I fell into a forest of legs where a boot stepped on my hand and in a stark moment it was clear that to lie there would deliver me from this world of striving and disconnection from which I had gained nothing and learned less and the life would seep out of me in a way that would not even require the exercise of free will but fingers raked my face and someone's knee drove into my side and I thought of Spaulding and whether she was safe and when I attempted to push off the ground another foot pressed against my calf grinding my leg into the pavement and as I tried to shift my hips and rise a knee thudded in my chest and sent me rolling and sirens shrieked and the whinny of a horse set off screams and the crowd heaved through the street as one organism and just as I thought I was going to be trampled two hands lifted me and I saw it was a fat man in a tee shirt that said *Fuck Tha Police* and he shoved me into the current of the mob as it whirled and eddied up Third Avenue and I was able to limp away from the hullabaloo.

Adrenaline had lit a pain-immolating fire that now began to subside and I noticed my leg ached at both the calf and knee. My pants were torn. My fingers were scraped and sore and covered in blood that I realized was from a cut on my face. I folded my jacket and held it to my cheek to stanch the bleeding. When I realized I had nearly been trampled to death my knees began to shake. I needed to settle down. Tomorrow was the first day of chemotherapy. I leaned against a car and took deep breaths. I stretched my legs and arched my back. After a couple of minutes my nervous system regained some equilibrium. A call to Spaulding didn't go through. A dead zone. Was all this the result of my exhortation to be bold?

I shambled toward Brooklyn and hoped she was all right.

A hot shower and a glass of ice water. A bandage on my jaw. Beached on the sofa staring at the bookshelves I tried not to think about what was going to happen tomorrow. To distract myself I thought of all the writers Spaulding had yet to experience, all the books I could pass along. Did she know Frank O'Hara? Had she read "The Day Lady Died"? I needed to act before it was too late. She had the courage to pitch herself into the heart of a roiling mob yet I was paralyzed. More than that, she had the courage to reach across the chasm of age and propriety that separated us to try to forge a connection. It was inspiring. It was unmooring. I wanted Spaulding but were we supposed to get married and move to Westchester? And it wasn't as if I could quit my job and run away with her. To do what? Travel around the country until I became too sick and then waste away and die in a desert motel in Arizona? I was having chemotherapy in the morning!

This entire train of thought was ridiculous. What had she done, pecked me in a taxicab? While she was drunk! Spaulding and I hardly knew one another. Was I now simply projecting pathetic hopes of salvation on a convenient screen? Whatever it was, I couldn't control it. Unable to read or watch television and tormented by a vision of Spaulding devoured by that mob, images of my death mixed with sexual fantasies of the most lubricious kind in a phantasmagoric mash-up of coffins, female breasts, and weeping mourners. This reverie abruptly ceased with the rapping of agitated knuckles against my door.

Through the peephole: My neighbor, the pit bull of Dubrovnik. I opened the door.

Bogdan was average height but with a weight lifter's build. His dense black coif was the grooming equivalent of free jazz and he sported the kind of thick mustache favored by old-school dictators. His pupils looked as if an artist using a brush with a single hair had painted them. He wore loose white trousers and his loudly patterned shirt caused havoc with my brain waves. Under this fashion calamity, an object bulged against the right side of his abdomen. I was pretty sure it wasn't a colostomy bag.

He was holding a covered tray.

"Pierogis," he said. "Dvotchka made." I had no idea who Dvotchka was but accepted the proffered gift and thanked him. It was difficult to discern why Bogdan could possibly have come brandishing a tray of dumplings. There was a moment of awkward silence during which I expected him to go away. It was at this juncture the emerald-green teardrop-shaped bottle of slivovitz he was holding came to my attention.

"I come in?" It would have been easy enough to claim I had another engagement but Bogdan was going to force this exchange at some point so best to get it over with. I waved him toward the living room. He asked if glasses were available and I fetched them from the kitchen.

We sat facing one another, Bogdan on the sofa, I on a wing chair. He sipped the slivovitz from a shot glass. Mine lay untouched on the coffee table next to the pierogis. Bogdan was not particularly adept at making conversation and the only thing we had in common was a shared wall, so after five minutes, all of which I had spent trying to find a way to get him to leave, he swallowed the pierogi he was chewing and came to the point of his visit.

"I want to buy your flat."

"Why would I sell?"

"Generous offer."

"Bogdan, the apartment isn't for sale."

"You have not heard offer." I exhaled and leaned back. He would not depart until he had made his pitch. "Please," he said, a word used as a placeholder, not as a request. Please in Bogdan's mouth meant I would pin your throat to the chair with my forearm if that was what it took to get you to listen. "Please."

He mentioned a figure well above market value. Slightly taken aback, it made me consider my stance for a moment. What he wanted to do was break through the walls, connect the apartments, and, in an ages-old New York tradition, create the enviable home he believed was his due.

"Why don't you move if you want a bigger place?" This was said in a tone meant to be affable but Bogdan's expression blackened. Rather than physically attacking, he remained in conversational mode, albeit a slightly strained version. In his temple a small vein pulsed like a poker tell.

"It would be better if I stayed in building."

"Then you're welcome to stay."

Although Bogdan had been my neighbor for over a year it was impossible to discern what he did for a living. That it was probably criminal was evident given the look of his confederates.

And Bogdan was of their ilk, a hulking predator escaped from the Balkans and roaming Brooklyn. He ran ringed fingers through the unruly mass on his head. Chest hair protruded from the neck of his white undershirt. He poured himself another shot and knocked it back. Then he rinsed the residue around in his mouth and displayed his teeth. It appeared to be a tic because it was hard to believe he would literally bare his fangs. Mouth coated with crimson liqueur, it looked like he'd been chewing flesh. This was not comforting.

"Jeremy." His voice, already low, now sounded as if it were emerging from a grave. And I'm certain it was the first time he had called me by my name. "Liberal proposal." I reiterated my opposition to vacating the premises. The offer on the table would have allowed me to move to a fancier place, something in Brooklyn Heights with a view of New York Harbor but, really, why bother? In what way was that going to help me finish a book of poems? Or live a longer life? Here is what would be engraved on my headstone:

Jeremy Best
Attorney/Poet
Angels Envied His Apartment

If I aggravated Bogdan enough I might be able to get him to kill me, thereby ending most of my problems. But upon reflection, if I was going to take the suicide route, a bottle of pills and a glass of whiskey seemed a lot cozier than being murdered by a Croatian gangster, although, given what I had said to Spaulding about self-annihilation, more than a little hypocritical. Bogdan nattered about my apartment for another five minutes and I nodded periodically so he would think I was paying attention. Then he raised his offer. Considerably.

"I have to get up early tomorrow, Bogdan. Thanks for the pierogis."

I walked toward the door. From his perch on the sofa, Bogdan regarded me through calculator eyes. He could have been weighing any number of things including how much he should spend on a blood diamond for his girlfriend or whether to have blini or boiled chicken for tomorrow's dinner, but likely he was considering how to eliminate me with as little fuss as possible. Ordinarily I would have looked away but I held his gaze and shrugged as if to say, what can I do? Kill me if you want, you're not getting this apartment.

A few more seconds elapsed before my neighbor rose to his feet and, grabbing the slivovitz, slowly moved toward me. Was he going to smash the bottle over my head, shards of glass and a wash of viscous liquid arcing through the gummy air? Suffocate me with hairy fingers then spread out in my living room, text his colleagues, and have a drug-fueled party over my corpse before tossing it in Sheepshead Bay to be consumed by flounder?

Bogdan stood directly in front of me. Although we were about the same height, his homicidal aspect made him seem considerably larger. The scent of tobacco and smoked fish became more intense with each hostile breath. Garnished with the bouquet of slivovitz, it was sickening.

"Good offer," he said. "Think about it."

When the door closed I collected myself. This had been a remarkably strange evening. Immediately I was delivered from my thoughts by the chirping phone. A text from Spaulding!

I'm in the back of a police car. What rhymes with misdemeanor? To the cleaner? Once you've seen her? Help!

A police car? What? Could this be true? Impossible to know. But the savoir-faire she displayed whether the situation was real or fictional was an undeniably attractive quality. I texted back:

In between her . . .

Spaulding had somehow found the path that led over the drawbridge and into the castle. For years its inner reaches had been hidden, protected, inaccessible. But getting involved with her could destroy my life. I needed to flee. From now on I would carry my passport.

SPAULDING
A Starving Prisoner Gorges Herself on Your Language

E ven after the quadruple espresso I was still pretty buzzed from the liquor and when I saw the cops converging on that guy right after I had told Mr. Best he should break a vase it seemed like a good time to make another kind of statement. So I exploded from the cab and hurled myself into the middle of the melee like some kickass roller derby chick. I didn't want to look over my shoulder to see if Mr. Best had followed me but I wanted him to. I wanted him to save me. But if I wanted him to save me why did I tell him about the mental hospital? All that would do was make him feel sorry for me. I didn't want to be his emotional charity case. I wanted him to love me the way a five year old loves cake.

The cops were waving nightsticks but they looked a little confused about using them when they saw me screaming my lungs out in front of the guy who had been knocked down. There must have been a dozen horses and these pulsing walls of sinew and muscle look even bigger and more powerful when they're surrounding you. The swirling crowd was all jacked up, twisted faces yelling DON'T YOU DARE TOUCH THAT GIRL LEAVE HER ALONE DAMMIT GET AWAY FROM HER MOTHERFUCKERS POLICE BRUTALITY!!! and I was screaming my guts out, too, and the fallen guy who I thought needed my protection was devoured by the crowd and an older cop who seriously needed to go on a diet grabbed me, cleared a space through the crowd, and threw me in the back of a police car.

Everything started to slow down as soon as he locked me in.

I looked up and down Third Avenue for any sign of Mr. Best but he was gone.

The mob stampeded. Cops reeled and gave chase. Horses floated through the crowd like great ships and I thought about books I read as a kid that had horses in them. Those horses were never in cities wading through angry swarms of humanity. They were meant for more beautiful things than herding masses of pissed-off people. Then I began to laugh at myself for thinking about storybook horses because I wasn't nine years old anymore. But the image of stallions running free made me remember the last time I was locked up and I started to bang my head against the glass. For what felt like a long time, I screamed for them to let me go, crying and yelling until it felt like a sandpaper cylinder was plunging my throat. No one paid any attention to me. It was like they had talked to my parents and all agreed I just needed to sit there and shut up.

My throat / is torn / I sink / into / the seat.

For twenty minutes I stewed as the spectacle continued to unfold. A police van materialized nearby and cops periodically packed it with handcuffed protesters. Already on a tight leash, how was I going to explain this one to Edward P and Harlee? The last of the throng streamed up the avenue and began to dissipate. The potbellied cop appeared and asked me for my father's name and address. It didn't occur to me to lie so I gave them to him. Then he unlocked the car door and told me to go back to Stonehaven.

Drowsy drunks in baggy suits and stoned preppies clotted the 12:35 back to Connecticut. In a row by myself, I stared out the window as the train rolled north through the dark tunnel.

Will you try to put your bonus in my partnership?

Sometimes you say words you want to retract the moment they're heard. The self-destructiveness. The humiliation and remorse. The sublime stupidity. After that question flew out of my mouth remaining in the cab was pointless. My continued presence would only decrease my chances of repairing the damage done to Mr. Best's opinion of me. Not to mention that I had barfed on his shoes. On his shoes! He was perfectly cool but it was hopeless. And then I kissed him in the cab? I had swallowed an entire tin of mints but what did my lips taste like? Coffee and sick? I disgusted myself. No wonder Mr. Best chose not to follow me. Is this what Dr. Margaret meant when she advised I approach social situations like a character named Spaulding? I don't think so. Unless that character was demented.

The whole fantasy was wrecked. I sank into the seat and tried to imagine some kind of future but all that appeared was a gray sameness of days, weeks, months, years of being captive in this body. I had an urge to call Dr. Margaret but it was late and my lack of impulse control had already made me hate myself enough for one night.

Why was I so interested in Mr. Best? Simple. A native New Yorker with divorced parents and artist's attitude, a poet stuck doing something he's not meant to do, he was some future version of me but with inner reserves I didn't possess because he had managed to thrive. Still, he was nearly twice my age and there was no point putting him in an untenable position. He was not into younger women. Either that or he was gay and after having given the possibility some thought I was pretty sure that was not the case.

It was a sweet shock when between the New Rochelle and Larchmont stations my smartphone coughed up one of his poems and a text that read: *In between her . . .* (his response to *What rhymes with misdemeanor?*). Despite my appalling behavior, Mr. Best was flirting back. Then another text: *Are you all right?* Immediately, I texted back that I had survived and was on my way to Connecticut.

Reading poems on a smartphone while riding a commuter

train surrounded by souses and sleepy prepsters was a far cry from a loaf of bread, a jug of wine, and thou but my insides quivered. As for Mr. Best, his talent shone. Between Larchmont and Stonehaven I read what he sent twenty times. This man bled talent and was completely miscast in the role of lawyer.

As the train swayed through Stamford, I texted,

In a bleak cell in Stonehaven a starving prisoner gorges herself on your language.
Yours, The Darkling.

Five minutes later I got an email from Mr. Best.

A week before Thanksgiving freshman year my Aunt Bren called to tell me that my mother had removed her clothes in the furniture department of Macy's on 34th Street and subsequently been taken to Bellevue where she was being held for observation, did I want to visit her?

His mother? Why was he writing me about his mother? I read on.

She had spent years trying to be an actress and was now performing her mad scene. In college and beyond parental parameters this awful business crawled from the swamp of my past like some kind of golem and threatened to claim primacy once again. This is why we have survival instincts. And these instincts were adamant: there was nothing to be done. I remained at school.
My divorced father, clued in to the catastrophe courtesy of Aunt Bren despite his ex officio status, refused to spring for a private clinic so she languished in Bellevue for three weeks until the medical staff deemed her fit to face the world. At this point the estimable Dr. Gumport had upped the antidepressants to a level appropriate for a mastodon and her affect, such as it was

after years of chemical dependency and alcohol, nearly disap-
peared. Christmas break was a pageant of cheerlessness and I
stayed at her apartment for only a few nights, preferring to couch
surf at a series of places that didn't feel like my mother's psy-
chotic projection. Caring for her was entirely beyond my ken, as
caring for me had been beyond hers. Such a deep fogginess
engulfed my mother that she didn't seem to mind.

This was not good. Mr. Best was telling me about his family
to push me away. Could there possibly be another reason?

Spring semester the calls slowed. Because my mother wasn't
constantly trying to track me down, when we did actually talk
we were able to have several civil and semi-coherent conversa-
tions. Asked how she was doing, my mother would tell me that
she was following Dr. Gumport's orders and even going for an
occasional visit to the Museum of Modern Art to look at her
favorite Rothkos or a walk in Central Park. So it was with more
than a little surprise that I heard again from Aunt Bren—it was
never good news when she called—that my mother had attacked
her wrists with a can opener and was going to be locked up
again, this time at the Payne-Whitney clinic, where Uncle
Barney was picking up the tab. Aunt Bren was convinced that my
mother didn't really want to kill herself, first because she used a
can opener—not the most efficient means of getting that partic-
ular job done—and second because she had called an ambulance
as soon as she mangled her veins. It was suggested that I visit
her; that maybe seeing me might lift her gloom. I didn't under-
stand why this should be the case since my presence never had a
positive effect the entire time we were actually living together
but this time guilt (if there is a more useless feeling, it has yet to
be discovered) won out.

Mrs. Best was far worse off than me. She sounded out of her

mind. I was only mildly depressed. I didn't know whether to keep reading. Maybe this ended in her being cured.

In a locked ward under the watchful eyes of several burly white-clad attendants we had our visit. Her face was slack and she slowly worked her jaw in a way I had never seen, as if there was a piece of gristle in there that refused to dissolve. They had her pretty doped up but she seemed to be listening when I told her how school was going and talked about the summer when a few friends and I were planning a trip to Alaska. There was nodding, some inappropriate laughter, and several unreadable facial expressions that led me to consider whether any of this information was actually being absorbed. After an uncomfortable hour spent wondering if this was some horrible vision of my own genetically predetermined future or if I would ever be in the same room with this person again, we said goodbye.

This time my mother's stay in the mental hospital was for nearly a month. When she was discharged the plan was for Aunt Bren and Uncle Barney to take her to their house in New Jersey for a few weeks. It was thought the surroundings would have a salutary effect and the three girls, my cousins, were all still living at home so she would have a lot of company. Everyone agreed this was an excellent idea.

Where everyone agrees something is an excellent idea disaster lurks. I didn't like where this was going, which was probably shock treatment. I checked the time. When did the train arrive in Stonehaven?

It was an exquisite May afternoon with no humidity and a brilliant blue sky when my aunt and uncle and I picked her up at the clinic and drove her back to the apartment to pack a bag. In her Stygian bedroom my mother folded clothes and placed them in a suitcase that I carried into the foyer. Emerging from

her lair, she squeezed Uncle Barney's forearm too tightly, dig-
ging her fingernails into his flesh, and thanked him for all his
help. While her sister and brother-in-law and her son—her
son!—looked on, my mother sailed inexorably across the living
room, gazing at the art on the walls, the books on the shelves,
the upright piano where she had banged out songs that sold
promise by the bushel and where I had endured years of les-
sons. She rested her hands on the sill overlooking the wide
avenue as if to give a speech, then before any of us could move
leaped out the window and fell to the sidewalk six stories
below.

Never give in, Spaulding. Never give in.

This was not easy to process but it certainly explained the
way he grabbed my arm when he told me killing yourself was
the cruelest thing you could ever do. I needed to apologize.
Immediately. In the few weeks I'd known Mr. Best information
about him was hard to come by and now he had thrust the key
in my face. It was probably why he wrote poems that rhymed.
Why he became a trusts and estates lawyer. Maybe it's even
why he wasn't married. When you're an eyewitness to your
mother flying out a window it's hard to see the universe as anything other than a place of total madness. Not to say someone
who survived that couldn't be a well-adjusted person who had
a long and happy life. But don't kid yourself.

There were no cabs at the Stonehaven station and it wasn't
like Edward P and Katrina had said to call any time day or
night and someone would whisk me home, so I began to walk
with all of this churning through my head. Did I remind Mr.
Best of his mother? There could be nothing worse.

At night the streets of Stonehaven are as quiet as the insides
of the dioramas at the Museum of Natural History that show
Native Americans or Eskimos. Not spooky quiet, either, but
the quiet of space, of nothing is going to ever happen. During

the day people take walks and kids ride their bikes and skateboards, but at night other than the occasional dog walker strolling languidly behind a purebred with a poop bag in one hand and a cell phone in the other there are no pedestrians. So it creeped me out when a figure appeared a few hundred yards behind me on Crooked Brook Lane.

A quick glance over my shoulder to see if he was walking a dog revealed this was not the case. Home was still over a dark mile away. It was hard to know if it was the persistent humidity or the escalating angst but my forehead was damp. I began walking faster. Wakefield Lane T-bones Crooked Brook and if the person continued down Crooked Brook my pulse might have slowed. But he followed me onto Wakefield. He was in my slipstream and had closed half the distance between us. It was after midnight and there were no streetlights. The large houses slept with eyes shut. My pace quickened. To knock at a front door and wake the residents would only produce embarrassment. The person behind me was probably innocent enough but I jogged past another five homes before I looked back. Whoever it was stood in the middle of the street and in the light of the indifferent moon he looked like the guy I had spotted from the taxi the day I arrived.

I started to run.

My Chucks flew. A rivulet of sweat knifed my temple. The guy had started running, too. Not running, actually, more like loping as if he were some kind of animal. Mad energy carried me like I was training for the Olympics but when I turned from Wakefield on to Farragut he was closer.

When I landed in Stonehaven a month earlier I didn't anticipate hiding facedown under a rhododendron in the middle of the night as a maniac sprinted past. The loamy smell of the rich, dark earth filled my nostrils. My forehead pressed the moist ground. A banshee yawp—*SOMEONE PLEASE HELP MEEEEE!*—would alert him to my location and I didn't want to use my phone because he might see the light. Something slimy moved against my hand and I shivered and swatted it away. When a couple of minutes went by and the only sound was a frenzy of cicadas, I tentatively stood up and looked around. The street was deserted. I took off. My feet slapped the pavement, arms pumped. And there he was veering from a lawn like a missile trying to intercept me.

This vio- / lent man / will kill / me if / he can.

The house loomed like an island. Downstairs the hall light blazed. I leaped from the road to the lawn but mistimed my jump and when the toe of my sneaker caught the curb I found myself sprawled on the grass. The footsteps were closer as I limped toward the front door. When I thrust my hand into my pocket it became immediately apparent that my wrist had been jammed when I fell because the pain that shot up my arm caught me completely by surprise. Cursing, I slid my hand into the pocket and extracted my key chain. I jammed a key into the lock but it was the wrong one. I could hear him panting. Nerves flayed, I maneuvered another key in the lock, twisted the knob, and as the door yielded I turned to look back. There was no one. The man had slipped off into the thick trees or privet hedges or to the darkness of a neighbor's yard.

I closed the door as quietly as I could. In the kitchen I checked to make sure the back door was locked. The house was dead quiet. Moonlight streamed through the gauzy curtains. I peered toward the backyard half expecting to see the monster's face in the window. But no one was there. My wrist throbbed. Upstairs I lay down. After a few minutes I began to think about Grendel. It was as if he had sprung from the pages of *Beowulf* and pursued me to my father's door.

—Spall?

My nervous system cartwheeled. Edward P was standing in the middle of the room in his pajamas. His eyes surveyed serene poet faces. I wanted to scream.

—When did you do this?

I considered reporting what just happened. But the man who was chasing me wasn't there at the end. The hallucinations I had experienced last winter after three days of not eating or sleeping threw me into a cyclone of doubt.

—Do you like it?

The question took him some time to answer.

—It's creative, he said. That's a word non-artists use when faced with something they are incapable of understanding. How are you feeling, he wanted to know.

—Fine. Why?

—These pictures are all taped up, right?

—They're glued.

—Does Katrina know?

—She just told me not to paint. And she's seen it. Do you know who any of these people are?

—Should I?

—They're poets, I said, with maybe a little too much emotion. It would have been good if I had inherited a little more of Edward P's lawman affect. It comes in handy when you want to drop to your knees and shriek.

—Okay, Spall, okay.

I thought about my time locked in the police car and the texts I received on the train ride home and being chased through the streets by . . . by . . . What was that? It was hard to concentrate on my father's face while he kept talking and I drifted in and out of the comforting tones. I thought about Mr. Best in the city, sitting at his desk, a glass of whiskey or cup of coffee beside him, music playing on the stereo. What kind of music did he listen to? He was a little old for indie rock. What about classical? He seemed pretty traditional. You can tell a lot about a person from their musical taste. Was there any way I could get him to show me his iTunes? I wanted to make him a mixtape but what if I chose all the wrong bands? In class he had used that phrase *jiving jazz quartet*. Maybe he liked jazz.

—Is something wrong?

—What?

He repeated the question. I told him someone had followed me from the station and was probably lurking outside right now preparing to kill us in our sleep. This must have triggered some kind of caveman response because he told me to wait a second and disappeared. I stared out the window into the darkness wondering if it would devour me until he came back in dad jeans and a golf shirt and told me to follow him.

Not until he was backing his Tesla out of the garage did I, slumped in the passenger seat, ask what we were doing.

—We're going to find this fellow, he said.

—And do what? I said. Shouldn't we call the police?

—By the time they get here he could vanish. And why didn't you tell me this the second you got home?

—I don't know.

Edward P's jaw was clenched, his head searchlighting side to side as he cruised slowly along Farragut Road. A breeze had picked up and twisted branches of old trees aggressively swayed over freshly cut lawns. Late-model cars lurked in driveways. But no humans presented themselves.

—What did he look like?

—Like he grew up around here, but with something wrong in the wiring.

—You express yourself well, Spall. A real way with words.

When he had something practical to do, Edward P was most in his element. He was on a mission. We drove up Farragut, turned onto Wakefield, and then onto Crooked Brook heading back toward the train station, but when there was no sign of my pursuer my father lost steam.

—Spall, he said, as we headed back to the house, this fellow who was chasing you, did he say anything?

—We didn't have a conversation.

—He just started chasing you?

—For no reason I could tell other than wanting to rape and murder me.

—Have you been taking the meds?

—Lower doses, but yes.

—Then don't take this the wrong way, please.

An imploring look came over his face, like he thought I might grasshopper out of the car or do some other kind of drama queeny thing.

—Uh-oh. What?

—Are you sure you really saw anyone?

The safe feeling curdled. My father was looking at me the way someone sizes up a feral dog. Is this thing going to bite? I wasn't going to bite. A sensation in my chest compressed my lungs before migrating to my throat where it made speech impossible. You're literally running for your life, you barely escape, and your father, your protector, the person who is supposed to be the impenetrable wall that keeps harm at bay, basically implies you've lost your mind or want attention.

—Yes, yes, I croaked. Someone was after me. Someone was there.

—Okay, he said, but not like he believed it.

—I don't know, I said. The crippling woe of being misunderstood was slowly eclipsed by feverish anger. Maybe it was my imagination. And what was I angry at? My father? My brain chemistry?

—Are you joking? Because if you're joking, it's not funny.

—There was a man. The next time I won't tell you. Maybe he'll kill us all.

So fur- / ther a- / way now / than I / once was.

In quiet frustration he exhaled but didn't say anything. For another ten minutes we drove around the neighborhood. It was two in the morning. Edward P was wiped and still working through the couple of Scotches he had downed at dinner. But from the way he looked at me there was some concern I was going to have another episode. Silence is the best strategy in these situations since trying to convince someone you're not insane is impossible. It was a tactical mistake to say anyone had been out there in the first place.

Back at the house I washed my face and peeled my clothes off. In gym shorts and a tee shirt I stood outside my door and listened. Edward P's door was closed. The door to Marshall's room was slightly ajar. He had fallen asleep with a reading light on and the script for the play he was doing on his chest. Standing at the closed window sealed off from the threat but not the consuming fear I looked toward the road. There was no one out there. But there had been. There had been.

I lay in bed and thought about Edward P and Hurricane Katrina and Marshall nestled in their beds and how safe they all felt. I wanted someone on top of me. To feel his weight, his thighs on my thighs, his stomach pressed against mine, to hear him breathe, smell him. I wanted him to protect me from everything out there and wondered if a fraction of this was possible with all the hookups and bad sex and date rapes a person had to endure.

I lost my virginity at a ski resort in France during spring break my junior year. I like the verb "lost" in that context. Like you left it behind a radiator. A girl at my school had invited me on holiday with her family and the guy was her older brother. His name was Massimo and he was a business student at the University of Turin. What do you do when someone tells you you're *Bella, bella* in this sexy Italian accent while he's licking your armpit? Mostly I remember trying not to laugh. He was sweet but inexperienced and the whole thing ended nearly as soon as it started. There was some pain but no drama. Massimo wanted to do it again the following night but I wasn't into it. I wanted to rest in Mr. Best's embrace.

The next morning Edward P awakened me. He was already in his work uniform of a blue suit, white shirt, and red tie. Sharp aftershave cut the cool morning air.

—Would you like to tell me what happened last night?

—Someone chased me.

—I just received a call from a man who said he was a New York City police officer.

It all came rushing back, the cab ride, the crowd, the massed horses surrounding me on Third Avenue. I told my father that I was trying to protect someone. In a moment of clarity that can occur in that instant between sleep and wakefulness it occurred to me that I had wanted to do something good. This I mentioned.

—Spall, he said, that's not your responsibility. You might've gotten killed. And those people you threw yourself in the middle of? They're the ones who'd murder us in our beds if they could. Now I don't think that's going to happen but let's be clear about what's real and what's a projection of an overactive imagination.

—Did you report what happened to the local police?

—I called them when we got home.

Was that true? Oh god, I don't know. When he left the room I lay on my side. Consumed with a deepening sense of the great distance between here and a future I cared about, there was a vast longing that seemed to take on corporal form and lie at my side, enveloping me, soft breath whispering isolation. Exhausted, there would be no rest. Homesick, I had no home. I thought about calling Gully but that was complicated. He had his own life and if all I ever did were bitch and moan he would dread hearing from me.

Ten minutes later I was still in bed when my father stuck his head in the room.

—Spall, let's go. We're going to miss the 8:25.

JEREMY
You Are Not Africa

Beth the Nurse inserted the needle into a plump vein in the back of my hand. In her early forties, she was a friendly woman to whom, because of my shaky emotional condition, I ascribed healing qualities. Beth told me they'd had good results with this protocol. At that moment I felt a deep love for Beth who, with her magic needles, was going to summon more life.

A transparent bag of industrial-strength cyclophosphamide dangled from an IV pole and the clear liquid flowed into my vein to begin its seek-and-destroy mission. *Rogue cells beware—you're going down!* (When thinking of my cancer cells, I was careful to maintain a posture of aggressive hostility.)

I had arrived in the oncologist's office pumped like a quarterback playing in his first Super Bowl, torqued, battle-ready. Give it to me, I implored. Whatever you have, I can take it. No, I can't just take it, I *want* it, okay? I fucking *want* it. That was what I was thinking as I prepared myself. In my head I was a Marine at Parris Island, *sir, yes, sir!* I was a paratrooper leaping from a plane, an astronaut blasting into space. All the images spinning through my mind were military because I was at war and would *not* be defeated.

This arduous mental activity occurred while I was seated in a green vinyl-covered chair from which I was not able to move for three hours. And I was not alone as the inner battle raged. I was in a room with five other people, three men and two women who ranged in age from their thirties to their seventies, none of whom were speaking to each other, all of whom were having chemotherapy, engaged in their own quiet battles.

Three hours.

Three long hours absorbing poison. But I brought a book and it was not just any book. It was Martin Gilbert's ("Magisterial," *The Guardian*) biography of Winston Churchill. A big, imposing hardcover, a bulky stack of pages suggestive of both Churchill's impressive physical form and the length of his ninety-one-year life. A Churchillian who had devoured his entire oeuvre, my father had given it to me as a high school graduation gift and it lay open on my lap. This book was a talisman, a Bible. Although Churchill had hardly been right about all the issues of his day, I always admired the man. To anyone facing long odds, his confidence was rousing.

I read several chapters and after an hour was ready for a break. But I couldn't go anywhere since I was pinned to the chemo bag. In the course of my voluminous post-diagnosis reading, I discovered that visualization is a popular new age healing technique. It was very simple. One conjured an image that would have a positive effect on one's state of mind. Then biology took over. This was a phenomenon known as the "mind-body connection" and it was making inroads with the medical community. For those who doubt the reality of the mind-body connection, I submit: A man is shown a picture of an attractive naked woman. He gets an erection. Case closed.

It's actually more complicated than that.

But not much.

I closed my eyes and imagined a scenario.

A beach, white sand and tropical, was invaded by cancerous gremlins that ran around screeching madly, drinking rum, smashing into each other, scratching, clawing, humping, humping, humping. A tsunami appeared in the distance. As the wave rolled toward the shore, it gained in size and force, building, growing, one could hear it, louder, *LOUDER*. By the time it smashed into the beach, it was overwhelming. The gremlins? Gasping. Choking. Drowning. Another wave appeared, more powerful than the first. The remaining gremlins, already soaked and decimated, cringed. Their pitiful remnants were carried out to the sea, dead, dead, dead, and vanquished forever.

When the cyclophosphamide drained out of its bag, Beth reloaded with fludarabine.

Drip, drip, drip.

More war. More gremlins, more waves.

Two hours later I was done. Beth gave me compazine to combat the nausea that, I was informed, would be arriving on the evening train. Flumes of toxicity flowing through battered pipes, I arrived at the office in the early afternoon.

My evening with Spaulding wrestled for primacy with abject fear over what havoc the chemotherapy might cause. It was impossible to concentrate. Had I done the right thing in telling her about my mother? All I wanted was to stop whatever was happening between us from going any further. If she thought I was whiny and self-pitying, so be it.

A sugar buzz seemed like a good way to counteract my pervasive sense of post-chemo entropy. I was biting into a peanut butter sandwich in the communal kitchen when my colleague Amanda Carr appeared. A litigator, Amanda was pale in the manner of someone born to wander the moors and ten pounds overweight but with the good sense to be wearing a loose-fitting skirt suit with a billowy white blouse. Her ginger hair was cut in the efficient style of a women's basketball coach. We greeted each other with the easy familiarity of combat veterans. Many late nights during our early tenure with the firm had seen us doing a pitiless partner's bidding over cold sausage pizza in the bowels of the night.

"What happened to your face?"

She dipped a spoon into a yogurt and waited. I had been so

absorbed in my health crisis I had completely forgotten that a souvenir of last night's events was taped to my cheek.

"A friend's cat. Bastard."

Amanda chuckled. Did she have a clue what was going on with me? Only if she was a mind reader. None of my colleagues had a clue because this was not the kind of news one shared in an email blast. Could I share this with Amanda? I could not.

"Best, I hate to ask."

Would I help fight world poverty and come to the African Horizons fundraiser, tickets were only several hundred dollars each, George Clooney was going to read a message from a jailed activist, and we'll all go home feeling better about ourselves.

It was a relief to consider Africa for a few seconds. Who wouldn't want to help? Global poverty was a nightmare. Unfortunately, the size and intractability of the problem meant the solution would not be found in our lifetimes and Amanda's cheerful obliviousness overrode the modest effects of the peanut butter. Her optimism in the face of such futility enervated me. Almost immediately my ghastly situation reasserted itself and came barreling down the veldt, displacing the elephants and lions and erupting once again at the center of my consciousness. One had to ration optimism. It wasn't as if an unlimited supply existed.

"Best . . . ?"

"Sorry, I was thinking about something else."

"How many tickets can I put you down for?"

"Two," I said, knowing I would not go.

Pleased with my altruism, Amanda removed a diet soda from the refrigerator and poured the contents into a glass. She took a sip and fixed her earnest eyes on me.

"It certainly puts our problems in perspective, doesn't it?"

"Our problems are nothing compared to those faced by Africans." I hoped that sounded sincere. I meant it although at the moment it was hard to care about Africa.

"You know the life expectancy for a male in Swaziland is thirty-three?"

That barely registered because Africa reminded me of Isabel. That's where she was going when we parted, to study polygamists. My thoughts rocketed back to Iowa City, the night she asked me to leave with her, and the timid decision I made. I couldn't taste the peanut butter, couldn't hear Amanda, such was the morass of self-loathing that engulfed me.

"Best, where are you? You're spacing out."

"Sorry, what?"

"Whatever problems you're having, you are not Africa."

Getting into the semantics of whether my situation was equivalent to the condition of Africa led to a blind alley and I wasn't looking for sympathy anyway. Had Amanda wanted to waste time gabbing about our fellow associates or parsing the latest perfidy of some partner I would have been happy to oblige but her line of conversation so disturbed my thoughts that I had to excuse myself.

"What's wrong with you?" Reetika stood at my desk with a hand on an angled hip, her extensive dance training at work. I was calculating the days I had left on Earth but told her everything was perfect. "You look like you have an upset stomach or something. Want a Rolaid?" I said thanks, but no. "Claude Vendler, Mrs. Vendler's nephew? He called again. He wants to talk about the sale of his aunt's home." I nodded and said I'd get back to him. When she asked if it would be all right to leave early for a theater audition I told her just get someone to cover. In gratitude (and with enviable confidence), she promised me house seats.

"Reetika," I said, "Nothing would please me more than you booking this job. Life is desperately short. Savor every ice cream cone."

"Do I look fat?"

"No, why?"

"Ice cream cones?"

"Take your pleasures. That's all I meant."

Claude Vendler lived in Arizona. In a brief phone conversation I reminded him the wheels of probate court grind at a leisurely pace. With considerable force he let it be known close attention would be paid to the distribution of assets. To announce he is no patsy, a certain kind of rube unaccustomed to dealing with lawyers often exhibits aggression. This hostile bumpkin was like a kidney stone. Politely, I told him I would be in touch.

A few minutes later I was on the phone with Dirk Trevelyan reporting the purloined Kandinsky had been tracked down and he only needed to write a check covering his wife's debts to recover it. He was thrilled and reiterated his gratitude. Was there anything he could do for me? Briefly, I thought about mentioning my fantasy of the Best Foundation—Benefactors welcome!—but was too distracted by everything else going on. We were saying our goodbyes when a spent-looking Spaulding shuffled into my office with several cut flowers in a ceramic coffee cup. She told me they were blue phlox from her brother's garden and apologized for the previous night. It was immediately clear that the email I sent, the sad story of my mother's self-destruction, guaranteed to push anyone away, had had the opposite effect.

"Why were you texting me from a police car?"

"I was totally out of control," Spaulding said.

Then she asked what had happened to my face. Automatically, I touched the bandage with my fingertips. I was going to repeat the lie about the cat scratch. Why let Spaulding know I had pursued her out of the cab like some misbegotten knight-errant, that my heroics had gotten me beaten and nearly trampled. Chemotherapy isn't exactly truth serum but the pounding the system takes can have other consequences. The flowers weakened my resolve.

"I ran after you and someone attacked me with a brick."

"Oh, no. I am so, so sorry."

"You didn't get hurt?"

"No, I'm fine. You really ran . . . I'm sorry to hear about your mother. You know, I was in Payne-Whitney, too." Not only had my gambit failed to push her away, it had released waves of empathy that now threatened to engulf me. "Does that sound like I read about her in the alumni magazine?"

"I hope the email didn't upset you." Upsetting her was the whole idea, that she would see me as too damaged to pursue and find someone more appropriate. But the sense of humor she displayed and her openness were bracing and volatile and entirely too attractive. Something burbled in my stomach. I willed the anti-nausea drug to work.

"No, it didn't upset me but I was upset for you. Did you write that whole thing last night?"

"It's from an aborted memoir. One more thing I couldn't finish."

The sweet perfume of the flowers was narcotic. I raised the coffee cup and pressed my nose to them, then placed it back on the desk. In the aridity of my office they were a mountain meadow.

"My father was super annoyed with me when I got home."

"You didn't tell him I was with you I hope."

Spaulding began to relate what had happened to her since we had last seen each other, the mob, the police, the hobo chasing her, and Ed's reaction to these adventures.

"That's awful," I commiserated.

"It was like a bad dream come to life."

I got up and walked around my desk. While I wrestled with a desire to hold her in a full embrace, I laid my hands gently on her shoulders. We stared intently into each other's eyes separated by the length of my forearms.

"Spaulding, I don't even know what to say. Are you safe up there?"

This was the moment Reetika chose to announce the arrival of the Farood sisters, who were ready to thrash out a disagreement over their mother's estate. I quickly released Spaulding and told my secretary, who stood in the doorway regarding me quizzically, to send the Faroods in. When Reetika retreated Spaulding apologized once again for last night and I said forget it, we all do silly things. The disappointment etched on her face when I ended our exchange cut deeper than my assailant's brick but it was nothing compared to my own. Her scent commingled with that of the blue phlox and lingered in the silken air.

SPAULDING
Drunk, Maybe, But Not Numb

The flowers were a miscalculation considering Mr. Best had barely looked at me since my drunken lunge in the taxi. It seemed like an excellent idea to back off. When some office errand brought me past his open door it was eyes straight ahead. At night I rode the train to Connecticut and tried to not think of ways to complicate my life. My encounter with the hobo had freaked me out so it wasn't like I could go for walks. Instead, I wrote or baked or helped Marshall in his garden. I still wasn't sure if Edward P was convinced that psycho steeplechase had happened but I knew Marshall believed me. He didn't want to go out either so we spent a lot of time together watching movies or writing in our journals. When Katrina wasn't around I let him try on my clothes.

The summer workshop at Barnard was a solid anchor and forced me to get some work done. I even managed to write a few poems that weren't awful. I brought a tray of homemade cookies to the class to help further erase any memories of my appalling debut. That was the positive. The negative was that in late July I was eating dinner with my mother and her boyfriend. Dodd was fervently vegan and had persuaded Harlee to embrace veganism so we were dining at Zen Yeah! (Yes, there was an exclamation point in the name of the restaurant) on Amsterdam Avenue. In the wake of my move to Connecticut I had suggested that the two of us have dinner one night a week. This was the second time Dodd had joined us. He was around my mother's age and had thinning gray hair he liked to run his fingers through. There was a little soul patch under his lower lip and he wore gold wire-rimmed glasses. He had the baggy look of someone who used to weigh a lot more. Going from the world of finance to the world of massage was more than just a career change. He altered his diet, started exercising, shed the pounds, began meditating, and in every way became a role model for my mother. Dodd was her guru. At our previous dinner he had delivered an entire speech about colon health. I'm still not sure what a colon does but my mother listened rapturously. When I had asked why we couldn't make these meals a mother/daughter experience, she said,

—Dodd's in my life now, Spaulding, so he's in yours, too.

How do you respond to that? Why was I meant to have a relationship with whomever it was she happened to be having sex with? Seriously. It's hard to say whether it was guilt, or habit, or residual affection for my mother that put me at the table for three in the corner of Zen Yeah! but there I was picking at something orange made from tempeh. To steel myself for the dinner I'd had several drinks. It was the first time I had touched alcohol since that night with Mr. Best but this time I calibrated it perfectly. Dodd had been telling us about a client he had worked on at the spa today who insisted on keeping all of his clothes on. It was hard to pay attention.

The frigid air raised goose bumps. Laughter from a nearby table scraped the inside of my skull. When Dodd excused himself to go to the bathroom my mother put her hand on mine. The flesh on her face was pallid. There was a piece of bulgur wheat between her front tooth and incisor. Who would take care of her?

—Spaulding, do you think you might need some rest?

—What, like sleep?

That look she gets when concern and understanding are on the menu. Like she's making her eyes get all damp on purpose.

—How's it going at your father's?

—It's going fine.

—He told me about an incident. You were chased.

—By some weird-ass hobo.

My mother breathed through her nose, pursed her lips, and straightened her back, staring at me the whole time like I was a particularly complicated stitch.

—Are you taking your meds?

—I'm winding down. And I'm talking to Dr. Margaret twice a week.

—You felt pretty rested when you left the clinic, didn't you?

—It's hard to tell the difference between rested and whacked out on pills, but, okay, where are you going with this?

—Your father and I were talking and we agree that maybe . . .

—You want me to go back there?

—No. We don't. Meema and Poppy are going on a two-week cruise in the Galapagos Islands and they've invited you to go with them.

Meema and Poppy were my mother's parents. They lived in Florida and I saw them every couple of years. My grandfather had been a top guy at a corporation and liked to golf and grumble about how Obama had destroyed America. My grandmother played solitaire and smoked a lot. There was no way I was going on a cruise with them.

—For, like, vacation?

—Exactly. And then you'd stay with them down in Tampa.

When she said this she clapped her hands together in delight, hoping I was with the program.

—No effing way.

—Honey, please.

Dodd returned from the bathroom and he likely wished there had been some kind of stomach situation that would have kept him away longer when I turned in his direction and said,

—So, Dodd, do you think I need to go on a cruise with my grandparents?

—It'll be so fun! Harlee chimed. All those giant turtles!

Dodd turned to my mother in mute surprise, his face asking, Do I answer this question? She had put him in a difficult situation. He laughed the way someone laughs when there is absolutely nothing funny.

—She could rest up before school.

—You seem okay to me, Spaulding, he said.

—Dodd, your degree is in massage, Harlee reminded him.

—Body workers aren't allowed to have opinions? I said.

—Your father told me what you did to your room, all those faces.

—What does that have to do with a South American cruise I'm not going on? And they're poets, Harlee. I showed the pictures to a lawyer at Dad's firm who's a published poet and he thought the whole thing belonged in the Whitney Biennial.

—Maybe the Payne-Whitney Biennial, my mother said.

It was as if a large Pyrex cube dropped from the ceiling and sealed us in. Diners' faces moved in animated conversation, but within our enclosure was only silence.

—Did those words really just come out of your mouth?

Dodd put his hand on my mother's forearm as if to quietly say shut the fuck up right now.

—Oh, Spaulding, you have to be able to laugh at yourself.

—You're one to talk about problems, Drunky.

The slap caught me by surprise. Harlee's aim was not good and she got me with more fingers than palm but it was humiliating. Instead of hitting her back I was standing on my chair holding a glass of water. I don't remember sliding back and stepping onto the chair but there I was. Everyone should stand on a chair in a crowded restaurant at least once. It's a view most people never get. Dodd's mortified face looked up at a tightrope artist slipping. Harlee hissed words obscured by the cinders flowing out of her mouth.

—May I have everyone's attention?

They gave it. A waiter with a tattoo sleeve stared open-mouthed. A pair of lesbian moms and their twin sons gaped. A guy around my age eating dinner with his girlfriend took out his phone and snapped my picture. Forty pairs of eyes were glued to the person playing the character named Spaulding. Did they think this was some kind of performance art? Was it? What was I doing? Besides incorrectly calibrating the vodka.

—I am battling mental illness, I announced. There were some expressions of shock, a few nods, and the lesbian couple applauded. And my mother—this is her right here—just smacked me in the face because I made fun of her drinking after she joked about my issues. Several people shot disapproving looks at Harlee. Well, I forgive. So let's drink to my mom.

I lifted the glass and sipped. A handful of the diners followed my lead.

—Thanks for your attention, everyone. By the way, she's in recovery now. I'm still dealing with mental health stuff but it's getting better.

The high / view is / I hope / a one / time thing.

The chair wobbled and I felt myself losing my center of gravity. For a moment it looked like I'd be splayed in the remains of Dodd's Tofurky but I regained my balance and lowered into the seat. Dodd had his hand on my mother's back. This is usually the point where a tear runs down someone's cheek but Harlee was displaying the emotion of an Easter Island statue. The audience went back to their dinners. They probably thought we were a family of actors cutting loose. A few of them stole glances at us but the show was over.

—You're the worst, Harlee said.

Never mind her betrayal, lack of understanding, or

soul-crushing cluelessness. I was horrible. Duly noted. But I swallowed this because I had made a ridiculous scene, didn't feel good about letting her provoke me, and was not going to give her more ammunition. I apologized for calling her Drunky and she apologized, too, although she wouldn't look at me.

There was a really awkward lull, what would be called a caesura if this were a poem instead of a horrible family incident. Then my mother said,

—Your father told me you were cited for disturbing the peace in the city. Seems like it's getting to be a habit.

—I don't want to talk about it.

—That's not acceptable.

—Neither is slapping me in the middle of Zen Yeah! But I'll tell you anyway. I helped someone who was about to get beat up by the police.

—You? Helped someone? She was incredulous.

—And you think that's something else I made up.

—Spall, I'm just saying. Don't be offended. We're all broken. Dodd, me, you. There's no shame in it. I really am sorry I slapped you.

And then she started crying. That threw the whole balance off. Dodd didn't know what to do. He rubbed Harlee's shoulder and looked at me with what felt like sympathy. It was too late.

When I discussed that evening with Dr. Margaret at our next session she said that whenever you find yourself standing on a chair in a restaurant you need to take a hard look at what led you to that point.

Yes, that was true. What was great about it, though, was that the numbness I would retreat into when life was overwhelming was not there in the restaurant. You don't get on a chair and say embarrassing things if you're numb. Drunk, maybe, but not numb.

Love was not going to save me. Love was only a substitute

for what your parents were supposed to provide and mine so consistently bungled. I longed to express all of this to Mr. Best, to write about the paradoxical impossibility and necessity of love. How was I supposed to convey these feelings without making a complete idiot of myself? Was that even possible, or was being a total idiot the whole idea?

JEREMY
In Want of a Country House

The field of trusts and estates presents ample opportunity for outright larceny. As clients are overtaken by the myriad indignities of age their minds will often cloud and the wily attorney, if endowed with a soupçon of unscrupulousness, can, with the mere adjustment of a comma, redirect amounts of money the size of the night sky. This was never my approach because greed is the least attractive of the deadly sins. The truth is, I had never done anything that could remotely be construed as unethical much less illicit

In the daisy chain of police states known as the Soviet Union, government-sanctioned writers were provided with dachas, country houses where they could retreat to ponder the important things Soviet writers pondered, like how to get toilet paper. While the stunted creative lives of these Eastern European artists were tragic, their real estate situation was enviable. What writer doesn't think he needs, strike that, *deserves* a dacha? Certainly every American one, and since the government didn't provide them, literary folk had to take matters into their own hands. In the rolling Berkshires Herman Melville rusticated at Arrowhead, Edith Wharton at The Mount, homes that burnished the reputations of their illustrious inhabitants. How is this relevant to anything other than early American property values? For the simple reason that I had been living in a one-bedroom apartment for five years and despite its proximity to the sylvan environs of Prospect Park found myself in want of a country house.

Nothing too grand, no sweeping lawn or lakefront required, just something appealing and in good condition less than three hours from the city that I could escape to on weekends. If the treatment worked and I lived, a house was something I could enjoy for decades. Were the Reaper's scythe to swing in my direction it would become The Best Colony, a retreat for writers, painters, poets, and artists of every stripe. I had set up foundations for clients and was intimately familiar with the ins and outs of the process. Dirk Trevelyan was only one of a number of potential benefactors I could approach to underwrite this project and a modest endowment would allow several artists at a time to avail themselves of the retreat. In years ahead it might come to rival Yaddo and MacDowell. As legacies go, it was one of which I could be proud. And if in the meantime it served as my country house, where was the harm?

This should have been something that demanded no monkey business on my part, but I had lost a lot of money in the most recent market crash and, motivated by the fear that has animated nearly all of my life choices, sold most of my stocks at a low point rather than patiently waiting for the inevitable uptick. There was not a great deal of cash on hand (and what there was had been marked for modest charitable contributions and street musicians). Circumstances required a shortcut.

The Montauk, N.Y., home of the recently deceased Brenda Vendler perfectly fit the bill: a saltbox that needed cosmetic work but sound as a Stickley chair. To sweeten the pot, the house sat on several acres with a pond and an old barn that could be turned into a writing studio. Several heirs were sprinkled around the country, all distant relatives; most of them, except for Claude, the one badgering me with hostile phone calls, unfamiliar with the housing market at the easternmost end of Long Island. There were funds in the estate that would be released to their grasping hands as quickly as the courts allowed. And Mrs. Vendler had appointed me her executor.

I reviewed the deed to double check that she actually owned the place and there were no liens against it. Then I went online and did a quick search of other properties for sale in the area. From this I was able to conclude that if the structure was not falling down it was significantly undervalued.

The plan: find a buyer to whom the house could be sold for less than market value, wait a year and a day (this was the time period during which an estate's executor could not own anything held in the estate), then buy it back, dealing my co-conspirator in for his trouble, and live out my days in Elysian splendor. This, let me be clear, is not against the law. Is it unethical? In a world where the riches generated by outright scams are calculated in the billions, the conclusion is clear. When this was done I would draft a letter to Claude Vendler apprising him that I had found a buyer.

And so on a Friday afternoon in early August, I found myself in a Middle Eastern restaurant on 1st Avenue in the shadow of the 59th Street Bridge seated across the table from my old college friend Margolis. At my office he had fallen into a long conversation with Reetika about the state of the contemporary theater from which I had to tear him away so we could walk to the restaurant. The two-time winner of a playwriting award at our alma mater, Margolis had graduated with lofty theatrical ambitions. Now an overpaid author of press releases for an international public relations concern with a specialty in disaster management, he had recently fled Los Angeles and transferred to their New York office. His marriage had collapsed and he was looking to begin life anew.

Margolis's crinkly hair was graying under a sun-bleached Mets cap that he did not remove during lunch. He wore frayed jeans, high-topped Nikes, and an old sweatshirt. Although rumor had it he had accumulated a large 401(k) in California, it looked like he might not have enough to pay for his share of the meal. I had ordered a falafel sandwich and Margolis was having hummus and lamb. He had been talking for fifteen minutes about the move from California, his job, and the perilous state of his career as a playwright.

"It's tough to get anything on in New York," he said. "My last production was at a theater in Wyoming. But now I've finished a new multimedia piece about the marriage of Henry VIII and Anne Boleyn."

"It sounds terrific," I said, taking another bite of falafel. Encouragement would put him in a more receptive mood.

"There's video, dance, shadow puppets, and the whole thing is going to be produced in a converted airplane hangar in Teterboro, New Jersey. Provided we get funding. You'll come." I assured him I would. He eventually ran out of things to tell me and asked what was new.

"I've written a collection of poetry," I said, purposely confusing the verb tense.

Margolis did not seem impressed. He sipped his iced tea. "Have you sold it yet?"

"It's coming out next year." I have no idea why I lied, other than my reflexive need to impress Margolis. Wanting to make it difficult for him to detect this prevarication should he immediately Google me, I dropped the following gem: "In France."

If his eyes could have flown from his head on springs they would have. Astonishment mixed with envy, chased by anger subtly downshifting to hostility before coming to rest at barely concealed resentment which he attempted to disguise with a half-smirk.

"*You* are publishing a collection of poetry? In *France*?" he said in a tone he might have used had I told him my dog could speak. Your *dog* can speak? Then quickly, "I didn't mean it like that. Congratulations, man, that's . . . amazing?" I thanked him and he asked if the poems had actually been composed in French.

I chortled modestly and told him they had not. I didn't want to be caught out in the event he asked me to say something in French, a language in which after *bonjour* I was more or less *perdu*. "Someone translated it."

"Why there and not here?" To this I offered what was an attempt at a Gallic shrug, intended to convey puzzlement at the inscrutability of the universe. "Just fucking amazing."

"Thank you," I said. He just nodded his head, entirely lost for words. To throw a lifeline, I asked where he was living.

"I'm renting a place in DUMBO. I don't like it," he said. "Too many art galleries. A man can't buy crackers."

"Margolis," I said, delicately probing, "Did your wife really get all the money?"

"Not all of it." He morosely stuck another piece of lamb into his mouth. He hadn't even asked what the poems were about, just happy to change the subject. I didn't blame him. Margolis was someone for whom the success of others ranked just behind lupus on The List of Things That Are Unendurable.

"Did she get the house?"

"I have about an hour of prime material on her," he said. "I've put it in King Henry's mouth. Yeah, she got the house, but my lawyer forced her to return my nuts, which she'd hung next to the wind chimes. Every time the Santa Anas blew they'd bang like castanets."

Although my thoughts immediately dove to my own nether regions and whatever cellular malevolence was percolating down there I wrenched them back to the restaurant, laughed politely, and asked if he was looking to buy a place on the East Coast. When he said that he was I explained the situation with Mrs. Vendler's saltbox and briefly outlined my plan.

"You could do a lot of things with that money."

I stared at him but he didn't make eye contact. He rubbed his chin then gazed at the crudely executed mural of the Pyramids on the wall across the room. Finally, he looked at me. "I don't have to do anything but hold on to the house for a year?"

"You do have to buy it, but I'll pay the mortgage."

"Besides that?"

I assured him the only requirement was that he agree to purchase the house then sell it to me at a tidy profit.

There were not a lot of people I could ask to do this. No one at work could be allowed to find out. My life was not dotted with old friends and there was no family on which to lean in this kind of situation. I needed Margolis to say yes. When the check came I grabbed it. Margolis asked what the catch was and I assured him there wasn't one. I hoped his skeptical look was more out of habit. He told me he would think it over but agreed to look at the Vendler place that Sunday.

Margolis thanked me for lunch and said, "Tell me about Reetika."

"My assistant? Smart, funny, a little desperate."

"We have a lot in common. Would you mind if I asked her out?"

The tender optimism implicit in this question was affecting. His career as a playwright (Anne Boleyn in a Teterboro airplane hangar?) was on the verge of crash landing in Dashed Hopes, a land where Reetika was fluent in the language. Still, the two of them persevered. Maybe they were perfect for each other.

"You should absolutely ask her out," I said. "Knock your socks off." We toasted to Montauk and the budding renaissance of the Margolis love life.

"By the way," Margolis said, "what's the timing on the deal?"

"Now."

"Doesn't it take a while to get a mortgage approved? I'm asking because I'm going fishing with some friends down in Mexico for two weeks and we're leaving next Friday."

"I can make some phone calls and get it expedited."

A televised Yankee game failed to distract me that night and although I was tempted to drown myself in a large whiskey I resisted the urge and sipped herbal tea instead. Lying between clean sheets my thoughts chased each other like monkeys—Was the chemo working? What to do if it failed? Should I confess my feelings to Spaulding? I was risking my job, my law license, any real means of making a living, but the threat of extinction had released me from my ethical moorings and just how far was I willing to go?—until finally sleep curtained my tired eyes and delivered black relief.

Dawn skidded in bright-eyed and I spent the better part of the glorious Brooklyn morning nauseated from the chemo and with a headache that gripped my skull like a badger. To reassert control of my spiraling existence, I put on clean khakis and a fresh oxford cloth shirt. At a corner deli I ordered a large coffee and with my notebook in hand made for Prospect Park. Over the next several hours I began to feel better and managed to get some writing done. When I left the park I passed an accordionist sporting jaunty facial hair seated on a wooden stool warbling the Stephen Foster song "Beautiful Dreamer." To his astonishment I added a fifty to the modest pile of bills in the shoebox displayed for that purpose.

On the walk home I stared at the sidewalk, diamond dust glinting in the late afternoon light, and thought about the word slake, how it included the noun lake and whether that was germane to its etymology. I failed to notice the person seated on the steps of my brownstone.

"Mr. Best."

She wore a short yellow cotton dress with a pearl-gray cardigan. Her sandals had delicate straps that wound like tendrils several inches above slender ankles. Her hair was tied in a thick ponytail from which several long curls had escaped and framed her pretty face. There was a trace of pink lip gloss on her mouth and her eyes were delicately shadowed in a manner foreign to most teenage girls. A small black purse on a gold chain hung from her shoulder. On her lap was the Moleskine notebook. In the pink light of the late afternoon she held up her phone and took my picture. Given all that was weighing on me I could not have been happier.

"Portrait of the artist," she said.

Immediately, I envisioned her father downloading the contents of her phone and his skull exploding when he saw my picture.

"You should ask someone before you do that," I said.

"I baked you a pecan pie." She reached down to the steps where an object covered in tin foil rested, picked it up, and presented it to me. "I hope I'm not being a pain." Her fingers absently played with a set of car keys. The nail polish had shifted from purple to deep blue since we had last met. One of my female neighbors, the squat proprietor of a candle shop with a rainbow flag prominently tattooed on her bicep, strutted toward us on the sidewalk. We nodded hello. She looked at Spaulding, then at me, and rolled her eyes before she entered the building.

"I want to apologize for my crimes." My expression must have conveyed that I had no idea what she was talking about. "For jumping out of the cab when you were doing me a favor. It was lame. And for harassing you on the Internet and making you read my emails and poems." Spaulding seemed genuinely contrite.

"I really don't mind." This was a considerable understatement since these interactions with Spaulding were my only source of joy, a commodity with which I had been extremely parsimonious. "I like it . . . Actually, I love it. And honestly, they were nothing compared to the email I sent you about my mother that I am now going to officially apologize for."

"Was it true?"

"Every word. Never mind that I should have kept it to myself. It must have seemed like a naked play for sympathy. Believe me, that wasn't how it was meant."

"I felt so close to you when I read it."

For a moment I thought she might cry. Gone were the self-assurance, the confidence and command. She embraced me and the sensation of her body against mine was the clearest window into a heartbreaking future that would never exist. My arms remained inert. I couldn't reveal that the confessional rawness of the email, its unpleasantness and deep unease, was intended to push her away. That Spaulding was standing on my stoop was indicative of how effective the plan had been. She released me and collected herself.

"Totally pathetic of me," I said.

"No, the opposite."

When she told me she needed to use the bathroom I handed over the keys to my apartment. "You're not coming up?" I gave her the pie, said thank you, and told her to please leave it on the kitchen table. I was going to enjoy what remained of the dwindling light and would wait for her on the sidewalk. She gave me a bemused look then marched up the steps and disappeared into the building. Had she stuck her breasts out as she passed me or did I imagine that? She didn't dress to accentuate them; her clothing choice, other than her sandals, was the standard poetry-slam-drama-club-loose-fitting-thrift-shop uniform that on an older woman bordered on cloying but draped on someone like Spaulding was whimsical. That some kind of dalliance figured in her plans was not a great leap. Or was it? Had I, in my overwrought state of mind, completely misinterpreted? Perhaps she was simply a pseudo-sophisticated teenage girl who thought I was famous—I *had* published—and was here simply as a fan or a student or a friend.

Beth the Nurse had warned me that chemotherapy was

unpredictable. There would be good days, she said, and less good ones. The weakness of the morning was gone and I felt fine, robust even. I allowed myself a sliver of optimism.

When five minutes elapsed and Spaulding hadn't returned I didn't even think about going up there. Never mind that she could have been doing anything: Rifling my medicine chest, photographing the rooms or my possessions, pictures that could find their way to some wretched blog along with captions and snarky comments. Preparing a video with her cell phone she could then upload to YouTube: *I'm standing here in the Brooklyn apartment of Jeremy Best aka Jinx Bell and if you're wondering why I'm not wearing a blouse . . .* She could have been making prank phone calls to Hong Kong. She could have a party; I wasn't going to move.

I texted: *What's taking so long?*

She texted: *B rt dn.*

Less than a minute later she was standing next to me with a copy of *The Dream Songs* by John Berryman. "I'm borrowing this," she announced. Her hair was dry so at least she hadn't taken a shower.

"You can have it."

"Really?"

I just wanted her to leave. "Yes, really. Now, Spaulding . . . "

"*Now, Spaulding*," she said, and twitched her hips, mocking what must have been the inadvertently officious tone of my voice.

A smile seeped onto my face. I wiped it off. "As much as I'd like to spend the evening chatting on the stoop . . ."

"Mr. Best, I have a problem and you need to help me."

"What with?"

"Do you have plans tonight?" In the moment it took me to formulate a lie, she said, "You don't, do you?"

"What is it you want?"

"Have you ever driven a Tesla?" I hadn't. Nor did the prospect hold the slightest interest and I said so. "I know, right?

They're so look-at-me. But here's the thing, my father and Hurricane Katrina are at some kind of college sailing team reunion so I liberated his. He never lets me get behind the wheel." She paused to gauge my reaction. I peered up and down the street. No Tesla in sight. Spaulding was entertaining, though, and there was no harm in playing her game for another second or two. Then, with mock innocence, "Never ever."

"I don't blame him."

"Just because I don't have a license?"

It was difficult to tell if Spaulding was telling the truth. Who knows if she was even staying with her father this weekend? She could have arrived by subway.

"You drove your father's Tesla here without a driver's license?"

"I'm a city kid. None of us have one." That part was probably accurate. I didn't get a driver's license until I was out of college. "Hey, the good news is I got a parking space on the street."

I wondered if she was a virgin and then upbraided myself for sexualizing her in even the most casual way (as if I hadn't already done it hundreds of times). But how was that to be avoided after she had arrived unbidden in my office, invited me to address her writing workshop, sent me her poems, kissed me in the back of a taxi, then turned up in front of my apartment in a summer dress armed with a pie and her libido primed for interstate adventure. *Interstate.* That hadn't even occurred to me. Was she really nineteen? Someone in my uncomfortable position could in a fugue of good intentions drive Spaulding home to Connecticut and conceivably be prosecuted for violating the Mann Act.

"Good luck," I said and began walking up the steps.

"Don't you at least want to see the car?" It would have been rude to not answer so I told her no, not really. "It's got a stick shift and I'm afraid to drive it back at night."

"It isn't dark yet. And honestly, I'm not even sure you have a car here, much less Ed's Tesla, if Ed even has a Tesla."

"I *swear* I do, okay? On my eyes. I heard that in a movie once. *On my eyes.* It's good, right?" There was no point in responding, but I told her yes, it was good. "Okay, look, I double swear his car is around the corner and it's getting dark and it's going to be totally dark in like half an hour." She was right about that. The sky had slid from cerulean to indigo since the time I'd been home. "Would you drive it back to Connecticut with me, please?"

"That's probably not a good idea."

"If you do I'll stop stalking you, okay?" Was this *stalking*? That hadn't occurred to me. Is it even possible to be stalked by someone to whom one has an entirely inappropriate erotic attraction? If she *was* actually stalking and not employing the verb with ironic intent it might have mitigated some of what churned in my viscera. "I swear I'll stop."

"What would we say to your father if he saw us pulling into the driveway?" I had already made the imaginative leap of getting into the car, the existence of which was still not real to me, and driving to Connecticut. How had she engineered that?

"I told you. They're not home." She managed to convey an extraordinary combination of pique and helplessness. "Please."

"Your best bet is to come clean, tell Ed you drove down here not to see me but to hang out in Brooklyn, and take the train back. Now, really, I have to go upstairs." I pivoted, fully intending to walk into the building.

"Are you all depressed because you have cancer?" This sentence arrived like a locomotive and pulped me. Not on the surface, however, where the skin remained intact. My entire body contracted as if in retreat from itself but I remained placid. "I totally don't blame you."

Telling someone you have cancer is the bad version of announcing a move to another city or a divorce. The message is that life will be different from this point and the person who is receiving the information, for better or worse, will never look at you the way they did before. I asked her to please not mention it to Ed.

Her head cocked and her face turned slightly sideways so she appeared to regard me skeptically. "You really have cancer?" I nodded. "Spaulding, you are such a tool." Her use of the third person imbued what was otherwise an uncomfortable moment with a certain loopy charm.

"If you didn't think so why did you ask?"

"The books?" Oh, the books. Those literary pom-poms, execrable cheerleaders to the afflicted. "They were on your kitchen table and I figured they were for research or something and so I wanted to make you laugh." She made a pistol with her hand, held it to her temple, and said, "Bang."

"Lay off the suicide gags."

"Sorry. Shit!"

"Those books *are* for research."

The querying look again. She smiled like I was the one joking. "So you're not sick?"

"No, I am."

Again, her face went full fathom five. "I'm a complete jackhole," she announced. "Forgive me, please? I'll stop bothering you since whenever we're together I'm apologizing for something. You don't have to drive me back to Connecticut or anything. I'm so sorry. That's a total suck-fest." Her pose had dissolved with such alacrity it caught me by surprise. There was no reason for me to do anything but say goodnight and disappear into my building.

The Tesla—it was red, the red of red flags, of warnings—was parked obliquely in the space on Union Street where it had attracted the attention of several neighborhood kids. In the front fender was a small dent. Spaulding noticed me clocking it.

"I grazed a light post."

She tossed me the keys. I snatched them out of the air with the sportiness that comes from bad decisions rashly made. I slid into the high-tech womb. My left hand gripped the leather-trimmed steering wheel while my right palm found its way to the smooth head of the stick shift. From the passenger seat she beamed at me as if I was Cancer Boy and she the Make-A-Wish Foundation. Was that pity? Sudden-onset resentment, while nowhere in the *Physicians' Desk Reference*, was not a pleasant sensation. For a moment I thought about getting out of the car and leaving her to navigate back to Connecticut solo. But the previous weeks had been so fraught that Spaulding and her father's Tesla here in Brooklyn suddenly took on the quality of a lark. Offense inexplicably gave way to exhilaration. Incoherence and contradiction were afoot and these were the bane of any trusts and estates attorney intent on keeping his job. But how much longer would my world be woven from tangible assets, probate courts, and disgruntled family members? This was a new country and its customs mysterious.

The Tesla darted through nervous traffic as we merged onto I-95. While I concentrated on not exceeding the speed limit Spaulding asked about my prognosis. I told her everything was going to be fine. Why did I lie? Because this was too much to hand someone who had more than enough problems of her own.

"Have you ever been married?"

"Spaulding, please don't take this the wrong way, but I've already shared too much about my personal life."

It was not my intention but Spaulding seemed offended. That couldn't be helped. Eighteen-wheelers eclipsed the Tesla. Cars careened past like pinballs. I drove like I drafted a will: with great circumspection. Although the Tesla handled nimbly, I wasn't going to open the engine up and be stopped by the police only to find Spaulding didn't know where the registration was. While it is an axiom that materialism is the ruin of Western civilization, the sense of sheer power rumbling beneath what I prayed were still healthy testicles sent sparks of kundalini shooting skyward where they fired in my brain.

As we passed Pelham, she rested her hand on my shoulder and said, "If you have cancer, Mr. Best, why not quit being a lawyer? You're an amazing poet. Everyone in the class wanted to marry you including the teacher. When you're done with the treatment you should hit the road, suck the marrow from the bone."

"Good image."

In Connecticut we glided beneath a blooming canopy of old-growth trees, their leafy branches offering a gently swaying benediction to the well-heeled wheeling below, and past large Colonials and mock-Tudors framed by meticulously maintained hedges and lawns.

"If you could do one thing before you die, what would it be?"

"I'd go back to Rome."

"Then go."

"Spaulding, I'm having chemotherapy."

"Stop acting like you're going to die. Never give in. Your words."

The force of her delivery stilled me. To be hectored by this sprite was disorienting. Her message, though, was essential. For the moment it was all she had to say. Together we brooded.

Mr. Best guided the Tesla into the garage and turned the engine off. I sat there desperately hoping he would try to seduce me but he jumped out of the car like the seat had suddenly caught fire. He was waiting for me on the driveway.

—Are you going to be okay?

—Sure, I said. Do you want to come in for a while?

—I need to get back to the city.

Usually I would have made some kind of bantering remark but I had totally put my foot in it with the cancer thing. He had humored me by taking this drive so it was time to admit defeat.

—Do you want me to call you a cab?

He asked how far the train station was and I told him it was a couple of miles. He said, it's a pleasant night, I think I'll walk and asked for directions. Then he waved over his shoulder and departed like a guy in an action movie who had just saved civilization.

Empty houses have strange personalities and it always creeped me out to come back to one. I was an apartment kid. If it wasn't for my mother and Dodd I would have been in the city now. But it was only until dorms opened in the fall so I needed to deal. The old wood groaned. Despite the heat, I shivered.

I stuck a frozen mac and cheese in the microwave. Waiting for the carbs to defrost, I went into Edward P's first-floor study to lose myself in *Middlemarch*. The room looked like something from a hundred years ago if you ignored the computer on the desk. The worn rug made it feel like an old slipper. There was dark wood paneling, an upholstered easy chair the size of a bear, and volume after volume of big hardback books on the stained wood shelves. Only some of them, ones with embossed gold lettering, were law books. When Edward P was younger, maybe he read a lot. Or maybe he just bought the books so he could sit among them and bask in their glow. On one wall was a painting of a tall ship in full sail and on another was a nautical map of the New England coast.

When I was a kid, Edward P used to take me sailing. Cruising along, I'd be enjoying myself as much as I was capable but then a chop would rise and without fail I would get seasick. He would try to pretend he wasn't annoyed with me, his lame daughter, but it was pretty easy to tell he wanted to toss me overboard. It had been years since we were on the water. Gully had invited me to visit Seattle and go sailing with him. A sentence from one of his emails read,

You can tack and come about and let a fresh wind fill your sails.

It's cheesy, sure, but I knew what he meant. He loved me absent all judgment, the only kind of real love.

In his senior year Edward P's sailing team won the Ivy League title. He had a bunch of sports trophies in the house but this one, a schooner the size of a hubcap made out of cast iron and mounted on a marble plinth, rested on his desk. I lifted it. The thing must have weighed at least twenty pounds. It seemed to contain the weight of his existence, the two wives, the four children, the law career, and the knowledge that more than half his life had passed. Jesus, Spaulding, I thought, it's a sailing trophy. Lighten up. I cracked *Middlemarch*.

Tight-assed and deluded Mr. Casaubon was saying something patronizing to the unbelievably patient Dorothea Brooke when I looked up and saw hulking in the doorway the man who had chased me home from the train station.

The hobo was standing less than fifteen feet from me.

Beneath his tangled hair were the most pained eyes. There was no point screaming because the house was empty. Then an odd thought cropped up. Can reducing prescribed doses of medication cause disturbing cognitive side effects? Maybe this was a hallucination. I rose from the chair.

—My Dad's upstairs. You'd better leave.

He just stared, like he knew it wasn't true.

—And he's got a gun, I said, also a lie. What do you want?

There was no answer to that question either. Was he even real?

—I can give you some food, but then you have to go.

He lurched toward me. French doors opened to the backyard but fear nailed me to the floor. When he got close enough for me to notice his stink I knew I was going to be murdered. I regained control of my muscles and tried to run past him toward the entrance hall but sticky hands grabbed me. His bedraggled face flushed and the pupils of those pinwheels swirled. The mangy fur of his eyebrows flew off in weird directions, fluid leaked from one nostril giving sheen to the skin just above his chewed-up mustache. There was a two-inch scar along his jawline that looked like a souvenir from a knife fight. I hoped he wasn't going to use a knife. I didn't want to get stabbed to death. He smelled horrid, like urine and spoiled lunchmeat. His foul breath contaminated my neck as he twisted my arm and forced me to the floor. I was on my side and he was trying to roll me onto my back. He was holding his forearm against my shoulder and when he forced one of his legs through mine he had the leverage to force my shoulders against the floor and I was thinking please don't rape me, please don't rape me just kill me when I felt his hands around my throat and his dirty fingernails dug into my flesh and his thumbs pressed and I closed my eyes so I wouldn't have to look into the hideous face when I heard a loud whack like a rock striking pavement and his body went slack.

I was afraid to look.

But when I did, Mr. Best was standing over me holding my father's sailing trophy, panting, red-faced. The hobo was still. Mr. Best kicked him off me with a feral look that trashed any memory of the lawyer who constructed graceful conversational sentences and wrote poetry. I scrambled up and tried to suck air into my lungs. The stink was worse than before. I collapsed in a chair. My hands, my legs, everything shook. I closed my eyes and tried to calm down. When I opened them Mr. Best was breathing heavily. He started to cough and his face colored. But the spasm receded as quickly as it arrived. He squatted next to the guy and pressed two fingers to his neck.

—He's dead.

Those were the first words Mr. Best had spoken since he had arrived. Then he asked if I was all right.

—I think so.

—Are you really here with me in this room?

Mr. Best gave me the strangest look. —Yes, yes, I'm here, he said.

JEREMY
Literary Monsters

In one place was an aspiring poet with an inflated view of Jeremy Best. In the other, an empty Brooklyn apartment next door to a Croatian sociopath. It was still relatively early. How pleasant, to have a nonalcoholic beverage and share some conversation. Why had I refused Spaulding's invitation? When I passed the haggard man on the street I thought of her alone in the house and the story she had told me about being pursued. Now there was a cadaver on the floor and I towered above it, the unlikeliest of champions. Perhaps the universe was not devoid of patterns. I dreamed a version of this the night before we met. Attacked on a beach, I beat the Minotaur to death with a club. Had this been prophesied like an ancient Greek myth? In this story, I was Theseus.

Spaulding was seated in a chair, lungs heaving. Without looking up, she said, "Do you want me to say I did it?" She was brave—it was one of many qualities that drew me to her—but on first blush the offer seemed outlandish. If the man was dead she could suffer the, the, what exactly? There wasn't a lot that could happen from a legal perspective. This creature had attacked, the story would go, and she vanquished him. It was inspirational. But I couldn't let her take responsibility. The cowardice inherent in that act would reflect remarkably badly on me and Spaulding's good opinion meant a lot.

"I can't allow that. Your father's going to be on the warpath if he finds out you . . ."

She interrupted, "What about when he finds out *you*? You're not supposed to be here. Let me do this, please." She rose from the chair, took my hand. Her irises shone. In them I saw my reflection. It didn't matter that Spaulding Simonson was nineteen. Her soul was as old as the elements.

A shot of energy surged through me and I kissed her. She maneuvered her body against mine, her pelvis pressing into my thigh. The smell of her hair wired to the blood in my groin. The night air crackled. My unsettling, unhelpful, and until now successfully suppressed attraction to Spaulding broke from its subterranean holding pen and jack-in-the-boxed to the surface. Her lips parted and my tongue darted into her mouth.

If there hadn't been a dead man nearby I could have gone further, despite the seismic ramifications. Here is a terrible thing to admit: I wanted to take her right there on the rug, throw her down, rip her panties off, and thrust myself into her as if an act of brutish rutting would somehow in its completeness narcotize me into a state of blissful purity. Please understand, I'm not saying this was a good plan. Even though my nervous system was in a state of hyperstimulation, I was not insane. Having sex in her father's den next to a corpse would have been an extremely bad decision under any circumstances but these are the things that go through an honest person's head.

When I released Spaulding from my grip she clung a moment longer. "This is so totally wrong." While it was impossible to know whether she was referring to the kiss or the corpse, both qualified and it was hard to disagree either way. Spaulding looked at the prostrate homeless man and asked if I was certain he was dead. The body had not twitched. I nodded. Spaulding sniffled, touched two fingertips to her forehead, and then began to sob, which endeared her to me even more. This went on for about thirty seconds, at which point the weeping subsided and she wiped her tears away with the heels of her hands. "Maybe we did him a favor. His life was awful. We should call the police."

Together we sat in the large reading chair, our thighs touching, the corpse still splayed in front of us.

"How are we going to explain my presence?"

Spaulding thought about this. Her eyes moved from me toward the body then to the dark yard. After a deep inhale of breath followed by a long slow release she said, "You should go."

"I'm not going to leave you by yourself."

In law school one learns about contracts, torts, and the Constitution, but nothing about dealing with a dead body. So to say I was out of my depth would be to considerably understate the situation. The first option was to put the corpse in the car and deposit it in a wooded area. The problems: a) we could be discovered driving with a dead body in the trunk or b) observed unloading the cargo. Further, my nerves couldn't be trusted to drive the car in this situation. The second option was dismembering the body, dissolving it with lime or acid, and burying the results in the backyard. In other words, this was not going to happen. The first two options were terrible and there was no good third one. How had I arrived at this juncture? Contemplating an affair with the managing partner's daughter, exploring a morally murky real estate transaction, and now pondering the disposal of a corpse? Had I become unhinged by the proximity of my own death? And was that necessarily a bad thing?

"I'm going upstairs to scrub the stank off."

When she left the room I kneeled down next to the intruder's body and rifled his pockets. There was a beat-up leather wallet. In it was a wrinkled five-dollar bill and a library card that identified this man as Karl Bannerman. A library card! What were his interests? His tastes? Mysteries? True crime? Perhaps he read poetry.

In the hope that fresh air would help me organize my thoughts, I stepped outside. The idea that this horror show had been foretold in any way and that Karl Bannerman's presence had some cosmic significance made no sense. He was nothing more than a malign coincidence, bad luck, a random actor. Standing in the backyard staring at the Simonson house, I knew the rest of my time on Earth was going to be spent writhing on a spit, wracked by self-recrimination so deep it would throttle the ability to feel anything else. Nothing prepared one for having taken a life. It was unendurable. How much was I supposed to tolerate before being reduced to a gibbering jumble? How much could anyone withstand before he looked to the uncaring heavens and cried uncle? The night itself was tightening around me. There was a sick feeling in my gut. I didn't know whether it was bile dripping or the chemo. I had taken the anti-nausea pills but there were no chemicals that could be prescribed to dampen the dread that had come to permeate everything.

When I returned to the scene it was immediately apparent something was amiss. Nothing moved. The air in the room was perfectly still. And the body was no longer there. The place Karl Bannerman had lain was empty, the only remnant of his presence a small bloodstain barely discernible on the rug. Had he gone upstairs? Was Spaulding there now? I charged into the foyer and noticed the front door was open. When I looked down the street he was bounding through the shadows.

Relief washed over me, quickly followed by terror. He was still out there, getting ready to do God knows what. I raced upstairs to tell Spaulding. After she got over her shock at the corpse's zombielike reanimation and retreat, I suggested we return to the city together. It was a testament to my vestigial fear of Ed Simonson's wrath and the effect it would have on my hopes for a partnership that this sense won out over my fear of the marauding hobo and I insisted we walk to the station to avoid a cab driver seeing the two of us together. Somewhere in my discombobulated condition I was still worried about the partnership.

"You can't be serious," she said. "I'm not walking."

"I'll protect you," I said.

In an act I could not have previously imagined (these were starting to accumulate) I took a stainless steel carving knife from a kitchen drawer and stuck it in my belt like a samurai. My successful defense of Spaulding made me slightly giddy. I would handle whatever further randomness the universe had in store by stabbing it.

"You're really going to take a kitchen knife?"

"Unless Ed has a gun."

When Spaulding realized I was completely serious, we locked the house and fled into the troubled night.

Khakis and an oxford cloth shirt were the perfect uniform if one had nearly killed a homeless man in suburban Connecticut and wanted to remain anonymous. Other than the carving knife at my hip, obscured by the untucked shirt, I looked like any other local out for an evening stroll. Spaulding had changed into a pale blue dress that hung loosely on her as we tramped toward the train. Cars drove past and no one gave us a second look. The evening was cool and starlit. A breeze carried a salt tang. The forested acres leaned oppressively close. Somewhere the intruder lurked.

"I had a dream where I killed a Minotaur," I said. "That's what was going through my mind when I thought he was dead on the floor. My Minotaur."

"Really? In my head I called him Grendel."

"You've read *Beowulf*?"

"We did a section in English called Literary Monsters. *Beowulf*, *Frankenstein*, the Hulk from Marvel Comics."

The mix of bliss and terror was wholly new. How could I not be smitten with someone who after nearly being murdered references *Beowulf*? Putting my arm around Spaulding, I held her to me. It took nearly an hour to navigate to the distant train station. On the empty platform Spaulding and I stood at a distance from each other, so in the event someone else was to arrive they would not think we were together.

There was a pay phone adjacent to the locked station and miraculously, it worked. I called the local police and reported the incident. I let them know Spaulding had gone into the city and would be available to file a report on Monday. When they asked my name I told them I was Ezra Pound.

A gleaming sedan rolled into the parking lot and a well-dressed couple around my age emerged from the backseat. They ascended the steps to the platform as if it was a victory stand where laurel wreaths would garland their broad shoulders. The pool of station light in which they posed lent their tall blondness an Aryan quality. His hair was a little long but perfectly groomed and hers was held back with a white band wide as a baby's wrist. He whispered in her ear and she laughed delightedly, the wittiest thing she'd ever heard. They could have been siblings but the way she adjusted the collar on his jacket then smoothed it with her palm told a more intimate story.

How I would have liked to trade places with this pair of golden retrievers. To have wrapped myself in the comfort they exuded, to have drawn their aggressive health around me like a protective cloak, to have tasted their candied concupiscence and been satisfied and needed nothing more, to have merged with them, been absorbed by them, to have become them was all and everything in the precious minute that had brought us together on the train platform.

Spaulding stood twenty yards away with her back to me. The effortless togetherness of these show dogs was something we could never experience and the sadness of that realization caused an ache that was wholly unanticipated. I wanted to run to her, hold her, kiss her again and again. Be bold. Be bold! It was a taunt to a man on a diving board who could not swim.

When the train arrived I discreetly slid the kitchen knife into a garbage can. The railroad car was only a third full. Spaulding took a seat several rows in front of me. Someone had left a copy of yesterday's *Wall Street Journal* and I pretended to read until we arrived at Grand Central Station. I walked to the subway with Spaulding in my wake and only when we got off the train in Brooklyn did she slip her arm in mine.

I closed the door behind us. Before turning the light on I listened for anything out of the ordinary. Faint city sounds, a car horn, a brief burst of Spanish on the street, the rattle of an ordinary evening. A wounded man stumbled thirty miles north of here or perhaps he lay dead in someone's woodpile and yet my overstimulated amygdala suggested I expected him to visit. I asked Spaulding if she wanted anything to eat or drink.

"I want to take a shower."

I gave her a towel and told her she could sleep in my bed and I would sleep on the couch in the living room. In the kitchen, I filled a highball glass with ice and poured myself three fingers of single malt. Then I remembered I couldn't drink and despondently emptied the contents into the sink. I filled the glass with club soda and took a few sips. For a brief moment I was able to focus my tumbling thoughts on the imaginary burn of whiskey in my throat. To act like Spaulding wasn't standing in a nearby shower, rivulets of water running down her naked body as she soaped herself, inadvertently driving me into the same state of sexual wantonness that got me thrown out of graduate school, I turned on the radio and found a classical station. As the calming strains of Mozart washed over me, I sat at the table with my not-whiskey and proceeded to get a staggering hard-on. In spite of Dr. Tapper's dire prognosis my circulation remained excellent.

SPAULDING
Only Poets

Given what we had just been through I thought it would be okay if I borrowed his toothbrush, and while I brushed my teeth I wondered if it was possible that one of the worst nights ever could also lead to an entirely new way of being. My suicide flirtation again shown up for the bullshit it was, I was overcome with gratitude for having been spared, twice now if you're counting. My will to live was unabashed.

The streetlight smoldered beyond diaphanous curtains and cast a soft light on the framed photographs of the World Trade Center hanging on the wall. Any safe place can be violated.

I lay in bed wearing one of Mr. Best's tee shirts. The apartment was locked and he was in the next room but it's hard to feel safe after you've nearly been murdered. Despite my attempt to banish them, the events in Connecticut played in a relentless loop: the headlong run from the train station, prostrate in the bushes, face in the dirt, the fruitless late-night search with Edward P and his doubts about my sanity, and then the attack in the house, that horrible creature with his hands on me, and Mr. Best nearly killing him. This malevolent movie unspooled until my muscles stiffened and I was grinding my molars. I had an urge to reach for a Xanax but there weren't any. And wasn't I trying to be less of a chemistry set? Taking a deep breath, I attempted to unwind. The familiar calming rhythm, the rhyme that would save me, or at least fend off the crazy, was circling and preparing to land.

The next / room holds / the key / to my / demise.

Demise? What? Where did that come from? The Iambic Pentameter Strategy did not always work perfectly.

I tried again.

In a / new room / a girl / waits to / be born.

I wanted to burst through the wall and land on Mr. Best's lap, have him run his hands through my hair. I wanted to feel him get hard against my thigh, his tongue dancing with mine. But still I waited. On the street two guys were singing "Happy Birthday" to someone named Saffron, their voices marinated in liquor.

After I'd been lying in his bed for ten minutes with the lights out the fear was like a wild animal thrashing in a rickety cage. Trying to get at me, teeth gnashing, claws outstretched, wild-eyed. The terrifying images kept cycling through my brain and I became more and more unnerved. Why wasn't Mr. Best in here with me? He had kissed me earlier in the evening so I knew he was attracted to me. And since I had been through something utterly horrible, didn't I deserve some comfort? And didn't he deserve it, too? He had done the hard part, literally saving my life. Why couldn't he just lie here next to me and make everything stop vibrating? I wanted to bury my face in his neck, to hold him even if we didn't have sex, but I wasn't going to leave the bedroom because I didn't want to make this about my needs. He had no family, no one he could depend on while he was trying to get well. The least I could do was not be the cause of more problems. But it was impossible to be alone. Perhaps it would be all right if I told him I was famished. We had skipped dinner. It made sense that I'd need food and if I said that he wouldn't think I was an emotional basket case.

—I don't feel like being by myself.

Mr. Best was hunched at the small kitchen table, a laptop open in front of him. He looked totally exhausted, as if the events of the evening had physically diminished him. But when he saw me he straightened his spine.

—I don't blame you.

—Are you hungry?

At a local market, the kind with ten varieties of lettuce, we bought some chicken—yes, chicken, because I didn't want to throw myself at him in his kitchen and he was still shell-shocked and all I had done was cause drama (and he had more than enough of that) so, yes, chicken—and new potatoes and some green beans that I could sauté with garlic. Mr. Best bought a large bottle of fresh-squeezed berry juice because he was on a new health regimen. We were quiet on the way back to the apartment, both of us wiped out from the evening, and the only words we exchanged were the kind you can't remember because there's a sense that you're becoming more comfortable, more at ease, drawing closer and closer so the words become detached from their meaning as they float in the air all around you and quietly connect into a net that keeps the animating energy from lifting you both off the sidewalk.

While I seasoned the chicken I kept sneaking glances at Mr. Best at the kitchen table futzing on his laptop but he didn't seem to notice. A desire to get to know him better, this savior, this poet and shield, fought with a fleeting sense of decorum that told me to leave him alone. But decorum never stands a chance with me. When I wondered if he would mind if I asked him a personal question, he told me to go ahead.

—You don't have to tell me if you don't want but this thing you have? How serious is it?

—It's serious.

—You have great hair. Really super thick.

—Thanks.

—Doesn't chemo make it fall out?

—Not always. When's the chicken going to be ready? It smells great.

He closed his laptop and checked the stove. It was easy to see I had gone as far as Mr. Best was going to allow me to go right now. Neither of us said anything for a while. He just stood by the stove and stared at the kitchen timer. When he had his back to me I took a close look to see if I could notice anything different since he had started treatment. It was hard to tell. He didn't look gaunt but you don't lose weight instantly. And his coloring looked all right, not haggard or yellow, just maybe a little tired, understandable since it had been a super-stressful evening. When I realized what I was doing my chest got tight because that was the moment the whole situation sunk in. I was examining him. It was clinical, but it also felt sexual, and the whole sensation left me lightheaded. My nerves tingled, not because I didn't think I belonged in this apartment but because I thought I did. At least I was pretty sure I thought I did. It was difficult to know. Was life without meds going to make me overthink everything?

He was looking at the chicken through the oven window. I rose, refilled my glass, and sat down again. I took a glug of the wine, so refined. Some of it dribbled down my chin and I wiped it with the heel of my hand. The kitchen timer shattered the silence. Mr. Best was taking the food out of the oven and placing it on the counter when I came up behind him and put my arms around his waist. He turned around expressionless and I began to stammer another apology when he smiled and that smile let me in and held me and crooned comfort and belief in me. It was confidence and resignation, connection and isolation, defeat and victory, possibility and nothingness, all of the complexity that only poets can put into words. He touched my chin and kissed me lightly. He opened his lips and I slid my tongue into his mouth. When his hands cupped my ass my doubts evaporated and I grabbed the hem of my dress and lifted it over my head. I stood in front of him in my bra and panties and I could feel he was already hard so I pulled his zipper down. He unfastened my bra and covered my breasts with soft kisses while I caressed his cock. I lifted my thigh and he split my fig and we had sex standing up in the kitchen. He supported my legs with supple hands and I came and then I came again and he came. He kissed my lips and my eyelids and my neck and my nipples. I remember thinking, Jesus, that took long enough, but it was worth the wait.

—Spaulding, he said, I don't think you should call me Mr. Best anymore.

I started laughing because, really, what can you do when someone you've just had sex with for the first time tells you that?

He started laughing, too, and for a few seconds I forgot he was supposed to be sick, and that I was almost murdered, and there might be blood on the carpet in Stonehaven, and the Tesla had a dent in it. With his body next to mine, his chest rising and falling in easy rhythm, his tired eyes clear, it was impossible to remember any of that.

—Jeremy sounds weird, I said. But if you insist.

He kissed me.

—I'm afraid I do.

There was chocolate chip ice cream in the freezer and we put scoops on slices of the homemade pecan pie I had brought that afternoon. He turned a radio on. Classical music played as we sat naked at the kitchen table. Jeremy told me about the year he spent as a student living in Rome, his first attempts at writing poems, and the unexpected detail that he'd never had a serious girlfriend. When there was a pause in the conversation, I said,

—Was this a time-killer?

—What do you mean?

—You said, and I'm quoting, Sex is nothing but a time-killer, something you do when the conversation is exhausted.

—When did I say that?

—That night in the cab.

—When you're trying to be clever and failing, sometimes bullshit comes out. That's not how I feel. Look, when I jumped out of the cab and ran into the crowd in my lawyer costume and some guy cold-cocked me, I lay there in the street and for a moment I thought, why get up? If I stay on the ground all my problems will end under the feet of that mob. But I wanted to know that you were safe. Don't read too much into what I just said. What I'm telling you is someone had to act like an adult. And I failed.

An unfamiliar sensation gripped me. It's hard to know what to call it because certain words can get you in trouble, yet at that moment I was more intertwined and allied, yes, totally allied, with another human being than ever before.

—Why didn't you tell me this?

He kissed my neck and said he'd be right back. I watched him go. Good shoulders that tapered into a trim waist and a compact ass. Lightly muscled like a dancer. A lightly muscled poet. And his manhandle was beautiful, too. It swayed as he walked back into the room a moment later holding a small object. He sat next to me so our shoulders touched and showed me a green carving the size of my open hand. It was a seated child with the head of an elephant.

—A friend of mine gave this to me. It's a Hindu god called Ganesh.

—He's cute. Is this jade?

—Soapstone. It's not worth a lot of money or anything. I kept it for luck.

—How's your luck been?

—Abysmal. Maybe it'll work better for you.

He handed over the figurine. It was heavier than I had expected. When I put it on the table I noticed it was anatomically correct.

—He's an uninhibited little elephant-boy-god, isn't he?

Jeremy agreed that Ganesh was pretty freewheeling and led me to the bedroom. There was sex again and this time his tongue traced patterns between my legs and I shuddered and came and came and came.

JEREMY
Remover of Obstacles

M y sleep was not untroubled and as I fought for consciousness in the early Brooklyn light I remembered there was a dangerous lunatic wandering Connecticut, traces of his presence were probably in Ed Simonson's house, and the chemotherapy was starting to make me unsteady. But the attack had been reported, it would take a forensic team to uncover anything, and as for the chemo, I could only hope it was working.

Spaulding was sleeping on her side, facing me. Not only was this tableau entirely unplanned, assiduous attempts had been made to avoid it. That is not entirely true. The truth is that my will had incrementally crumbled and now that she was curled up warm in my bed, all of my protestations, hesitations, and fears seemed pointless. Her father or her mother would be expecting her but that could be sorted out later. The collapse of my resolve was not surprising, only that it had taken so long. Days without Spaulding were an endless stream of anodyne tasks peppered with intimations of mortality. To deny small joys no longer made sense.

When she stirred I gently touched her shoulder. The sharp intake of breath startled me. She contracted and made an involuntary noise, somewhere between a squeal and a grunt.

"You scared me."

"I only touched you with my fingertips."

"Remember what happened last night?"

"You're right. I'm a dunce."

Spaulding had dealt with the situation admirably and left-over fragments of fear and confusion were understandable. She was hungry so I scrambled some eggs. Draped in one of my old tee shirts, she sat at the kitchen table sipping orange juice and inspected the Ganesh.

"He's supposed to be the remover of obstacles."

"Are you Hindu or something?"

"I'm not religious."

"At all?"

"When we die, we die," I said as I handed her a plate of eggs. I served myself and sat across from her.

"Okay, so. We should go to Chinatown."

"What's in Chinatown?"

"There's this healer down on Mott Street. I swear he cured my mother of alcoholism." This information was imparted in the awestruck tone of one who had witnessed a miracle. "I went with her, the two of us. The guy said he could cure any-thing."

"I'm not in the market for some kind of woo-woo cancer cure."

"How do you know it's woo-woo?"

"I'll think about it, okay?" She grunted and told me that was something her parents would say.

I spooned shade-grown Sumatran into a large press while Spaulding tapped on her phone. The silence was unwelcome so, although it was none of my business, I asked what she was doing. She told me she was texting her father to inform him she had stayed with a friend from her writing workshop. The idea of deceiving Ed bothered me but I was on a new path and did not suggest she do otherwise.

"Is this a real Andy Warhol?"

Spaulding stood by the fireplace in the living room with her hands on her hips and scrutinized the lithograph. I told her it was. "Who's the subject?"

"That would be my father."

"Really? Your father knew Andy Warhol?"

"He did legal work for him. Sometimes they socialized." Spaulding waited. She wanted to hear more.

"It sounds like he was cool."

"In the most superficial way. A week before I was going to leave for college he accused me of siding with my mother in the divorce and told me he wouldn't be contributing a penny to my tuition. So his timing wasn't that cool. And he did ruin my mother's life but I didn't take sides. I got that he was gay, that he'd been repressing it for years and needed to be true to his nature. But it didn't make him noble and that's how he wanted me to think of him."

"So why did you hang his portrait?"

"Because it's a Warhol? I don't know. That's a really good question. It's the only thing he ever gave me, other than a biography of Winston Churchill." My feelings about my father were not entirely resolved and I didn't want to explore the surge of emotion I was experiencing. "Let's not talk about this."

Spaulding wandered around the apartment, trailing eros. Without asking she put a Pixies CD in the player and sank into the sofa with *The Collected Works of Allen Ginsberg* on her lap. I asked if she'd ever read Frank O'Hara.

"Who?"

"He's a poet who wrote a lot about New York City."

I handed her a paperback copy of *Lunch Poems*.

"Read this instead of Ginsberg. No one better captures New York City. Killed by a dune buggy on Fire Island."

"That's so random."

"He was forty."

I wanted to tell Spaulding that he was a curator at the Museum of Modern Art who would take walks during his lunch break then return to the office where he would coax poems about what he'd seen from an old Royal typewriter. That a high school teacher gave me this book and it was one of the reasons I became a poet. But I began to feel like I might start to cry again. What was at the root of these waterworks? My father? The uncertain nature of my illness? Or was it the dawning realization that after years of believing it to be impossible and nearly giving up hope someone could see what I saw, apprehend it the same way, that she was for me and because I wasn't dead yet there was still time to do something about it.

Spaulding closed the Ginsberg volume and opened the O'Hara. One leg crossed over the other, she flexed her toes. As the Pixies' jittering yip filled the apartment I fell to my knees and from sheer gratitude covered her feet with kisses. She giggled.

"Don't tell me you're a foot guy."

"No," I said, as she slipped the tee shirt over her head and my kisses migrated from her toes up her ankles to her calves, knees, thighs, pussy, stomach, ribcage, breasts, neck, ear, cheek, and lips and I swept Frank O'Hara out of the way.

In my obsession over last night, the most astonishing occurrence of all was elided: Spaulding had offered to cover for me. No one in my life had ever done anything so selfless. Yet Spaulding Simonson stared death in its rheumy eye and offered herself up. Had I not gone back to the house, Karl Bannerman would have killed her. Contrary to my dire view of myself, I had acted courageously. Dragon vanquished, maiden saved. The sensation of well-being I experienced was further intensified by the earthquake of my orgasm.

Whether because I was uncomfortable with this valiant role or with anything resembling actual intimacy, when we finished a familiar visitor arrived in the form of guilt and the condition of Karl Bannerman took on fresh urgency. Since I had nearly killed him, I wanted to know that he was getting medical attention.

After sluicing several cups of coffee down my throat I did an Internet search of every hospital in a ten-mile radius of Stonehaven. I told Spaulding that it was important from a moral perspective to find out if this man had survived. Maybe it was more paranoia but it didn't seem like a good idea to call the hospitals from my phone. When I mentioned I needed to go out for a few minutes and explained why, she did not tell me it was unreasonable and announced she would come too.

At an Arab-run store on Court Street I purchased a disposable cell phone, the kind favored by drug dealers and terrorists, and as Sunday morning Carroll Gardens ebbed and flowed around us called the two hospitals in the Stonehaven area. Neither would give me the information. We began to walk back to the apartment.

"Best. Freeze." The voice was an assault. I froze. Across the street a school playground with Sunday morning kids cavorting on monkey bars. Ahead of me an old lady walking a small dog.

I slowly turned my head and saw—Margolis? He wore a frayed tee shirt, cargo shorts, and sandals.

"Do I look like a land baron?"

My expression must have been one of almost cartoonish incredulity since he immediately asked if I had forgotten our expedition to Montauk this morning.

"The house. Yes, yes, the house." My head nodded violently.

"I'm Spaulding."

In my nervous attack I had completely forgotten she was there.

With feigned élan I declaimed, "Spaulding, yes. This is Margolis." He gave me a quizzical look then greeted her the way someone might greet a maid cleaning a hotel room to which they had returned after having forgotten a pair of sunglasses. Ordinarily this would have bothered me—Couldn't he have been friendlier? Why the snobby reaction? Was he judging me for being with someone Spaulding's age?—but under the circumstances it barely registered.

"Spaulding's father and I work together. She was in the neighborhood and dropped by to say hello." It was difficult to tell whether Margolis believed me. I asked Spaulding if she would give us a moment. Without a word she strode to a nearby shop window and feigned interest in a display of artisanal cheese. I told Margolis not to refer to our putative business transaction.

"Do you really work with her father?" His eyebrow rose to a nearby treetop.

"Yes."

Margolis did not press further. It would have been easy enough to make an excuse, to claim work or a mild illness, but this was an excellent day to not be home. We picked up the pale green Volkswagen Beetle I kept at a nearby garage and headed toward Long Island, Margolis in the passenger seat, Spaulding in back staring out the window with an enviable aura of blithe unconcern. Fifteen minutes into the ride her eyes closed and she fell asleep.

In the manner of many people in the public relations industry, Margolis was a chatterbox, which largely relieved me of the need to talk for most of the two-and-a-half-hour ride from Brooklyn. Had he actually engaged me instead of merely jabbering, what would I have said?

The last eight years, three in law school and five at Thatcher, Sturgess & Simonson, were spent toeing the line, penned in by expectations and the wrong kind of ambition, but the uncertainty of the diagnosis and my newly fragile sense of the future had released me from these tethers. Not only had I nearly killed a dangerous man, I was pursuing an illicit real estate scheme and the boss's daughter lay curled in the backseat. As a slave to the circumspect world of trusts and estates my only outlet had been poetry. Now I was a gangster.

The house was on a bluff overlooking Fort Pond Bay. To say that it needed work would have been a considerable understatement. Although Mrs. Vendler was a woman of some means, none had been placed in service of home maintenance because what the listings would have called her charming saltbox had not been touched since the Cuban Missile Crisis. The most recent home improvement was the bomb shelter in the basement built by the late Mr. Vendler in 1962 and stocked with hundreds of cans of superannuated baked beans and a camp stove with which he presumably intended to heat them. Spaulding, Margolis, and I peered around the room from the doorway.

"This is creepy, Jeremy. I can't be in creepy places," Spaulding said, and disappeared.

I tried to imagine the Vendlers huddled here as bombs rained down. They wanted to persevere in their subterranean hidey-hole yet it would have been nuclear winter above. People are eager to cling to life in the most appalling circumstances imaginable. Human beings seem incapable of accepting the simple fact that their existence must come to an end, but not me. I understood. There was no way to predict how the treatment would go, yet my life had a clock on it and the only gamble was playing a long game because what if there turned out to be no long game?

Margolis lifted a can of baked beans off the massive stack.

"Can you imagine," he said, "down here with your loved ones waiting for a nuclear attack to begin, all there is to eat is baked beans, you don't know whether you're going to live or die, and everyone's farting."

"A massive gas attack."

"A fart-fest in the face of doom."

Margolis was seized with a fit of laughter. His shoulders heaved and he pinched the bridge of his nose between his thumb and forefinger to bring himself back under control. There was nothing amusing about the image he had invoked because it was entirely too close to my own condition: Terrifying, yet still somehow ridiculous. And while others would continue to view Jeremy Best as a circumspect trusts and estates attorney, I would know the bitter truth. We headed up the basement stairs.

The house was built nearly a hundred years ago and the doors and ceilings were low. The old-growth elms and birches in the yard allowed little sunlight to penetrate the shadowed interior. The furniture was bulky and dark. On the first floor there was a living room that faced the front yard, a dining room with a formal dining table, and a gloomy kitchen that featured an ancient black stove with one working burner. Upstairs were four bedrooms each with a wallpaper motif from a different conflict—Revolutionary War, Civil War, World War I, and the master bedroom was, eccentrically, the Napoleonic Wars, which I could discern from the word Borodino in Cyrillic-style script near the molding. Through the master bedroom window I could see a garden in the backyard, untended and overgrown. Spaulding was photographing it with her phone.

It was easy to picture the transfiguration of the Vendlers' spread into an artists' colony; playwrights, painters, and composers working in their studios, wandering the grounds; a discreet kitchen staff preparing meals for delivery to poets' doors; novelists holding forth during evening gatherings in the dining room. The Vendler heirs would get their money. No one was stealing. At least that's what I told myself.

To one side of the house behind a copse of trees a swimming pool was half filled with murky rainwater. Mosquitoes lurked virulently, buzzing an ominous hum. It appeared as if no one had swum in the pool for years and in the absence of humans a colony of frogs had moved in. They floated, swam, and leaped along the slate tiles that bordered the fetid water. The frogs appeared to have been there from time immemorial. We stood beside the brackish depths.

186 · SETH GREENLAND

"I'm sleeping with Reetika."

"Congratulations," I said. "I have cancer."

"That isn't funny."

"I'm not joking."

This revelation was received with bewildered silence. While waiting for Margolis to respond, I looked up and saw an oriole with a worm hanging from her beak glide to a branch in a nearby oak tree. She hopped along the branch for a few inches then landed in a nest where she would feed it to her hatchlings that in turn would enact the same scene with their own offspring. After Margolis recovered his ability to speak he offered the usual nostrums served to those we believe to be goners while silently praising whatever deity he worshiped for sparing him.

"Are you going to be all right?"

"Sure, sure," I said. "But we need to address the situation with this house."

I pointed out the bird's nest. There was no point in being a downer and it gave us a chance to shift the discourse. Margolis asked if the sale of the house to him and then from him to me was, strictly speaking, kosher. I said we were, strictly speaking, in a gray area, a not entirely accurate assessment. I glanced toward the house. Above us the oriole took flight again, beating her wings, free. The wisdom of the deal had begun to fray, but swept up in the power of my action I pushed ahead.

"There's a reason we're not putting anything on paper or in emails. I'm prohibited from buying property from the estate, but you can buy something and sell it to me."

"Is there any way this could . . ."

"Not unless one of Mrs. Vendler's relatives showed up and wanted the house, and I'm sending them all checks as soon as we close."

"If I buy it."

Rather than look at Margolis—no one liked pressure—I searched the sky for the oriole and after a moment started to feel dizzy. The sensation quickly passed but I was reminded of the poison coursing through my veins, the transitory quality of the entire tableau.

"With what you'd make you could produce your theater piece."

Margolis appeared to be considering how to tell me the second thoughts he was having and his essentially risk-averse nature were not going to allow him to proceed.

"All right," he said. "Let's do it."

We clasped hands and patted each other on the back. Margolis whooped and for a few seconds I felt like Leonard Nimoy at a *Star Trek* convention.

The rumble of a cranky motor could be heard putt-putting nearby. Spaulding appeared from around the side of the house riding an old lawn mower. There was no vestige of the near disaster yesterday, no sense she had been battered and nearly killed. This was Spaulding triumphant. Replete with possibility, the personification of a future receding before us, her golden image shone inside a frame of profuse grass and deciduous trees all set against the blue dome of late summer. When the image became diffuse I realized tears were forming in my eyes for the second time today. It had been years since I had cried but ever since I'd heard those violinists in Central Park play the Bartok Duo this abiding sadness was never far away.

Back in Brooklyn we dropped Spaulding off at the subway. Margolis waited in the car when I got out to say goodbye.

"It's important we not call or text," I said.

"No electronic trail. Totally."

"Are you going to be okay?"

"My tooth kind of hurts. Kiss me anyway?"

I did. We threw our arms around each other and then she disappeared into the subway.

Spaulding went back to Connecticut and for the next several days did not come to the office. I expedited Margolis's mortgage and by the oiling of certain gears was able to generate the papers and get them signed and notarized in what had to be the fastest time on record. While I was preoccupied with logistics I thought a lot about Spaulding and my overcautious request that we not call or text. Yes, the disaster in Iowa had been caused by an electronic trail, but so what if it happened again? I was going to be dead anyway.

But what if that wasn't true? If the treatment worked and I lived? The law is clear when it comes to the matter of trusts and estates attorneys and self-dealing: It is *verboten*. This was the kind of ethically challenged behavior that had cost my father his law career. Why hadn't this realization crystallized earlier? Had I allowed the stress I was under to turn me into a younger version of him? That was horrifying. Fear had blinded me to this but the situation had changed. What if I were found out? Exposed. Prosecuted. Disbarred. My life would crumble. I would have no job, my prospects would be dismal, and it was impossible to know how Spaulding would react. And the only person whose opinion mattered, the only one, was Spaulding.

It was imperative that I immediately reverse course and put a stop to the sale of the house. The papers had already been submitted. I couldn't just submit them and un-submit them without attracting attention. It would look erratic. Margolis had to do it and he was in Mexico. I frantically tried to reach him but this proved impossible. My only hope was that the two weeks would pass quietly and when he returned we could clean up the mess I had created. Anne Boleyn and Henry VIII would have to find another source of funding.

At the office I maintained a placid exterior but was desperate with worry. Drafting an amendment to a document my heart would begin to thud and I needed to walk around the block to restore a sense of equilibrium.

"Margolis," I nearly screamed into the phone, "this is the

seventh message I'm leaving. We need to fix this. Call me immediately."

I had just come back from my latest walkabout. It was mid-afternoon and the thermometer was north of ninety. My forehead was still moist from the exertion and the air conditioning in the office made my skin clammy. I daubed the perspiration with a handkerchief. When I looked up Reetika was standing in the doorway staring at me with maternal concern.

"I heard yelling," she said. "Is everything all right?"

"Has Margolis called you since he's been away?"

"He's out of cell phone range."

"I know he's out of cell phone range," I said, perhaps with too much emphasis. "If you hear from him, please tell him to contact me."

"You're not really a yeller, Jeremy. Are you sure there's no problem?"

It would have been a relief to have unburdened myself to Reetika. To enumerate my misdeeds, receive absolution, and use her as a sounding board in my effort to conjure a less crazy-making, more satisfying future. But while we may have been together in the same physical space, I was alone. A fresh trickle of perspiration ran down my back.

"Everything is fine."

I took your car out of the garage, I bumped into a light post, and I'm really sorry, okay? It was stupid, I shouldn't have done it, and I'll pay.

Edward P and I were standing next to the Tesla in the parking lot of the Metro-North station in Stonehaven. The dent in the fender glared accusingly. My tooth nagged. My father was calibrating his response. One of the advantages of being considered mental is loved ones aren't so quick to scream at you.

—That's a couple of thousand at least.

—I said I was sorry.

And now I had to bring Edward P into the loop and tell him that far from being a boring place, Stonehaven had its own homicidal maniac. I hadn't imagined it. The house wasn't safe and he needed to be clued in.

—Look, Dad, the hobo that followed me home from the train station tried to strangle me last night. I know that sounds hysterical but it's true. And my tooth is bothering me.

I delivered an edited version of what had happened, leaving out the part about Jeremy swinging the sailing trophy like a mace. As Edward P listened, I could tell he was trying to determine whether or not this had actually occurred, but it must have been convincing because after asking me a couple of questions that seemed more reflexive than anything else (What time did it happen? and What did he look like?) we drove to the Stonehaven Police Department, where I gave a description of the attacker to Officer Felix, a curt cop with a flattop that you could have landed a helicopter on. When he asked me why the man had fled, I told him a dog's bark scared him, and no one questioned it.

Officer Felix checked the log from that night. He eyed me.

—There was a call from a Mr. Ezra Pound reporting the assault.

—The poet? my father said.

—I told this man at the train station, I said. He called.

—Why didn't you call? Edward P asked.

—Because I was too freaked out. God! Why does it matter?

—Why did he say he was Ezra Pound?

—Maybe because that was his name. Why are you asking me all these questions? Shouldn't you be asking if I'm all right?

—Are you?

—No. I'm in a police station, I was attacked, and I don't even know if you think it happened.

—Spall, calm down, okay? I believe you. And your welfare is the priority here.

I told the whole mostly true story again from beginning to end, again leaving out Jeremy's participation. I still wasn't sure whether or not my father believed me. Maybe he thought I *thought* it happened but it was really just something I imagined. Officer Felix said he would be in touch.

When we got back to the house I took Edward P into the den and stood over the rug.

—See this? I said, pointing.

—He looked down. What, Spall? I don't see anything.

I dropped to my knees and pointed to several red stains.

—This is blood, okay? You can have some police lab guy out here and run a test if you don't believe me. Don't wash these stains. They're evidence.

When I went upstairs, he was thoroughly confused. For all I knew he thought the marks on the rug were cranberry juice and his was daughter insane.

No phone calls, no texts, the night was nearly impossible. I painted my gums with Anbesol, swallowed two aspirin, and tried to sleep. My muscles tensed with each creak in the old house. Every car that drove past ferried a murderer to a victim. I threw the light blanket off and stared at the dead poets' faces, wondering how any of them managed to survive. Somehow, I tumbled into sleep. The next morning my tooth throbbed. I lay in bed, trying to marshal the energy required to live. Sylvia Plath's pretty blondness stared back at me from her place on the wall between photographs of Sara Teasdale and Vachel Lindsay at the nexus of the suicide section. I tried to block out the pain.

When I was in sixth grade my math teacher, Mr. McCloy, had recommended *The Bell Jar*. If you missed the oddball detail in that last sentence, it's this: Math Teacher. The book was one that every private-school girl read by the time she went to college but I was eleven. An English teacher might have recommended it purely as a fine novel but a math teacher could only have suggested this particular book as a prescription for what he believed, accurately, to be ailing me. I was a good math student but quiet, and on the rare times I spoke in class it was to ask questions like, "If the universe can't be measured, why bother to have math?" Mr. McCloy took sadistic delight in calling to the blackboard girls who did not shine in his classroom. He couldn't get me that way, so instead he recommended *The Bell Jar*.

At breakfast, when Edward P saw I couldn't bite down he instructed Katrina to get me to a dentist immediately. It turned out to be an impacted wisdom tooth and the dentist sent me to an oral surgeon who for good measure extracted all four of them. The next two days were spent on my back in front of the television with an ice pack fashionably strapped to my face. With my grotesquely swollen cheeks, I looked like a clinically depressed chipmunk. I didn't trust myself to text Jeremy because the painkillers that had been prescribed might have made me too truthful.

By early evening on my second day of confinement I was feeling much better. Outside the bedroom window fading fingers of vermillion and umber stretched along the horizon. Marshall and I were watching a YouTube video of a kid smoking a bong on a treadmill when I looked up and saw Edward P standing in the doorway.

We took Katrina's BMW because the Tesla was being repaired. In the car he asked about the writing workshop and I told him it had ended the previous week.

—Go well?

—Definitely.

He never asked to read anything I'd written. I was used to it. I wished it didn't matter.

Edward P was a fast driver and we were humming along. An SUV materialized in the opposite lane. My father's phone vibrated. He glanced at it and as he texted a reply the car began to swerve.

—Dad . . .

The SUV driver leaned on his horn and my father corrected course before a collision.

—We have to get milk on the way home.

—You realize you could get us killed texting while you drive.

—I've managed to avoid that so far.

—Katrina couldn't wait ten minutes to hear back from you?

—You of all people shouldn't tell me what to do, he said, maybe because it came out with the wrong tone.

We rode in dissatisfied quiet.

The first sign of autumn occurred in the August heat when whispers of color started to show up in the trees, the early yellows and browns. The towering maples and elms were less threatening now, the pines more benign. None seemed like they were leaning toward me anymore.

At the Stamford Police Department, a middle-aged black woman sat at a desk in the reception area reading a celebrity magazine. Edward P said, The Simonsons are here, like we were at a cotillion. She picked up a phone and repeated this to the person on the other end then told us to take a seat. After a brief wait a man in a gray suit came out and said he was Detective Yee. He was a tall, thin Asian who walked with a slight hitch and we followed him down a dimly lit hall, the fluorescent light greening our faces. We stopped at a gray metal door with a window in it. Detective Yee asked me to take a look in the room.

—Is that the man who assaulted you?

At a table, his hands shackled behind him, was a scraggly guy with a beard who appeared to be in his twenties. You've seen him on the F train, you've seen him pushing a shopping cart loaded with his belongings in Riverside Park. My Grendel.

—We picked him up an hour ago, the detective said.

—Edward P asked, Who is he?

—Karl Bannerman. His father is a doctor in Fairfield. We think he's got some form of schizophrenia. When I asked him about your case, he pretty much admitted it but since it looks like he's mentally ill, he could admit to killing Jesus. That's why we want you to ID him.

—Spall, is this the guy?

It was, but I hesitated. Now that I saw my monster chained in a police station, I didn't want to have any part in making more trouble for him. He looked like he had bugs crawling on his brain. They were going to stick him in an institution, probably forever. Did it matter what I said? I was stricken with an overwhelming sense of empathy for him, his condition, the broken life that looked beyond repair.

—Can we get the guy who was with you to ID him? This was Detective Yee and it took a moment before I realized the question was addressed to me.

—What guy?

—Bannerman gave a statement and said there was a guy with you that attacked him.

—Spall? My father looked at me.

—He's got a lump on the top of his head the size of a golf ball and a laceration as well, Yee said.

—I was alone.

—Looks like someone hit him, Yee said.

The detective's tone was neutral but it felt like an accusation. I felt myself seizing up but desperately didn't want my father to have any inkling I hadn't been alone in the house. My jaw started to hurt. It had been hours since I had taken a painkiller. They both looked at me. Again my father asked if anyone else was there.

—He's crazy, I said, pointing toward Karl Bannerman. You can't possibly believe what he says.

The truth was that we were both crazy, just varying shades. Through luck, mostly, I was not the kind of batshit insane that Karl Bannerman appeared to be. But presenting as "normal" was a challenge. At that moment it was a struggle I was winning. I stared them down, the two men, my father and Detective Yee, who I was pretty convinced didn't believe me.

—Spall, are you sure you were alone?

—Who would I have been with? And by the way, Detective Yee, his blood is on our rug. You guys can do a test.

Detective Yee said he would get a technician out there to do that. Edward P thanked him and we left.

My father knew something had occurred at the house but wasn't remotely certain what it was and lacked the confidence to press. The sick son of a local doctor had been crowned, but by whom? It was all too confusing for Edward P and as I looked over at him driving his second wife's car, staring silently at the road, and trying to think about sailing or clients or whether he remembered to get the 0% fat milk his wife required or had accidentally purchased the 2% kind, I knew he wanted nothing more than to take refuge from the dark carnival that was his only daughter. I wanted that for him, too.

—Spall, I am really truly sorry. I should not have doubted you. Honestly, there's no excuse. It's my job to protect you and I dropped the ball. That could have been Katrina in the house or the boys and you took the hit for the family. I wish you had come to the reunion.

—You were doing so well there, Dad, with the apology and everything. But even if I had gone to the reunion, you still didn't believe me, did you? And that sucks.

—What do you want me to do? I already apologized.

—Nothing, I said.

Back in my room, I removed the Ganesh from my purse and placed it on the nightstand. Then I lay on the bed and stared at a cluster of early 20th-century American poets on the ceiling. The collection of faces shifted and dissolved into one huge set of features and murmured, *Spaulding, flee Connecticut.* My mother's apartment was no-man's-land. There was Gully in Seattle and that was a definite maybe but how would I get there? I didn't have money for a plane ticket and I couldn't expect my brother to support me while I looked for a job, something I was bound to be terrible at. College awaited but it was going to be a challenge to hang on for the few weeks before the semester started. The turn life had taken made it increasingly difficult to see myself as a student in September. And none of this mattered anyway because what I needed wasn't Gully, or college, or a job. I needed to be with Jeremy.

JEREMY
A Single Organism of Happiness

A biblical plague of summer associates descended on the better firms of New York City every June. From the most prestigious law schools in the land, these sparkle-eyed, business-suited beginners spent their summer vacations in the purview of starched legions that had already blazed the path. They swarmed to firms large and small that competed with one another to overpay the neophytes in the hope that the more promising ones, the ones best suited to the high-end rough-and-tumble of our profession, would carry pleasant memories back to campus and so return when they graduated. Their tenure was a long seduction of cocktail-fueled outings to baseball games, concerts in Central Park, and leisurely boat rides like the one I was on. The section of the craft I occupied was called the fore. Or maybe it was the aft. Who cared, really? I hated jargon. It kept people from having a genuine connection. Let's just say this: Location-wise, I was on the upper deck, above the revelry whose festive hum and drone mixed with the head-splitting beats of electronic dance music.

In the morning I had gone to the hospital for a scan that would reveal whether or not the treatment was working. The results would be available early next week. I needed a drink and so, given the circumstances, decided to allow myself a "cheat day." The chemo made me more susceptible to alcohol than usual. Slightly buzzed, I stood on the upper deck of a large motor yacht cruising past the Statue of Liberty, sipped my second whiskey sour, and, contrary to my prohibition of communication, attempted to compose a text to Spaulding.

As the sun narrowed in on New Jersey, pockets of genetic-lottery-winning summer associates mingled on the lower deck. Most of the Thatcher, Sturgess & Simonson partners and associates were on the cruise (the only acceptable excuse was a court-related deadline the following morning) so my presence was not required below.

There: A circle of lion cubs riveted by the story told by a handsome lacrosse star. Soon-to-be law school graduates, the coiled studs and alpha girls, shoulders thrown back, smiled perfectly. The sun's dying rays bathed unlined faces in amber flame, eyes wide mirrors that reflected the disappearing light, everything possibility, a rising road that would go on forever and ever warm in the glow of an always afternoon.

There: Reetika, laughing with several of the paralegals. Was she telling her audience about the nascent romance? She had thanked me profusely for introducing her to Margolis. He gave her all of his plays. In one night she read them ecstatically, convinced of his genius.

Partners preened, associates aspired, and all attempted to impress. Did I want to be here on this seductive summer evening to partake in the orgy of ambition? No, I did not. Rome beckoned. There was a passport in my pocket. And now this pivotal point that found me standing above my current life, surveying everyone below: I would, I could, I should, but I was so cowed by the existence I had chosen, so emotionally hemmed in, so terrified of leaving a digital information trail, that I couldn't allow myself to have what I desperately wanted which was not a partnership but for Spaulding Simonson to accompany me. I missed being with her, the sense of adventure she brought, that feeling I had of being stupidly alive when we were together. Why did I need to deprive myself?

The text: *Spaulding . . .*

Uncharacteristically, that's where it ended. The words would not come. All of this was stirring my pot when I sensed Pratt's presence. He took a swig from the bottle of Heineken he was holding.

"That girl with the polka-dot blouse?" He pointed to a summer associate in a fitted gray suit with reddish hair that fell to the middle of her back. "She's working in corporate. NYU Law." I watched a tugboat make for Brooklyn and wished I were on it. Pratt took another swig of beer. "Think she's a spinner?" With cells possibly multiplying in who knows how many vital organs and my complete fixation on Spaulding, the sexual proclivities of this particular summer associate were not a subject of the slightest interest right now and I hoped my non-responsiveness would send Pratt back to the lower deck. But he would not be deterred. "Best."

"What?" I nearly shouted. I hoped he would ascribe my tone to a wish to be heard over the engines of the boat, the party chatter, and the music. Though annoyed with the intrusion, it was important Pratt not think my decibel level was about him. I suddenly realized I was high and didn't want my dissonance to leak out.

"I asked if you think Miss Polka Dots is a spinner?"

"Why don't you ask her?"

If Pratt was disturbed by my refusal to pick up the conversational ball, he didn't show it. Instead, he withdrew two cigars from the inside pocket of his suit jacket and offered me one. When I declined, he shrugged and slipped it back into his pocket. He lit the other, took a deep draw, and exhaled a blur of smoke so dense it momentarily obscured several of the buildings south of 14th Street. That my cancerous lungs were rotting in the shadow of this smug smokestack was unbearable. It would have been hard to find someone more satisfied with his lot in life than Kevin Pratt. He was handsome, successful, and brimming with vigor. I willed a seagull to crap on his gelled head.

"We missed you at the African Horizons benefit, Jeremy."
This was our colleague Amanda Carr. She sipped a vodka and
tonic as she emerged from whatever they call the steps on a
boat. "George Clooney was super inspiring."

"Family in town," I lied. "Sorry about that."

"But thanks for your contribution."

Ordinarily I would have analyzed Amanda's tone for the next
five minutes. Was it sarcastic or sincere? Had I strengthened a
friendship or lost a supporter? But my mind no longer worked
in the usual way. While the two of them discussed a pending case
my attention was drawn to the lower deck and a familiar nimbus
of blond hair. Spaulding was in deep conversation with several
summer associates. She gesticulated with ringed fingers and
pointed toward somewhere in Manhattan. Their eyes followed
the languid movement of her hand as if under a spell. Talking to
these frat boys in suits and ties clutching plastic beer cups like
they were at a Delta Chi Epsilon mixer, she wore a sleeveless
dress with a floral print and sneakers. Her weight was on her left
leg. She angled her right foot behind her and the tip of her toe
touched the deck. The gulls cut back and made for the eastern
horizon. The boat hit a wave and juddered but Spaulding held
her pose. When she drained the can of soda she was holding, the
harbor breeze rippled her hair. Then she turned her head and
glanced in my direction. I didn't know whether to give an insou-
ciant salute and risk Pratt asking questions or ignore her. I felt
transparent, exposed, exhilarated. The annual summer associate
cruise was no place for this kind of perturbation.

Amanda excused herself and joined a pair of nearby colleagues. Pratt turned his attention to the revelers below.

"Did you ever take a good look at Ed's daughter?"

Quickly, I said, "No. Why?"

"I'd like to fuck her."

"You didn't really just say that."

"Seriously? Wouldn't you?"

"Kevin, for God's sake . . ."

"I'd like to bend her over the custom-built credenza I'm going to get when I make partner and shove my rock-hard cock right up her sweet little ass."

"You need to apologize."

"Best, are you gay?"

"Apologize, Pratt."

"Blow me."

Only when my fist collided with his chin did Pratt understand what was happening. His head snapped to the side, my class ring sliced his cheek, and I cut my knuckle on his incisor. There was no real buildup, no significant escalation of tension leading to catharsis, just stimuli and explosion. It was a reaction brought on by the volubility of my emotional state and the sudden rupture of the membrane between impulse and deed. Although I had nearly killed someone less than a week earlier, never in my life had I acted to defend anyone's honor, and I can only attribute it to my upset at the imminence of death, a desire for repentance, and a heretofore-unacknowledged taste for violence unleashed in Connecticut. And I was drunk. Because I had caught him entirely by surprise, Pratt staggered back. My nerves jangled like a tambourine and I noticed my drink was gone.

"What the fuck, Best?" He touched his cheek, looked at the smudge of blood on his fingers, incredulous. I shook my injured hand to ease the pain. "You realize if I hit you back I would kill you." He had held on to his beer.

"Stay away from her, Pratt." My hand throbbed. Had I just slugged a fellow associate? Associates did not punch each other. Braining Spaulding's assailant had emboldened me but this was self-destructive. "Hey, I'm really sorry, okay?" One of my legs started to shake. Pratt took out a handkerchief and held it to his cheek.

Our fracas had drawn the attention of Amanda and the

other attorneys, who looked at us unclear whether we were fooling around or about to tear each other to shreds. To his credit, Pratt forced a sodden smile and they turned back to their conversation.

"Jesus, you dick. Are you drunk?"

"I already apologized. I should not have done that."

"No shit." He spat on the deck. His saliva was flecked with blood.

"But she's had some problems."

Pratt put his arm around my shoulder and pulled me to him, bro-style. "You're such a faggot. If you could punch harder I'd have thrown your ass overboard."

Laughing hollowly because it was easier than further engaging with Pratt's repartee, I inhaled the fresh harbor air. My chest expanded and my heart ceased fibrillating. I exhaled through my nostrils. Another drink would have been useful but a trip to the bar required moving and my knees couldn't be trusted not to buckle. I looked toward Manhattan. There was a slight movement in my peripheral vision. Had Spaulding tried to signal me?

"What was that?" Amanda said. She had returned to our conversation.

"We were just messing around," Pratt said. "Best was showing me his stuff." He shadowboxed in my direction and I tried to grin.

"You guys up for some dinner at the Charcuterie?" This was a restaurant that had recently opened in the meatpacking district. It was impossible to get a table. People waited for months. It had been an unavoidable topic of conversation at the office, where the lawyers, most of whom were liberal arts majors, channeled their need for culture toward a religious interest in food preparation.

"Thanks but I'm meeting an old friend later," I lied (again).

Why didn't I want to go with them? I needed to make up

with Pratt. He could tell the partnership committee I had punched him. Amanda was a witness. She could corroborate his story and that would destroy my chances. And they weren't bad people. Intelligent, successful, personable. Amanda was engaged to a banker in Boston and he was going to move to New York in the fall. They were looking for a co-op on the Upper East Side. Pratt was the kind of guy who remembered your birthday. Both had gone from college to law school to Thatcher, Sturgess & Simonson as if they were on a conveyor belt that would take them into relaxed-fit clothing, quiet pension years, and death. Were they alive to the possibilities of the universe? Had they ever known what it was like to burn incandescently? To exist in a larger, all-encompassing way that would allow them to transcend their flavorless days spent in pursuit of an ersatz happiness and exist in a more vibrant reality, alert to the lamentations of the cosmos and their brief time as vessels of consciousness?

Oh, please. Did I? Not to put too fine a point on it but no. At least not until Spaulding had walked into my life. But I judged them, the Amandas and the Pratts and the rest of my oblivious colleagues, and who was I to do that? What transcending was I doing? Talk all you want about transcendence, it is even more difficult than finishing a poetry collection and apparently I couldn't do that either. Amanda migrated toward the lower deck. Pratt and I were alone.

His fist drove into my stomach before I could react. I bent forward fully expecting a blow to my head that would send me reeling into the harbor. Pratt laughed as I struggled to breathe.

"If I wasn't up for partner, I would totally fucking kick your ass," he announced, standing over me drunkenly relishing what he had wrought. Then he departed in a haze of satisfaction, ire, and hops. My stomach ached. Blood oozed from the back of my hand so I pressed it against my lips. When I managed to stand upright I glanced toward where Spaulding had been but she had vanished. The urge to look for her was interrupted when strong fingers squeezed my shoulder. I looked over and saw Ed Simonson's ruddy face. Would this cruise never end? His veined hand gripped a Scotch and soda. What was he doing on this deck and shouldn't he have been mingling with the summer associates? Was this going to be about Spaulding?

"What did you say to Trevelyan?"

It was difficult to discern the angle of the Raptor's attack. His expression was, as usual, impossible to read.

"What do you mean?"

"Why do you think I sent you up there back in June?"

Because Trevelyan had been fleeced by his wife and his anger was assumed to be seismic and possibly uncontrolled and it was just the kind of cataclysmic and potentially hostile emotional climate a partner would use his seniority to avoid.

I said, "Because it was a trusts and estates matter?"

"That's what you thought?" Where was he going with this? My mouth was dry. On the lower deck, knots of eager summer interns kissed up to partners. Pratt and Amanda stood at the railing with fresh drinks. Spaulding was nowhere in evidence. Several seconds passed. Ed seemed in no hurry. My wounded hand was still leaking and I shoved it in my pocket.

The Raptor booms, intent insidious / Expression open, heart perfidious.

"It's your poise, Jeremy. The man was understandably distressed and you are Mr. Even Keel. I don't know what the hell you told him, but he was impressed."

"Really?" I tried to keep my voice from leaping a register. This was semi-successful. What would Ed think if he knew Mr. Even Keel had just smacked Kevin Pratt? That he was having an affair with Spaulding, looting a client's estate, and had nearly killed a homeless person in the Simonson den.

"He's pretty damn persnickety." Simonson turned toward

the skyline. My nervous eyes dutifully followed. "The city's changed a lot since I moved here. Our business has changed a lot, too." Ed had always been professional toward me, guarded, never chummy. Now he appeared genuinely wistful, as if he was revealing something he didn't display to non-partners. "My father and grandfather were both attorneys. Back then, when they were working, you made partner and you were set for life. The partners looked after each other like family, all-for-one sort of thing. But that's gone to shit." With two fingers he massaged the side of his neck. I thought about Dr. Tapper's examination room, the strange mixture of brightness and fear. "Christ, who chose this godawful music?"

"Someone evil."

The Raptor shook his head in dismay. Together we suffered the relentless beat. At that moment, I felt a singular and altogether unfamiliar closeness to him.

"These days, it's all about alliances. Who's going to protect you, who can you protect, and what benefit redounds to you from whatever action you take. Do you follow me?"

"I think so."

"The partnership meeting is next week." I nodded. He swirled the ice in his glass and observed the summer associates, the associates, the partners, all in a web of ambition, calculation, and systemic anxiety. I had the barely containable urge to tell him that I loved his daughter even though I might be dying and she had become important to me in a way I did not expect him to understand. Instead, I gazed toward the horizon with what I hoped was a commanding and confident look that contained just the right degree of supplication. "Keep it up."

It was not the Simonson style to bestow an endorsement, but that was as close as he would get. Whatever my ambivalence about being an attorney, and my gnawing concern that this path on which I had been traveling was entirely wrong for me, the financial security inherent in a partnership—however compromised the institution had become—was welcome. Never mind that my concern in this area was already beginning to seem vestigial.

"Ed, there is one thing," I said. He was done with me already so his look was impatient, get on with it. "When you asked me how I was, I misspoke. I may actually have a serious health problem and you should be aware of it."

"Then tell me."

"I'm being treated for cancer."

He asked me how serious it was and I told him what I knew.

"I've started chemotherapy. The doctor said that we'd know pretty soon whether or not it's working."

The depth of the breath he took expanded his chest to the point where the fabric on his white shirt pushed against the buttons. "I'm sorry to hear that, but you've got to hang in there."

It would be hard to feel further from another human being than I felt from Ed Simonson at that moment. Our bond over the dreadful music a distant memory, it was as if all the emptiness of time and space separated us and we each floated cold and alone in the unforgiving void. When Ed saw I was not going to do a conversational save and reassure him I'd be returned to glowing health in no time he cleared his throat and said, "You're not going to die, Best. A little chemo, some rest, you'll be fine. Look at me. I drink too much, have high blood pressure, a second wife who won't let me lie down on the weekends, and I'll tell you this, I'm not going anywhere. Screw that cancer, all right?"

"Screw it."

"That's the spirit."

He awkwardly pawed my shoulder and for a second I thought he might try to pull me into a one-armed hug, but mercifully, that did not occur. He nodded again, repeated that I should take care of myself, made an excuse about having to talk to the summer associates, and departed.

I began to text.

* * *

Spaulding looked pleased when she slid into the backseat of the Lincoln Town Car. I asked where she had been this week. Did I sound relaxed? In my excitement at seeing her, perhaps my engine was revving a little too fast.

"This is going to sound crazy."

"You're just sensitive," I said.

"But that's exactly what it's been like for me."

"It's why I was so paranoid about leaving an electronic trail. No more of that."

I asked where she had been this week. Did I sound relaxed? In my excitement at seeing her, perhaps my engine was revving a little too fast. There was a twinge of pain in my ribs from Pratt's blow. I concentrated on that as she told me about her wisdom teeth.

"I'd offer you a Vicodin, but since I'm trying to be chemical-free I tossed them," she proudly informed me before looking out the rear window, presumably to double-check whether anyone had seen her get in the car. I asked if there was any news in Connecticut and she told me about Karl Bannerman.

"So he's all right?"

"It depends what you mean by all right. The detective said he was schizophrenic."

"Does your father know that I was up there?"

"I didn't tell him."

In this age of oversharing, her keeping my presence secret was remarkable. I squeezed her hand and she returned the pressure. To soothe my nerves, I began to talk about schizophrenia, which has two meanings. The first is a psychological condition where one suffers from social isolation and there can be hallucinations and delusions.

"That actually sounds kind of familiar," she said. "You know, when I saw him sitting in that room in the police station I felt this strange kind of kinship with him, like we were related or something."

"The second definition of schizophrenia," I said, "is the coexistence of contradictory or incompatible elements."

"Like the way someone can be a lawyer and a poet," she said.

"Like the way someone can give in to an impulse that can be totally self-destructive, but in every other sense is glorious."

Karl Bannerman's fate was terrifying, but the electric notion of contradictory ideas being somehow reconcilable, along with Spaulding's presence, put me into a hopeful mood. Pratt had slugged me and I survived. Even the chemotherapy didn't seem insurmountable.

"Are you hungry?" Spaulding asked. "Should we get dinner?"

"We can get it on the plane."

She looked at me, incredulous.

"On the plane? Where are we going?"

"To Rome."

"When?"

"Now. Tonight."

"Are you serious?"

"Do you still carry your passport?"

She rummaged in her purse and there it was. The corners of her mouth rose to form a thrilled smile. Spaulding texted her father and advised him she needed a few more days off because of her surgery and was going to spend them at her mother's apartment.

Dirk Trevelyan's jet was at Westchester Airport, a G6 with a pilot, a co-pilot, and a stewardess. The smooth flight allowed for several hours of uninterrupted sleep. A taxi to a *pensione* in Trastevere. A top-floor room overlooking a quiet street.

The effects of the chemotherapy were becoming more evident, creakiness in my bones, a slight diminishment of energy, some accumulation of hair in the shower drain, but not enough that anyone would notice. At least I hoped that was the case. Either way, I determined to carry on.

Picture the two of us in a little Fiat. We bought prosciutto, cheese, and bread and rode to the Palatine Hill for a picnic. Above the faded rose, sienna, and terra-cotta of the cityscape we spread a blanket on a patch of grass in the shadow of an ancient temple. A restoration crew was erecting a scaffold around the structure, which reminded me today was not a holiday. I had sent an email telling Reetika to inform everyone I was taking a few days off.

Palatine Hill overlooked the Forum, one of the more vexing of the ancient sites. The word itself connoted grand esplanade, a place of imposing proportions where weighty people interacted and great events occurred. Yet to the unschooled eye, the Forum was a pile of old stones. Gone was the lively and bumptious atmosphere that characterized this central gathering place at the height of the Republic. At twenty, when days of good health seemed endless, it was difficult for me to imagine the existence of the people who had animated this landmark. Oh, I could picture them like sandaled actors in an old movie but the full scope of their lives lived out against the city eluded me. But now these ghostly Romans were palpable and their passage into memory suddenly relevant.

Why was I bedeviled by Decline and Fall thoughts when we had come for a picnic? Because now I could imagine being one with every Roman soldier, citizen, aristocrat, slave, painter, sculptor, traveler, and priest, of a piece with every person who only existed in memory, and this was not a pleasant thought.

Spaulding reclined, her fingers linked behind her head, eyes closed. A platoon of ants was approaching the remains of the bread and with a godlike hand I swept them away. In the distance a few tourists wandered around snapping pictures of the ruins. Her right hand closed and she rolled onto her side and curled up. I stroked her shoulder and she mumbled something unintelligible in her sleep and bit her lower lip. By the time a fleck of saliva appeared at the corner of her mouth I was overcome by a feeling of the purest gratitude because I was not alone.

In the afternoon we drove through easy streets past the monument of Vittorio Emanuele II, through the shadow of the black-domed brooding Pantheon, down the Via Veneto where decades earlier eager paparazzi shot shimmering black and whites of glamorous starlets, to the Church of Santa Maria della Concezione dei Cappuccini.

Thirteen years had passed since I first encountered the unusual contents of its dim environs on a damp winter day. As we walked through the nave, Spaulding observed the stained glass, lugubrious paintings, dark shades, and suffering, and asked why we were here.

"You'll see."

I handed the bespectacled old nun stationed at the door to the crypt ten euros and beckoned Spaulding to follow. The crypt was a warren of tiny chapels decorated, and yes, that would be the word, *decorated* with the old white bones of thousands of monks all of whom donated their mortal remains to the glory of this display.

Spaulding shivered and when I placed my hand on the small of her back to guide her along she spun away. Every visitor should experience the crypt her own way, so I chose not to say anything.

We wandered beneath archways constructed of human skulls, masses of bones stacked like logs, walls decorated with geometric patterns assembled from fibulas and tibias, full standing skeletons that looked ready to ambulate, through the

Crypt of the Resurrection, the Crypt of the Skulls, the Crypt of the Pelvis, the Crypt of Leg Bones and Thigh Bones, and the Crypt of Three Skeletons where the center skeleton held a scythe in one hand and a scale in the other. The effect was at once overwhelming, horrific, and, in its whimsically crafted sheer fantastic abundance of death, darkly hilarious. Did the catacombs resonate with her? The place was macabre but Spaulding's sense of humor ran in a dark direction. Being here was life affirming, wasn't it? *Memento mori* and all that.

"It's as if the world's most morbid interior decorator was given free rein," I said.

"Why did you take me here?"

We were standing in the Crypt of the Skulls surrounded by mounds of exquisitely arranged craniums. Thousands of empty eye sockets stared. Row upon row of teeth grinned. The centerpiece of the dimly lit chamber was a massive church door constructed entirely of skulls. In front of this were arrayed the skeletons of three monks in dusty brown cassocks, all standing, facing the tourists and pilgrims and looking for all the world as if they were going to start singing. Arching over this jolly trio was a giant cap festooned with a pair of Mickey Mouse ears designed in keeping with the prevailing cranial motif. Flanking this display were two smaller skulled arches, each occupied by languidly reclining skeletons, their cassock-cloaked limbs arranged in casual dishabille. Once one became accustomed to the idea that these were the remnants of men who had lived and breathed, eaten, shat, loved God, fought, prayed, and died, the utterly lunatic nature of the display was disarming. I told Spaulding I thought she'd like it.

"It's awful."

The knowing look, the groan, the eye roll, the usual Spaulding reaction that would cut through all of the death imagery and turn it into a laughter-in-the-void moment did not come. Instead, she was upset. I tried to comfort her but she pushed me away and then she was gone. When I caught up with her on the sidewalk, she was livid.

"What is wrong with you?"

"What are you talking about?"

"I get it, Jeremy. Life is fleeting. We're all going to die. Forgive me if I'm not so accepting of that right now, okay?" When I put my hand on her shoulder she shoved it away. Then she started to cry. Not loudly or histrionically, but with quiet sorrow that rendered me mute and helpless. She sat down on the steps of the church and I sat next to her. Across the street an old lady hobbled along on a cane. A gaggle of uniformed schoolchildren fluttered past us into the church.

"I thought you'd love the catacombs," I said. Spaulding didn't react. I tried again. "I'm sorry if they upset you." Still nothing. Is this what happens when a person spends too much time in his own head? The whole idea of this trip was to connect and already I had made a hash of it.

A youthful mother in a stylish dress walked past pushing a pram. Her hair was bobbed and she looked to be in her late twenties. She wore sunglasses and a chic bag was slung over her shoulder.

"*Mi scusi*," Spaulding said, no longer crying. "*Avete un fazzoletto?*"

"*Ho questo cosa*," the woman said and smiled. She reached into the pram and pulled out a plastic container. Opening it, she took out a baby wipe and handed it to Spaulding, who daubed her face. "*Qualunque cosa sia non puo essere cosi male. L'amore è difficile.*" The woman smiled and resumed her stroll.

"You speak Italian?"

"*Un po'.* I studied it in school." Spaulding folded the baby wipe into a neat square and stuck it in her purse. Without looking at me she said, "First of all, you don't even know if you're dying."

"That's true."

"So to bring me here to show you're cool with it . . . I don't know . . . it's a little premature, maybe? And totally fucked."

"You're right," I said. "I can see how you would think this place was a little over the top."

"Whoever thought of it must have been tripping. And please tell me how he convinced anyone to go along with the plan." I could see she had been more upset than angry. "Don't you want to buy a souvenir?" she said. "A nice femur for your desk?"

"Ha ha."

"But I didn't see a gift shop," she said with mock innocence.

Death had begun to terrify me and perhaps taking Spaulding to the crypts was my attempt to weaken its power. Going alone was not something I could have done. Was it fair to drag her along? Another time and it would have been a lark, but not that day. I was sorry and said so again, but she had already collected herself and was walking toward the Fiat.

"We're going to the Capitoline Museum," she said. "There's something you need to see."

It turned out that Spaulding had visited the museum complex with her class from boarding school and remembered it well. We parked near the Piazza del Campidoglio and I followed her past a throng of tourists and into a neoclassical building, through the soaring foyer, and up the wide stairs. We turned right and skirted sculptures of the infants Romulus and Remus suckling a she-wolf, Roman soldiers wielding swords, gods and mortals nude, standing, sitting, reclining, their physiques perfectly articulated, and then we were in front of a statue of a goddess. Her serene face, smooth hands, and feet carved from black onyx. Arms outstretched, wrapped in a marble cloak. But this was not the smooth marble cloak that clothed a nearby emperor. This cloak was adorned with the fruit of the Earth, apples, pears, grapes cut from marble.

"Do you get it?" Spaulding said. At a loss, I stared at the statue. Jet-black face, supplicant hands, she looked like nothing else in the gallery. "She's a fertility goddess."

"Ah," I said.

"She's beautiful, right?"

"Exquisite."

"Life, Jeremy, okay?"

"Yes," I said. She punched me in the arm. "Yes."

"*Tu non sei ancora morto*. You're not dead yet."

Spaulding was wearing the clothes she wore back in New York so we found a store nearby and bought a pale yellow skirt and two linen blouses, cream and mint green, and a linen jacket. A brown leather satchel caught my eye. It was perfect for manuscripts and I pictured myself carrying pages in it as I traveled. In a fit of optimism, I bought that, too.

At ten o'clock that evening the Piazza del Popolo was dotted with tourists strolling back to their hotels. We had consumed a rack of lamb with a 2011 Montepulciano (my last "cheat day") and were walking it off. On the sidewalk a Senegalese vendor displayed counterfeit Rolexes on a folding table. As a gag, I bought one for Spaulding and she slipped it on her wrist.

"Now I'm classy," she said.

"This watch is connected to the heart of the universe," I said. "When it stops running, time stops. And everything remains exactly how it was at that second for all eternity. Like a poem."

"But only when it stops because if it's running . . ."

"Then it's just some made-in-China piece of crap."

"And when it stops?"

"It's a poetry watch."

"A poetry watch? That is an epic name for a fake Rolex."

We drove south on Via del Corso. The car windows were rolled down, the night air warm on our skin. I was sated from the dinner and feeling expansive.

"Have you ever seen a movie called *Gianni and the Pope*?"

"I don't think so."

"There's a scene that takes place on the banks of the Tiber and I want to show you where they shot it."

We cruised from Ponte Sisto in the southern end of the city all the way north to Ponte Milvio. I drove slowly and peered toward the river. Cars, trucks, and Vespas flowed past us. For half an hour we looked but the physical site appeared to have evaporated with the era of the film. When I wasn't able to find the place a strange emptiness came over me like the sour feeling one gets after missing a train, the sense that everything was moving further away. Why did I want to show Spaulding a location from a film she hadn't seen in the first place? I expressed my disappointment and aimed the Fiat back toward the center of the city.

"Hey, don't worry," she said. "It's only make-believe."

She pointed out a low-slung building on the other side of the river and said it looked like a giant pastry. The wind ruffled her hair as she examined her new wristwatch. That we couldn't find what we were looking for didn't matter to her at all. We were at a red light near Piazza Bainsizza when she asked me to pull over. I turned onto a side street and parked.

"You have to stay in the car. And don't look." Spaulding climbed out and disappeared. Pop music played in a nearby apartment. There was a sidewalk café on the corner and several couples lingered at tables. My gloom dissipated. It didn't matter that I couldn't find where the scene had been shot. This was plenty.

After a moment, I heard, "Now back up really slowly, like, one foot." I had no idea what she was doing but released the brake, shifted into reverse, and inched backward. "Okay, that's great." Then she was in the passenger seat.

"What just happened?"

Spaulding beamed and held up her wrist to show me the now-squashed fake Rolex. The headlights of a passing car illuminated a miniature constellation in the cracked glass of the newly minted poetry watch. For less than a second, tiny dots of light glistened. The time was 11:14.

Sunday in the Villa Borghese we sat on a bench and ate shaved ice. Skateboarders wearing Vans, tee shirts, and baggy shorts slalomed through musicians stationed behind open instrument cases dusted with coins and bills. A pair of skinny kids bashed out a punk tune on beat-up acoustic guitars while a four-man African drum circle traded rhythms. A flaxen-haired harpist who looked like she had wafted in from a Wagner opera intently tuned her instrument. A Roman family was having a picnic, grilling sausages on a hibachi. Grandparents, aunts, uncles drank wine and older kids chased each other while cherubic toddlers in bright outfits rolled in the grass. Shirtless teenaged boys played pickup basketball, their muscles slick with sweat. A vendor sold roasted chestnuts to an older couple who didn't look up when a six-foot transvestite wearing a silver lamé dress and wielding a wand glided by on spangled roller skates. A child ran past us holding a yellow balloon on a string.

"Look at that little goofball," Spaulding said. She laughed and I thought, How many more times will I see the color yellow?

I gave money to the guitarists and the drum circle, then placed a wad of euros into the harpist's upturned hat. Spaulding was surprised at the amount but I told her someone had to let the harpists of the world know that what they did was important. Spaulding was wearing her broken watch and before we left the Villa Borghese, I saw her glance at it. The tiniest gestures made me the happiest.

Dirk's plane was waiting for us at Fiumicino Airport.

* * *

Because we were never on European time I didn't have any

jet lag and woke up Monday refreshed and marveling at the vagaries of chemotherapy. It was one of those late-summer New York days when the mercury hits ninety-five by ten in the morning. I was at my desk catching up on work. Spaulding and I had returned the night before and stayed together at my apartment. That morning I had gotten on the scale and noticed I had dropped five pounds. Determined to put the weight back on, I ate a bacon cheeseburger for lunch that I chased with a chocolate milkshake and was polishing off a blueberry muffin when Reetika came into my office to tell me she had an audition and Ed Simonson wanted to see me.

Pratt and I had not encountered each other since the dust-up on the boat and he looked considerably less jovial than usual when I passed him on my way to Ed's office. We nodded frosty hellos, our friendship suspended.

Ed was seated at his desk reviewing a document, half-glasses on his nose. It would be difficult to calculate the scope of his wrath if he knew I had spent the past several days with his daughter in Italy. Spaulding had told him she was staying with her mother and there was no indication he was any the wiser. I sat on the sofa. He made a note on the document, removed his glasses, and rose. With a folder and the document in his hand he walked around the desk and settled into a chair opposite me. On the low glass table between us was a book of photographs, *Schooners: A Celebration of Sailing*. He laid the folder on it.

"This is your partnership pay package."

It had happened. Years of intense and concentrated work dealing with the high-stakes minutiae of demanding clients' lives had resulted in admission to the inner circle of a major New York law firm and all of the enviable perks that accompanied it.

"Thank you." My throat felt papery. I was overwhelmed. "I'm grateful."

"You'll find the key to your new office with a view of the river in there as well. But before you open the folder I want to show you something else." He handed me the document.

Civic Court of Suffolk County, New York State

Claude Vendler v. Thatcher, Sturgess & Simonson and Jeremy Best

My stomach rotated. The scheme had blown up before I could walk it back and the blast would shatter everything. It had been a horrible mistake, one that I already recognized and had tried to undo and now it would cost my job, my partnership, and whatever shrinking future remained. Ed was toying with me. Why had he bothered with the partnership ruse? He was a sadist. I noticed there were crumbs on my shirt and brushed them off. If I told him the cancer had rendered me momentarily *non compos mentis* but I had tried to correct my blunder would he be willing to overlook it?

"You'll observe the plaintiff hasn't just named you as a defendant but the firm as well." To plead cancer was beneath me. There was nothing for me to do at this point other than accept the consequences. For some things there are no excuses. As I prepared to samurai on my sword, Ed continued, "But we're not going to ask you to resign." What? The physical laws of the universe were being contravened. Had I misread the Raptor yet again? "This morning I called Dirk Trevelyan. I don't have to tell you what our relationship with him means to the firm. He said if you were to depart he would take his business elsewhere."

Dirk Trevelyan would be my savior? The tones of love and legacy and Diogenes in a giant pot vibrated far longer than I suspected.

"So, where does that leave us?"

"The sums involved here aren't great. I'll assign the Vendler estate to Pratt. He can sell it at the market rate and if the firm has to kick in a few shekels to sweeten the pot we will. I'm certain we'll be able to get Claude Vendler to drop the suit. I'll want you to look me in the eye and give me your word this was a one-time, not-to-be-repeated indiscretion. You understand how a law firm works, Jeremy. Trust. It's all we have to sell. If our clients can't trust us we'll be out of business pretty damn quick."

I could only nod. There was nothing to add.

"But there's another matter." Ed opened a desk drawer and produced a glassine envelope that held a Mark Cross pen with the monogrammed initials *J.B.* "I found this in my Tesla. It's yours, isn't it?" I said that it was. "Were you by any chance in my car?"

In the pregnant silence my cell phone began to trill. Once, twice, three times.

"Do you want to get that?"

"I'll call them back." Without looking at who had called, I silenced the ringer.

There are crossroads in life where the choice one makes will signify a tectonic shift in one's existence. If I wanted that partnership so badly, I could lie. Say I had given the pen to Spaulding as a gift. Deny everything.

"Yes, I was in your car." I could barely breathe.

Ed's face slackened. This was not what he wanted to hear.

"Keeping in mind that your entire future is at stake, would you like to describe the circumstances?" The perspiration that had been confined to my palms now glissaded down my sides and back. Slumped into the couch I studied the acoustic tiles on the ceiling. Why was I stalling? Fear? Habit? I searched for the right way to tell Ed what was going on, to find some fragment of honor in my misbehavior. "As your colleague and boss, Jeremy, as your friend, I am asking you a direct question. The pen? The car? Again, please describe the circumstances."

Raptor Ed wears might too tightly / I lick his trophies, ignite politely.

"Spaulding and I were in Rome." He regarded me clinically

for a moment, trying to ascertain whether or not this was a delusion. On the surface it must have sounded preposterous. My expression remained impassive.

"Rome, Italy?" The truth of what I was saying spread through Ed's mind like a tincture in a well. The stupefaction that overcame him gave me no pleasure. His mouth moved but for a few seconds words did not come. He stared at me, trying to make sense of it. "Spaulding went to Italy with you?"

"We got back last night."

"In what capacity did she go?"

"This might not make sense to you."

"In what capacity?"

"We're comrades. We love each other."

"You love each other?" The mocking tone he employed in no way vitiated the force of his rage. His breathing appeared labored. "She was in a mental hospital."

"If I thought she was unstable, I never would have . . ."

"Did you tell her you were going to die? That's a good line. She's a nineteen-year-old girl, Best. Nineteen. With serious emotional problems. She tried to kill herself."

Ed's fury was understandable and any attempt to mitigate it would be futile but I did not let that stop me.

"Spaulding's healthier than you think she is. She's admirable and tough and she's a lot better now than she was last year."

"Which you know because you're a doctor? She was ripe to be taken advantage of and, congratulations, that's what you did."

"She's an adult."

"So are you and you should have known better. You were going to be a partner, set for life, and you threw it away."

"I'm resigning."

"You're damn right. And Dirk Trevelyan can go fuck himself." With that pronouncement, Ed was exhausted, the emotion dissipated, replaced by a weariness that came from the realization that there were situations beyond his understanding. He was silent for a few moments. Then: "I would appreciate it if you kept this whole thing quiet. Will you at least agree to that?"

"Yes. And, Ed, I apologize for the pain this is causing you. But I don't regret it."

Five years had drawn to a mortifying close. No Champagne corks popping, no valedictory cake consumed with happy colleagues, no heartfelt speeches. There would be the usual workplace gossip as my former colleagues attempted to ascertain the exact nature of what had occurred. Circumspect in all things, the Raptor would leave them guessing and soon enough what had happened to me would cease to be of interest. As I strode through the office several of the assistants looked up from their desks. I stared straight ahead. It didn't take long to pack up my office.

While I was waiting at the elevator, I checked my phone messages. My oncologist had left word. I returned the call.

It started as a drizzle but the skies purpled and Manhattan was suffused with a lurid apocalyptic light. The windows of the buildings glowed and the structures themselves seemed to thrum in anticipation. Rain splattered the street, swelled the gutters. Umbrellas were hoisted. Taxicabs plowed through the squall, all of them full. Pedestrians huddled under awnings and in doorways as the downpour intensified. Along the sidewalk I strolled, clutching a plastic-wrapped box filled with my personal effects, the only figure moving through the cloudburst. Rain ran off my head, streaked my face, and soaked the suit I would never wear again. I splashed through puddles, shoes ruined. How many more times would rain begin and end? How many times would it soak me to my skin? I lifted my face and opened my mouth to taste the world.

SPAULDING
And Then It Got Weird

I t was around three in the afternoon when Marshall's text
arrived.
*Where have you been? Opening night is tonight and we're
performing the show for a week. You better be there.*

Immediately, I texted back that I wouldn't miss it. I had just
returned from Chinatown where I had visited the healer I had
told Jeremy about, the one my mother claimed had cured her.
I described Jeremy's condition to him as best I could and he
gave me a bag of leaves and twigs to boil.

—Drink glass every night for one month, he said. Cure disease.

On the subway ride uptown I spent the entire time reading
about cancer researchers in Geneva who were getting awesome
results with gene manipulation. The rain had stopped and on
the sidewalk pedestrians danced around puddles. I was going
to tell Jeremy I'd fly to Switzerland with him if he wanted since
I knew my way around and could be his guide. But his office
was empty, the desk clean, and it was clear he had left for good
when I noticed the poetry shelf was gone. Reetika was at an
audition and no one else I asked seemed to know what had
happened.

My call went direct to message. When I texted no answer
came back. I took refuge in the office of an attorney who was
on vacation. With her door closed, I settled in, went on the
Internet, and continued investigating alternative therapies. If
what Jeremy was doing didn't work, I wanted him to be aware

of the options. It all felt like something from the kind of science fiction movie that made me anxious so to calm myself, I tried to transform the remedies into a poem.

"Better"

Nutritional supplements
Electromagnetic shark
Cartilage, insulin
Therapy, gene
Therapy, and photodynamic
Therapy, pig
Enzymes and coffee
Enemas
You die in
The End

It wasn't good enough to be set in stone but arranging the words in a discernible pattern made them slightly less scary. As for the last two lines, well, to everything there is a season and that's not science fiction. I printed out fifty pages of my research, put the poem on top, and slid the contents into an envelope. At five Edward P's secretary called to say he'd like to see me.

My father looked up when I entered his office. I asked if he had fired Jeremy and without answering he told me to close the door and have a seat. I dropped onto the couch and waited. Edward P didn't say anything so I repeated the question.

—He was engaged in illegal activities, Spaulding.

—I don't believe you.

—Well, you can ask him yourself although I wish you wouldn't.

He sounded like he wasn't mad but it was easy to see he was making a major effort to control himself. Then something totally bizarre happened: The door opened and my mother walked in.

—Hi, Spall. Boy, it's humid out there.

My father got out from behind his desk and embraced my mother. As far as I knew, the two of them hadn't been in the same room since they got divorced but now they were united in alarm about my dysfunction. Everything has an upside, I guess. My mother sat near me on the couch and my father dropped into a chair across from us. They both stared at me.

—What are you doing here, Harlee?

—Your father asked me to come.

—Spall, my father began.

—Is this an intervention?

—Not at all, my mother said.

—We think the stress you're under is causing you to make some bad decisions.

—Duly noted, I said.

—Jeremy told me the two of you went to Rome.

This was unexpected but since they already knew I didn't deny it. Harlee and Edward P exchanged a glance.

—We're not sure you're ready to go to college, my mother said. Emotionally, Spall. We all know what a terrific student you are.

—We want you to take a drug test.

My head pivoted between the two parental poles.

—Please, tell me this is a joke. When some crazy hobo was chasing me through Stonehaven, you didn't believe me. He broke into our house and you didn't protect me. Jeremy saved my life, Dad, literally. Did you know that?

—What do you mean?

There was no point keeping it quiet now and I told them the whole story, the journey to Brooklyn in the Tesla, Jeremy bringing me back to Connecticut, and how he saved my life when schizo Karl Bannerman attacked.

—I'm sorry I took your car, but Jeremy's a hero, okay? A real one, the kind they wrote sagas about in the Middle Ages. He didn't want to come back to Stonehaven with me. I made him. And if he hadn't I'd be dead.

That one sat for a few seconds, ticking away, waiting for someone to touch it. Neither of them did.

—Spaulding, when your father told me you had flitted off to Europe . . .

—I didn't *flit* off.

—We don't want to rehash old stuff, my father said, but frankly, for all we know you could be smoking crack.

—Smoking crack? Seriously? The person I'm closest to in the world might be dying.

—That's probably bullshit.

—It's not. And I don't want to talk to you about it because you'll probably tell me it's something I've imagined in my sick brain. *Spall*, you're going to say, Urinate in that jar then go on a cruise with Meema and Poppy and then maybe you should go back to the clinic for a tune-up. Well . . . no. No, no, and no. Thanks for all you've done. I really appreciate it, I do, I'm not being sarcastic, but why don't the two of you use this opportunity to get reacquainted because now I'm leaving.

And then it got weird.

When he grabbed my arm I screamed, not a sound usually heard in a Manhattan law office. My mother looked like she had been punched and my father reacted like he had suddenly found himself holding a scorpion. In sprung rhythm I was out the door, through the reception area, down the stairs to the lobby, and out into the street. The temperature was still in the nineties and the wet sidewalks were sardined with overheated people.

My phone vibrated. A text from my mother.

Spaulding, please come back. ☺

I won't comment on the emoticon. There should be a word for when you love someone but can't be around her. I would text back later when I wasn't running. At 51st Street I got on the subway.

Jeremy buzzed me in when I rang his bell. I walked up the stairs and opened his door without knocking. I was about to unbutton my blouse so I could take a shower when I saw him seated at the kitchen table with a sketchy-looking guy. There were documents on the table between them. The lecherous appraisal the stranger gave me was not welcome.

—Bogdan's buying my apartment, Jeremy said.

I filled a glass with cold water. Before drinking, I pressed it to my forehead. As they continued to pore over the papers it occurred to me that my parents or someone representing them might show up here. I asked Jeremy when the two of them were done to come meet me at the Japanese restaurant down the street.

There was no way I would move back in with my mother and I couldn't go to Connecticut. And it wasn't as if I could just pitch a tent at Jeremy's either, especially given what he was dealing with. And he had just sold his apartment.

Begin / with qui - / et mind /
if goal / is cool / and calm.

I was eating soba noodles when he sat down. In five minutes we brought each other up-to-date on what had occurred since this morning. I got a little breathless discussing the encounter with my parents. He put his hand on mine and told me not to worry, I'd be all right. That seemed far-fetched. Then I handed him the envelope with all of my research.

—You should read this, I said. It's about all kinds of treatments.

—You're incredibly sweet to do that. If you want, you can stay with me.

—You just sold your apartment.

—First, he said, you don't sell an apartment and then immediately vacate the premises. I have the place for a while.

He called the waitress over and ordered a glass of iced

green tea. It was nearly eight o'clock but the sky was still light. The restaurant was filling up.

—I'm driving to Montauk after dinner. Want to come?

The Volkswagen had a good sound system and I found a radio station that played the kind of ambient hip-hop you trance out to. The temperature cooled off once we were out of Brooklyn and there wasn't much traffic on the L.I.E. Jeremy was quiet. The last time we went to Montauk, I had slept most of the way. But I was awake now. I was so awake I thought I'd never sleep again. Had I just broken up with my parents? Was there a way back and did I even want to find it? My thoughts were like birds' wings beating in a confined space. It probably wasn't the best time to have a meaningful exchange but I needed to hear Jeremy's voice. The geography of Long Island was mysterious to me so I asked him to tell me about it.

—Look at your right palm with your pointer finger aimed straight away and then separate your thumb as far as you can. Your pointer finger is the coast of New York and Connecticut. Your thumb is Long Island.

I flexed my hand and he squeezed the coast and the upstate part of New York, too. Instantly, I felt better. Air coursed through the car and it seemed to cleanse the stink of the day, all the bad stuff that had happened. I didn't want to ask him questions like what his plans were so mostly I just looked out the window and listened to the music while Jeremy told me about Montauk.

—It's not glitzy like the Hamptons and the crowd that goes there in the summer is looking for the sun and the sky and the surf and the cliffs. The houses are weathered. They've survived hurricanes and blizzards and persevered. The ocean can be rowdy, even in the summer when the beaches are stippled with families.

—Stipple is a great verb but I don't think I could just drop it into a conversation.

—The beach is stippled and on a calm day maybe the water is dappled.

—Stipple and Dapple sounds like a law firm.

—But even if the water looks calm there are rude currents, this wild aliveness teeming just below the surface.

That's how Jeremy described it as we approached on the road from Amagansett: This wild aliveness.

—Stipple, Dapple, and Rude, he said. Pretty good.

—*That's* the law firm, I said.

Past Great Peconic Bay and Napeague, beyond a long sandy neck the land expands and the borders of Montauk stretch from the ocean to the Long Island Sound. The shops that lined Route 27 were dark when we drove through the quiet village. We checked into a surfer motel called the East Deck. It was important to him that we be able to hear the ocean.

The room was basic, a large bed, a couple of chairs, a desk, and a set of drawers. But it had sheets, towels, and a roof, and most important, no one knew we were there. Jeremy brought two bags in from the car, a large canvas suitcase on rollers and the leather bag he bought in Rome. When we unpacked, I put the Ganesh on the dresser.

In the morning we walked into town and drank coffee and ate eggs and hash browns. My phone had been off since yesterday. I turned it on and saw there were seven messages from my parents.

I texted my father,

Please don't worry. Taking a little vacation.

Thirty seconds later I received this: *Where are you?* I texted back *I'm all right* and copied Harlee. Then I turned the phone off again. I felt bad about it but also believed they might try and have me committed so a time-out was necessary.

When we walked back to the East Deck, Jeremy asked me what I was going to do today.

—Be with you, I said.

—I have to finish these poems, he said. I need enough good ones for a collection. I don't know how much time I have or how long it's going to take me but this morning I need to write.

—I understand.

—I know you've jettisoned your life to come out here. Any time you want to go back . . .

—No one made me.

At the beach surfers in their black sheaths floated like giant water bugs. I panicked when I realized I had forgotten to take my meds for two days. The doses were way lower than they had been but now I was going to do without them entirely. The situation with my parents was nuts, my own mental health was improving but still felt a little tenuous, then there was the assault in Connecticut that for all I knew had left me with post-traumatic stress disorder. All things considered, I was a rock.

A boy and girl around my age stood ankle-deep in the surf flinging a football back and forth. They were my contemporaries yet entirely different from me, so blithe and carefree in this paradise. I was the apple-bearing snake, carrier of knowledge, prophet of exile eyeing these innocents at the shore. Around me little children played under the gaze of watchful parents who lay on towels or sat in chairs sheltered by colorful umbrellas. A mother was slathering a patient boy in sunscreen; a father affixed water wings to the chubby legs of his baby daughter. Parents believe they can protect you from what the universe has in store but they're no better than some Indian elephant god when it comes to keeping the really bad stuff away.

In the village I bought a hot plate and a teakettle. That afternoon I put a batch of the Chinatown leaves and twigs into the boiling water. After a couple of minutes the room had filled with a nasty funk. I poured the viscous potion into a cup and offered it to Jeremy, who tried not to gag. It looked and smelled like something from a toxic dump. He took a few sips before emptying it in the bathroom sink.

—You did a good deed, he said, but I'm afraid this stuff is going to kill me.

SpauldingS1@gmail.com
EPSimonson@TSSLAW.com; harleeyoga@msn.com

Dear Parents, I know how worried you are about me and given how I've behaved in the past that is totally understandable. While I am still kind of a mess, I am no longer an unhealthy, self-destructive mess. I appreciate the good things you have done for me. Have faith that I will be all right. You will, too. Your daughter, Spaulding

Jeremy was seated on the bed with his laptop open. It was noon and I had just returned from the beach. When I asked him what he was doing he said he was working on a will.

—That's what you were doing the day we met, I said.

—This one isn't Mrs. Vendler's. Are you sure you want to be here?

—Stop acting like you kidnapped me.

We walked to the Sandpiper Café in the village. The bright room was crowded and we sat in the back. A waitress came over and took our order. Her name was Sharon, she was twenty-one, from Dublin, and working here for the summer. Her cheeriness seemed so real. I wondered what traumas she endured. A father who drank, a boyfriend who hit her, no one escaped. And yet she processed what the universe served, rose in the morning and showed up for work. I ordered a tuna melt and Jeremy got a fish sandwich and a milkshake.

—Are you going to tell me what's going on with you?

—I thought we had agreed to not talk about that.

—It's not an unreasonable demand.

—All right, one question. What do you want to know?

—What did your doctor say?

—We're all dying, Spaulding.

—I know that. But we're not all dying soon. I've been reading about these alternative treatments that sound . . .

—Please stay off the Internet. My whole professional life has been spent with this. I prepare people for their final voyage, that's what I do. I see them at check-in and stamp their passport. I wave goodbye and tell them to have a good trip.

—It's that easy?

—How's your tuna melt?

I told him it was the best tuna melt I'd ever had even though it wasn't, but I thought it would be healing for him to hear something positive. He smiled and I noticed the dark circles under his eyes. Was he thinner than he had looked a week earlier?

When the sun beats against your eyelids and you open your eyes, everything is washed out. This is the opposite of how I felt. The strangled shouts of children sad at summer's end and the crying of gulls. The pavement hot on the soles of my feet as I walked to and from the beach. The pungent smell of sunscreen. The rough feeling of sand on skin. Everything madly vivid. I swam and sunbathed and wrote snatches of verse in my notebook. We met up for lunch and after we ate Jeremy gave me driving lessons. Arranged in the Volkswagen's passenger seat wearing a baseball cap and dark sunglasses, he sat quietly, occasionally reminding me to speed up or activate the turn signal. It was the kind of experience a person usually takes for granted, but I would let my eyes wander from the road to Jeremy and try not to think about driving alone.

We drove up Route 27 to the lighthouse, then back around the airport and over to Fort Pond Bay. There was a seafood restaurant on the Sound and sometimes we stopped there and ate mussels and French fries. Jeremy didn't have much of an appetite but he liked to watch me eat.

Late one afternoon, Jeremy told me to turn left on Captain Barrett Road. It looked familiar and when he asked me to pull over I realized we were in front of the house he had been planning to buy. There was a For Sale sign on the lawn.

—I used to talk about the "psychological acuity" required to write good poetry and now I think, "How remarkably pretentious," because I understood nothing.

—That isn't true.

—It is. Promise me you won't lead someone else's life. That you'll lead your own.

—I promise.

Jeremy got out of the car and walked onto the property. He stood on the grass and looked at the house. I sidled up to him and without saying anything he slid his arm around my waist. Anyone driving past would have thought we were the proud new owners.

—Can I help you?

A man was walking toward us. He had been in the backyard. Around my father's age and overweight, he was dressed in shorts and a burnt-orange tee shirt with Lone Butte Casino emblazoned across the chest.

—We were just admiring the place, Jeremy said. Who are you?

—The owner, the man replied. One of 'em anyway.

—What's your name?

—Who wants to know?

—Ezra Pound.

—I'm Claude Vendler. My aunt left us this place. Some New York lawyer was trying to screw us out of it but here I am.

—I happen to know that lawyer.

—You know Jeremy Best?

—And he regrets what he did.

—You can tell him Claude Vendler says he's a worthless son of a bitch.

—He already knows. But I'll give him the message.

—He knows? What the hell does that mean?

—It means he's aware of it, he feels terrible, and I'm sure he'd appreciate your forgiveness.

—I'll think about that. The place is for sale. You interested?

—Used to be, Jeremy said. But not anymore.

The sunlight flared in the windows of the house, turning them into pockets of blinding fire. I squinted and looked away. Claude Vendler said goodbye and sauntered in the direction he'd come from. Back in the car, I didn't start the engine.

—Did you really do what that guy said?

—It's a little more complicated than that, but I'm not proud of myself. Some people, Spaulding, when they get sick they become saintly. I don't want to destroy your illusions but I'm not one of those people. The whole plan was a mistake. I didn't want you to know about it so I tried to fix what I'd done. Before I was able to do that your father found out. I don't want to keep anything from you.

I turned the key in the ignition, looked both ways, and guided the car back on the road. For five minutes I drove and neither of us said a word. I reached over and squeezed Jeremy's hand. He didn't say anything else, just looked away and stared out the window. The car was so quiet I could hear my phone vibrating and because I thought it was probably my parents I wasn't going to look. Something made me pull it out of my pocket. A text from Marshall.

Tomorrow night is final performance. U coming?

The summer was nearly over and recent events had conspired to make me completely flake on Marshall's play. My first thought was that Edward P had put him up to sending the text to trap me back in Connecticut but Marshall would never allow himself to be party to a plot like that and I was ashamed of myself for having even had the thought. It was misery to not see his performance. How was that supposed to reflect the new and improved me? Marshall probably wouldn't care that much but I felt like a big hypocrite. I told Jeremy about the play.

—Would you let me borrow the car and drive to Connecticut?

—I'll take you there.

The next afternoon we drove to Port Jefferson on the north shore and boarded the ferry to Bridgeport. I asked Jeremy to stop at a store so I could buy a gift for Marshall and then we navigated to the local high school where the Southern Connecticut Community Players' production of the original show *Planet Fire* was being performed.

The school was a sprawling old two-story brick structure surrounded by acres of pristine athletic fields. Joggers loped around the running track, the tennis courts were busy, and a brook bubbled along in front of the campus. I asked him to let me out of the Volkswagen at a distant point in the crowded lot.

—Where are you going? I asked.

Jeremy had gotten out of the car and was walking beside me.

—I didn't come all this way not to see the show.

—What if we run into my father and his wife?

—What if we do?

Willing myself to be invisible, I tugged a sun hat low over my eyes. Jeremy was wearing a baseball cap and he did the same.

—We look like really bad spies, he said.

The lobby was packed, every mother, father, sister, brother, aunt, and uncle who hadn't made it during the run of the show there to see the massive cast on the closing night. We purchased tickets, were handed programs, and keeping our eyes straight ahead found seats in the back of the auditorium. There I slouched and waited for the show to start. Families filed past, friends greeted each other, teenaged couples held hands. While my eyes darted around the room looking for trouble,

Jeremy was examining the program like it held the key to the universe.

—This was an excellent idea, he said. I could use a little entertainment.

Edward P and Katrina did not appear to be in the house. Soon the lights lowered, people powered down their smartphones, and the anticipatory hum faded. The stage was an old proscenium with a curtain of maroon velvet that parted to reveal at least fifty kids ranging in age from elementary school through college all in a series of bold creations. There were kids costumed as trees, oil derricks, and various animals; there was a coral reef comprised of three girls, schools of fish, and one little boy who I'm pretty sure was supposed to be a nuclear reactor. And Marshall, who looked like a shrub with his head sticking out of the plant life that wrapped his body, delicate branches shooting off his arms and a head-rig with greenery sprouting from it. He turned out to be one of the leads, which he had not bothered to tell me. The story involved a fish, a dog, a human, and a plant (Marshall) attempting to save the planet from environmental destruction. I pointed my brother out to Jeremy, who complimented his costume.

—If I didn't know he was a kid, I'd try to water him, he said.

There were lots of songs, some slapstick, a sad scene where rising ocean temperatures caused a family of dolphins to die, and several stretches where it was hard to tell what was going on other than Earth's fate hung in the balance, but it was all performed with tons of zippy carbonation and the audience, admittedly biased, laughed, sniffled, and clapped at the right moments.

Marshall had a big number called "Photosynthesis" where he was surrounded by all these forest trees and he sang and danced and clowned around like a pocket-sized Justin Timberlake. He looked incredibly at home up there and it made me so happy to see him and all of a sudden I was weepy, I'm not sure why, maybe because he so deserved to be happy, and I had to get a hold of myself before Jeremy noticed since it wasn't a depressing part of the show.

My brother was so excellent I almost forgot I was there incognito and when everyone jumped up at the end for the standing ovation I made sure to bend my knees a little so if I had somehow missed Edward P and Katrina my head wouldn't be high up enough for anyone to observe. Jeremy stood straight as a pine tree while he applauded, so I'm not sure why I bothered. I asked if he wouldn't mind waiting for me and to please keep a low profile when I snuck back to congratulate Marshall.

The backstage festivities were a mixture of cast, crew, and a few pushy family members who had bamboozled their way past the porous security. You were supposed to wait at the stage door for the actors to come out but I told the lady in charge I had to catch a train. I thought Marshall might have a seizure when he saw me. He was accepting congratulations on his performance from the nuclear reactor when his face froze. He ran toward me, nearly knocking over the coral reef.

—Why didn't you text me you were coming?

—You were so awesome, Marshall. Totally exclamation point amazing.

We hugged and then I reached into my purse for the present I had brought him.

—I can't stay long but I brought you these, I said, handing him a pair of ballet slippers.

Marshall looked around as if he was checking to see who was watching. But then he grabbed them, gave me another quick hug, and stuffed them in his leaves.

—Where are you going?

—I'm with a friend right now.

—Does he work for Dad?

—They told you?

—Take me with you.

—You know I can't do that. I don't have a long-term plan but I'm totally glad I came.

That feeling I had while watching Marshall dance around onstage came over me again but I was able to control it before he noticed. We yakked for another thirty seconds and then I told him I had to bounce. I congratulated him again, embraced him a third time, then zoomed toward the stage and escaped through the now-empty auditorium.

I burst through the heavy stained oak doors leading to the lobby and my eyes went right to Jeremy who was talking to Edward P and Katrina. Of course he was, because that is the thing I least wanted to happen. There were lots of people milling around so there was a slim chance nothing ridiculous would occur.

—Spaulding, Edward P said when I joined them. Nice to see you.

Let me unpack that. First, he only called me Spaulding when he was angry. Otherwise it was always "Spall" or some offhanded honey-like endearment. As for Nice to see you, here's the translation: If you think you're getting anything else after that performance in the office, forget it, you should be happy I'm saying hello.

—Nice to see you too, I said. Translation: Let's get through this without something horrible happening.

—We were just catching up with Jeremy.

—I saw your dad and stepmother and came over to say hello.

—That's great, I said, and greeted Katrina, whose smile was so brittle I thought it was going to snap and fall off her face.

—You see, Ed, we've been staying out in Montauk, where I spent summers when I was a kid, and Spaulding has been amazing. I keep asking if she wants to go back to the city, but . . .

—I'm not going back now.

—She wants to stay at the beach, Jeremy said.

—Your brothers have missed you, Edward P said, ignoring Jeremy.

—I missed them, too. I just saw Marshall backstage. How great was he?

When Jeremy put his arm around my waist I could see my father tense up. The feeling of his palm on my hip calmed me down.

—What about Barnard?

—I'm going to postpone school, I said.

—We've got to catch the last ferry, Jeremy said. Good to see you.

Jeremy offered his hand, but my father chose not to shake it.

—Spaulding, this is ludicrous, he said. Best is a criminal.

—Duly noted, I said.

—Not technically, Jeremy said.

—He knows he's not a saint, I said. Neither am I.

—Spaulding, you're a child. And whether or not Best is technically a criminal is irrelevant. He's morally reprehensible, my father hissed. Best, your nerve is astonishing.

This was not the kind of conversation that generally took place in the lobby of a summer theater production at a Connecticut high school and several people, alerted by the intensity of the exchange, were looking our way.

—Katrina put her hand on my father's arm. Ed, relax, she said.

He was getting red in the face and appeared to be struggling to control himself. It was hard not to feel my father's pain. He wanted what was best for me, or at least his idea of what that was, but the last time we had been in the same room he had implied that I belonged in a mental hospital. And just like at the office, he grabbed my arm.

—Let go of her, Ed, Jeremy said.

—Oh, fuck off, Best. We still haven't decided whether to press charges.

—Ed, Katrina implored, please don't make a scene.

—Can we get ice cream before the cast party? Marshall timed his arrival like a trapeze artist. He had scrubbed the makeup off his beaming face. Jeremy shook my brother's hand and complimented him on his performance, and that further intensified his glow. Katrina hugged him and Edward P dispensed some awkward praise. Marshall asked if Jeremy and I could join them.

—They'd love to, Marsh, but they have a ferry to catch, Katrina said.

We offered our congratulations one last time, said stiff goodnights, and escaped. When I looked back at the sallow light of the lobby, it felt like we were astronauts drifting away from one planet and toward another, better one.

—Thanks for talking to my father, I said after we had been driving for a few minutes.

—There's no reason to hide anything. You're really not going to college?

—Not now.

—I think you should go. I can take care of myself. It's not fair to expect you to hang around, Spaulding. You should be with people your age, going to clubs and writing workshops and reading the classics and staying up experimenting with whatever non-addictive drugs they're doing these days.

—I'm not going to tell you this again. I want to be with you.

* * *

The end of August arrived and after Labor Day weekend the crowds blew away like dandelion spores dispersed in the autumn wind. Classes had started at Barnard a week earlier. It was easy to picture the girls in their fall clothes walking to class in twos and threes, riding the subway to downtown concerts, sitting on benches in Riverside Park, pens poised over fresh paperbacks. What was difficult to picture was being among them. There was the world out there that was not worth paying attention to right now and there was the space between us that was everything.

One afternoon in late September when I came back to the motel to meet Jeremy for lunch he asked me to drive him to the post office. The collection was finished and he was sending it to an editor at Faber in London.

—They published Eliot, he said.

—Eliot who?

—Seriously?

—Sorry, that was lame.

My comedy ineptitude made me laugh and he laughed, too. As we walked out of the post office I heard the tiniest *clink* on the sidewalk, the sound a pebble would make glancing off a rock. Then Jeremy kneeled down.

—What are you doing? I asked.

—My class ring slipped off.

He stood up and slid it back on his finger. He smiled at me with what looked like guilt as if he was sorry I was witnessing this. I wanted to complain about the unfairness, to rant and rail and spit fire at the sky.

—Let's eat steak tonight, I said. And baked potatoes with sour cream and chives. And a cake. A whole cake. Jeremy brushed a lock of hair that had fallen over my eye but didn't say anything. Don't you want to give the finger to God, or the universe, or whatever concept is in charge for fucking everything up so royally?

—And give them the satisfaction?

I think what he meant was that a person should only do what everyone expects if it suits him. Let others whine about how unfair life is like it's such a surprise.

At the Sandpiper Café Jeremy seemed free, like a weight had been lifted, although he wasn't talking much. It was easy to get a window table because there were only a few other people in the place. Sharon was cheery as ever. She was flying back to Dublin in a couple of days but wasn't it a fine summer and she couldn't wait to come back next year. She drew a smiley face on the check and invited us to look her up if we were ever in Ireland.

Jeremy barely touched his clam chowder. I asked what he was going to work on now that he had finished his collection.

—I'm done, he said. That's it. I'm not writing anymore.

—Why not?

—Look outside, he said. Those are cumulonimbus clouds in an azure autumn sky.

—That's poetic, I said. Azure autumn alliteration and all that. He didn't smile.

—I don't want to struggle to describe things anymore. I want to let experience happen without the filter of intellect.

His skin was pallid and the circles under his eyes were lakes. A pair of local businessmen sat drinking coffee with some papers between them on the table. A mother and her son who was a little older than me were having lunch. No one paid attention to the quiet couple in the front.

We lingered in the café for a long time. After Jeremy paid the check we stood on the sidewalk. On the highway cars cruised east and west. A man in a Hawaiian shirt emerged from a hardware store with a shovel. An athletic-looking woman walked a sheepdog. The dog sniffed Jeremy's hand and he scratched the animal's snout.

—He likes you, the woman said.

—I used to walk dogs at an animal shelter, Jeremy said.

The woman said she thought that was a cool thing and continued on her way.

—You walked dogs for an animal shelter?

—I don't know why I stopped. It gets you out of your own head.

Jeremy shielded his eyes and watched the woman with the

sheepdog cross the street. I put my hand on his back and just stood on the sidewalk next to him. He pounded his chest and made a guttural sound. A violent cough shook his body and his face contorted in pain. He composed himself and squeezed my arm. Then he took out a vial of pills, opened it, and popped one in his mouth.

—What's that?

—Oxycontin.

The temperature was cooler than it would have been at this time a week earlier. Jeremy looked drained. Another cough wracked his chest. He covered his mouth with his hand and when he drew it away his palm was spattered with blood. I ran back into the restaurant to get some paper napkins. When I returned he was seated on a bench in front of the hardware store. I sat next to him so our legs touched. He wiped himself off and apologized. I put my arm over his shoulder and he leaned into me.

—Are you okay?

—I'm terrific.

Jeremy started to laugh, which was not what I expected. He coughed again and a little more blood came up.

He opened the napkin. —How would you describe this? he said. A spray of blood?

—A sheen?

—A mist? Blood mists the napkin? Can something mist a solid surface? A window, I suppose, but a window is transparent.

—What about a spew or a spurt?

—Too literal.

—And gross.

—What's a fresh way to describe it?

—Blood splashed the napkin?

—Good, but that's a lot of blood if it's splashing.

—I can't believe we're doing this, I said.

—What else is there to do?

—Stipples, I offered.

Jeremy smiled. Blood stipples the napkin. —Excellent, he said.

—Does your doctor know about this?

—The treatment didn't work.

Time isn't supposed to stop but I swear it stopped then. The external world froze and a well of inarticulate emotion flooded my senses. Heart and lungs, nothing stirred. Even the wind seemed to hold its breath. Then sound and movement sputtered back, feeling returned, and life pushed relentlessly forward. I took Jeremy's hand and held it. There was nothing else to do. We looked at each other and he shook his head, the way a person would when a comedian tells a bad joke.

—What about alternative medicine? Did you even read the stuff I gave you?

—I thought the poem you included was good.

—Fuck that, Jeremy. What about never give in? There are experimental treatments, alternative medicine, diets, science fiction shit they're coming up with. How can you just sit there and let your life slip away?

—Spaulding, I blood you.

—What?

—Sorry, that came out wrong, and he laughed.

—I blood you, too, I said.

That's what happens when you love someone. You "blood" them, if blood as a verb in my personal dictionary can be taken to mean "understand, comprehend, get them in your marrow and with unbridled affection, the deepest way we can absorb another human being."

Jeremy didn't want to go back to the motel room so the two of us ambled to the beach. The gulls in Montauk usually careered over the waves in dense flocks but that afternoon a single bird could be glimpsed, immobile, suspended like a grayish-white kite in the cool updraft. We huddled together on the sand. Jeremy put his arm around my shoulder. I thought about what led me here and a pattern began to emerge. It was the same impulse that found me in the audience for Marshall's play. There were people you cared about. Maybe not many, but there were a few and when you cared about them enough it hurt.

A fine mist started to fall. We huddled together and for another few minutes watched a surfer in the rough ocean, a guy around my brother Gully's age. As the swells undulated beneath him, he straddled his board, fearless and in complete control. The rain intensified and a wave rolled in and he looked over his shoulder and started to paddle. The wave lifted his board and he rose to his feet, thrusting his arms to steady himself. He shuffled forward then back as he rode the curl with supreme assurance until his foot slipped and the board shot out from under him and the wave crashed down and he disappeared beneath the churning water. When his head popped up, we walked back to the motel.

* * *

I found a furnished sublet in Williamsburg, two rooms on the third floor of a brownstone that belonged to a journalist. It was filled with books and had a big desk set against a window that overlooked the street. Three mornings a week I volunteered at an animal shelter where I took packs of dogs for walks. Like Jeremy said, it gets you out of your head.

The leather bag he purchased in Rome was filled with notebooks, the kind with marbled bindings that students use. I devoured them. He had been keeping a journal since high school. There were pages and pages of ideas for poems and novels, observations about friends and schoolmates, trips he'd taken, political opinions (progressive but with a conservative streak, he wrote pages about Winston Churchill), sketches about his clients, and lots of stories about women he'd been with. He'd even written about me and when I read those parts it was hard to not be able to thank him for getting so much of it right. We think words bring us close to people when they're gone but they're a comfort, not a substitute. Words can summon a memory but absence has no cure.

Gully checked in regularly. He invited me out to Seattle but leaving New York didn't seem like a good idea for me so I tried to convince him to come back here. He said maybe he'd visit next summer and in the meantime he was always willing to Skype.

I spent an afternoon recreating the Poets' Wall from my memory of the bedroom in Connecticut. I put Jeremy's picture in the American section. It was one I took in Rome. He was looking right at the camera, a great photo for a book jacket.

One day I met my mother for lunch at a restaurant in Chelsea and we patched things up as best we could. She and Dodd were getting married and I congratulated her. I meant it, too.

—How are you getting along, Spall?

—I'm all right. Jeremy left me enough money to live on for a while.

—I'm sorry I never met him. But maybe next time you'll find someone more appropriate.

—Sure, next time.

—How are you feeling?

—I was scratching granite so long my fingers were bleeding, I said. But not anymore.

She wasn't sure how to process that but to her credit didn't ask me if I needed some "rest." So, progress. The two of us have more work to do, but you can't accomplish everything over the course of a Cobb salad and coffee. We said goodbye on the sidewalk and after she got in a cab I vowed to be more generous in our relationship, to consider my mother as more than the sum of her bad decisions.

246 - SETH GREENLAND

* * *

New York Times, November 3, 2014
Poet and Lawyer Jeremy Best
*The poet and attorney Jeremy Best, who published under
the pen name Jinx Bell, died in Montauk, NY. Although Best
was little known in his lifetime, his work recently caused a
stir in the London literary world when several publishers vied
for his first collection,* Akbar Isn't Here. *Faber & Faber will
publish it next year and American and French editions are
planned.*

*Best was raised in Manhattan where he attended the
Dalton School. He earned his undergraduate degree at Sarah
Lawrence College and a law degree at Columbia. Best also
briefly attended the Iowa Writers' Workshop. At the time of
his death, he was an associate in the trusts and estates department of Thatcher, Sturgess & Simonson in Manhattan.
Managing partner Edward P. Simonson said, "Jeremy Best
was a superb trusts and estates attorney. He was honorable
and circumspect. We mourn his loss."*

*He assumed the pen name Jinx Bell after leaving graduate
school for reasons that remain obscure. Although his output
was small, his poems were published in* The Paris Review,
Poetry Magazine, Wagon Wheel Quarterly, *and* Black Clock.
*In the few times reviewers engaged with his work, he was
classified as a formalist or neo-Classicist. Ian Tiburon, the
chairman of the Creative Writing Program at Columbia, said,
"It's a mystery why he wasn't better known. Bell's work fuses
traditional metric forms with contemporary subject matter in
a pleasing and provocative way."*

*The industrialist Dirk Trevelyan, a client of Best's, has
endowed the establishment of the Best Prize that will carry
an award of one hundred thousand dollars and be granted
annually to an American poet.*

He had no survivors

Because Jeremy was indentified as a "formalist" or "neo-Classicist" I didn't think he would want to be remembered in blank verse.

"Elegy for Jeremy Best"

Jeremy Best gave up the ghost last night.
Known by the pen name of Jinx Bell,
He had reams of poetry still to write.

At trusts and estates he did excel,
Workdays filled with codicils and wills.
Less unswerving paths lead to a Nobel.

His unnerving verse gave London's critics thrills.
It's ironic all this posthumous acclaim.
Fate prematurely stilled his pointed quills,
But now discerning readers know his name.

For language J.B. held dominant affection,
He believed it must be what we most treasure.
The power, he said, to effect deepest connection

Is how we should ultimately take its measure.
In verse he sought solace from a lifetime of regret,
Elegant ordering of words his greatest pleasure.

Our interplay resembled a jiving jazz quartet.
Although the time we spent was too attenuated,
We soared to heights found mainly in Tibet.
In stars and planets our verbs forever conjugated.

* * *

In early December Edward P called and asked me out to dinner. He suggested the University Club, a place he used to take Gully and me when he lived there right after the divorce. I would have preferred something more casual but my father liked it and you have to make allowances for another person's quirks. When I arrived five minutes early he was at a corner table sipping a Scotch. He looked pleased to see me and the feeling was definitely mutual. I sat down and ordered a cranberry juice and soda. The conversation was a little awkward. We told each other what we'd each been doing and I asked about my brothers and Katrina. They were all fine. He wanted to talk about me.

—Spall, he said, You really do need a plan. I understand if you don't want to work at the firm, but I'd love to know, do you intend to go to school? Are you going to get a job?

—This is the plan.

—I don't understand.

—To live my own life.

—Spall, that's not a plan.

—My plan is don't rush me.

The best thing you could say about our conversation was that it didn't turn into an argument. I had resumed seeing Dr. Margaret, who told me she thought I was doing relatively well even though there was definitely room for improvement. We said goodbye on Fifth Avenue and agreed to do it again.

On a Tuesday around noon a few days before Christmas I was experimenting in tetrameter when there was a knock at my door. I peered through the peephole and was surprised to see Marshall standing there looking like a marshmallow in a puffy winter coat. It was an azure blue and he looked like a little piece of sky. I opened the door. Behind him was a small black suitcase on rollers.

—I ran away from home.

—No, you didn't.

—Can I stay here?

I told him to come in and we'd talk about it. We were seated in my living room drinking tea. Marshall still had his coat on. It was too big and made him seem younger than he was.

—You got here on the subway by yourself?

—I don't want to live with my parents anymore. They're freaks.

—You like your brother, don't you?

—He's four feet tall and thinks he's going to be a professional basketball player.

—The Connecticut Simonsons are as typical as families get. It would be great if you moved in with me but I've already caused enough problems for everyone.

—I think I'm depressed.

A year earlier I was lying on my side with a stomach full of pills waiting for an ambulance. But now my brother needed me, which was crazy.

—What do you love, Marshall?

—Stuff, you know. Movies, plays, music, reading . . . oh, and my garden, which is, like, dead now.

—Your garden's not dead. It's winter.

—It's dead.

—Listen, you're thirteen years old, you live in the suburbs with parents who don't really get you . . . you're totally normal.

—I don't feel normal.

—My therapist says that word has a pretty broad definition these days.

—Mine says that, too.

We finished our tea and an hour later the two of us were gliding across the skating rink in Prospect Park. What is it about skating? It's hard to be in a bad mood when you're sliding over a silvery surface of ice. The morning had been overcast but the skies shifted and sunlight poured through the clouds. All the local schools were on vacation so the rink was swarming with mothers and fathers and their bundled kids. Some swirled boldly like saucers while others stumbled around the ice. Reckless boys with red faces chased one another, long-legged girls in warm jackets and short dresses performed spins and arabesques. Enlivened by physical activity, Marshall zipped through the teeming scene while I just tried to not break an ankle.

He had a way of being joyful that I envied and desperately hoped he would never lose and you could see it on every inch of his graceful body that crisp December afternoon. From the way he pitched his head to the way he moved his gloved hands, my exuberant little brother was a shot of bliss. A feeling hits you, it comes out of nowhere—no idea it was even there—and there's nothing you can do. It made me so happy to watch him I thought I might start bawling.

When I sat down to rest he parked himself next to me and I gave him some money to buy hot dogs. We ate them and watched an older couple in Christmas sweaters gently navigate the rink.

—You know I blood you, right?

—I blood you, too.

What's great about Marshall is that he didn't even ask what it meant. He just understood. We skated for a couple of hours and then went to a café that served hot chocolate so thick you could stand a spoon in it. Marshall ordered a piece of lemon cake, his favorite. The skating had jazzed him up and he chattered about school and his parents and what a trial it all was. But the more he talked the more the positive effects of the afternoon began to dissipate. Not for me, because his company was so welcome, but my brother slowly deflated.

—Marshall, I said, you can talk to me whenever you want for as long as you want and I'll always listen.

That seemed to improve his mood. By the time he finished the cake he was less vexed. It's truly amazing the power of knowing someone, somewhere, is willing to listen to you for free, of knowing you're less alone than you think. Isn't that what everyone with a beating heart really wants? To know they're not alone. When it started to get dark and I told him he had to go back to Connecticut he was too tired to argue. We returned to my apartment to get his suitcase.

Marshall sat on the sofa with his jacket on his lap and the suitcase in front of him. I could tell he didn't want to leave.

—I have a going-away present for you, I said, and handed him the Ganesh.

—What's this?

—It's from India. I want you to have it.

—Why?

—Marshall, you don't ask why. You're just supposed to say thanks.

—Okay, thanks. But why?

—Jeremy gave it to me. It's for good luck.

—Was he lucky?

Marshall looked at me, waiting on the verdict. How do you respond to that? It was hard to know whether I'd live long enough, even if I made it to a hundred, to figure out the proper answer. I wanted to tell Marshall that luck wasn't everything, but that wasn't really true because without it you were screwed.

—That depends on how you define the word.

Together we rode to Grand Central Station on the subway. The car was crowded with people in bulky winter clothes, a lot of them weighed down with shopping bags laden with presents. There was a guy wearing a hat with antlers playing a guitar and singing an old pop song. He had a good voice but was doing the song in a funny way and people were laughing. When he passed the hat I gave him a few dollars and when

Marshall saw me do that he reached into his pocket and added a rumpled dollar bill to the modest pile.

At Grand Central Station I walked him to the platform to make sure he got on the right train.

—Can I visit again?

—Seriously? Whenever you want.

He kissed me on the cheek. Marshall's head was about an inch below mine and I thought, today is the last time he's going to be this size and the next time I see him he's going to be taller than me. That was hard to believe. It's weird the first time you realize you're watching someone grow up because it means you're not a kid anymore. We hugged goodbye and I gave him a jokey shove. When he turned and walked toward the train in his big marshmallow coat pulling the suitcase behind him that feeling came over me again. I was glad I didn't have to talk to anyone. Marshall took a window seat and waved at me, then he turned around and faced forward. I stayed on the platform until the train pulled away and I kept waving until it vanished.

THE END

ACKNOWLEDGMENTS

I want to express my gratitude to the colleagues, friends, and family who read drafts of this novel, offered advice, and generally provided the kind of help most authors depend on. To my first and best reader Susan Kaiser Greenland, who edited multiple drafts with the keenest of eyes, I am deeply thankful. Barry Blaustein, Jay Gordon, Drew Greenland, Sam Harper, David Kanter, Dinah Lenney, Tom Lutz, Sylvie Mouches, John Romano, and Diana Wagman did me the great favor of reading early drafts. Richard Kay provided details of the legal profession. I am grateful to my agents Sylvie Rabineau and Henry Dunow for their advice and friendship. And to my editor Kent Carroll, whose gracious manner and deft editorial pen brought the process to a satisfying conclusion. I thank them all.